TO DUST YOU
SHALL RETURN

TO DUST YOU SHALL RETURN

Donna Fletcher Crow

MOODY PRESS
CHICAGO

ISBN: 0-8024-2712-X

1 3 5 7 9 10 8 6 4 2

Printed in the United States of America

To Nancy Sawyer
in appreciation of
her many infinitely gracious welcomes
to her beautiful land

Miles 0   25   50   75
Kms 0   25   50   75

ENGLAND

Thames River
London
Medway River
KENT
Chatham
Ramsgate
Canterbury
Tunbridge Wells

Canterbury Cathedral

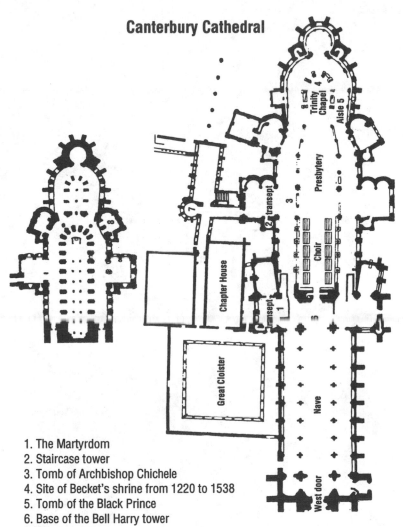

1. The Martyrdom
2. Staircase tower
3. Tomb of Archbishop Chichele
4. Site of Becket's shrine from 1220 to 1538
5. Tomb of the Black Prince
6. Base of the Bell Harry tower
7. Water tower

Crypt
8. St Gabriel's Chapel

1

Nonsense! Everyone of taste knows that true Gothic is the style in which God wishes to be worshiped." The Dowager Duchess of Aethelbert raised her chin, and her diamond choker twinkled in the glow of the candles on the table. "It is unthinkable that Canterbury Cathedral, the primary church of all England, should lag behind so many others in the land."

"Aunt Elfrida—" her nephew Charles, the sixth Viscount Danvers, leaned back in his chair and toyed with the stem of his Waterford crystal goblet "—if you are referring to the vandalism that has been perpetrated on Lichfield Cathedral—turning it into a French pastry—"

"Sir, I will have no such irreverence spoken at my dinner table."

The debate whirled around her, but Lady Antonia could not force her mind to follow it. It would have been so much more comfortable to consider the proposed restoration of Canterbury Cathedral than to pursue her own troubling thoughts, but she couldn't. That anything that seemed so right as her marriage to Charles could have been wrong . . .

"The Perpendicular Style is one of the glories—"

"Charles!" Agatha, Lord Danvers's long-faced older sister, pushed the last of her Pheasant Gitana to the back of her plate. "You force my patience past endurance. You really do. I did not summon you to Aethelsham to discuss Aunt Elfrida's architectural committee. Our sister Eleanor must be rescued from the clutches of this fortune hunter. And you must do it."

"Randolph Lansing—" Danvers began.

"Randolph Lansing is a perfectly respectable gentleman," the dowager duchess cut in. "He comes from an old family—very good stock. His people go back as far as mine. Almost. Of course, I'm descended from Joan, the Fair Maid of Kent, wife of Edward, Black Prince. But then we can't expect everyone to have royal blood. What would be the good of having it if they did?"

"How strong does Eleanor's attachment—" Charles tried again.

But the dowager duchess was not to be checked. "Randolph Lansing is a man of impeccable taste. I have appointed him chairman of my architectural restoration committee with the full blessing of the dean of the cathedral." She turned to the butler standing by the sideboard. "You may serve the soup, Soyer."

The bald, pigeon-chested butler removed the cover from an ornate silver tureen. A bright-eyed young footman stepped forward, but the maid, possibly intent on focusing the footman's attention on her soft brown curls, round blue eyes, and full pink lips, failed to move.

"Lily!" the butler reprimanded her.

The lace-capped head jerked to attention. Lily removed the first course plates.

Soyer ladled the thick, white Francatelli soup into flat bowls, and the footman handed them around.

Danvers took a deep breath and tried again to bring the conversation into focus. "Lansing may be a very fine society portrait painter, no matter what his views on church architecture, but I should like to be informed as to my youngest sister's feelings in the matter."

The dowager duchess sniffed. "Feelings! What do they have to say to anything? What does a girl of nineteen know of feelings?"

"For once Aunt Elfrida is quite right. Eleanor's feelings have nothing to say to the matter." Agatha gave her head a firm shake. Her dark hair was fashionably done up in a pearl torsade with tassels of pearl at the back and sides. Although the height of fashion, on Agatha it gave the unfortunate effect of a horse with its mane caught in a snowberry bush. "This is a matter of family honor."

Antonia had spoken hardly anything during the meal and had eaten less. The slices of sautéed pheasant smothered in a sherry sauce with bacon, onions, and tomatoes lay untouched on her plate. She hoped Aunt Elfrida's excellent cook wouldn't be offended, but she simply couldn't force anything past the lump in her throat.

She looked at Charles. The precise tucking of his linen shirt shone beneath the black velvet collar of his dinner jacket. His unruly dark locks gleamed with the dressing Hardy had given them with macassar oil, the latest fashion in men's toiletries, in an attempt to keep them in place. How could she have done such an unforgivable thing to that man?

"Charles, you must stop Eleanor from doing irreparable harm to herself and to the family," Agatha persisted.

"Poppycock! What Eleanor must do is to bring him up to scratch. And if the girl can't do it, *you* must bring him to the point, Charles. You shall speak to him when you attend the architectural committee meeting."

Danvers made a sound deep in his throat and reached for his wine goblet.

The dowager duchess bore on. "It's all very well for you to sit there grinding your teeth, young man. But you are now the head of this family. For quite obvious reasons Eleanor chose to live with me rather than Agatha when

11

your father went abroad. So you must do your duty. And it is your duty to see to it that Eleanor marries Randolph Lansing."

During the exchange, Lily moved down the table removing plates. She was apparently unprepared to find a plate still full, for her hand jerked when removing Antonia's. A large portion of Gitana sauce slopped onto the crisp, linen damask square that covered Tonia's lap.

Soyer was so quick to remove the soiled napkin and replace it with a fresh one that no one might have noticed the mishap had not the action caught the dowager duchess's sharp eye.

"Lily! What is the matter with you, girl?"

"Sorry, ma'am." The servant dipped a curtsy and fled the room with the still-dripping plate.

"Speak to her, Soyer. If she doesn't improve, you'll have to dismiss her."

"Very good, madam." He inclined his bald head and, the soup-serving concluded, led the tureen-bearing footman from the room.

"Don't be too hard on the girl, Aunt Elfrida," Danvers said. "She was probably thrown off stride by our argument."

"Fiddle-faddle!" The dowager duchess sniffed. "Well-trained servants never hear anything their betters say. Besides, I was not arguing. I was simply telling you what shall be done for the good of us all."

"I'd think twice about dismissing the girl," Agatha said. "It's impossible to get good servants these days. Why, only yesterday at the Society to Rescue Fallen Women a lady was telling about her servant who comes in drunk."

"Poor management. And if you mean that Catherine Bacon, I've known her since we were girls. She doesn't manage her household any better now than she managed her pony cart and kittens then. You won't find any of *my* servants misbehaving. Strictest propriety. Always. Anything less reflects sloth and bad breeding on the family. There's far too much French blood about. It all started with William the Conqueror."

Charles held up his hand to stop the tirade. "Yes, Aunt Elfrida, you've favored us with your views of history. I'll speak with Lansing. And maybe Antonia can have a word with Eleanor. They've always gotten along famously. Haven't you, Tonia?" When there was no answer, he cleared his throat. "I say, Tonia, you and Eleanor—"

Antonia gave a small start that was really more a shiver. "Oh! What? Sorry. Oh, yes, I'll talk to Nelly."

It was unfortunate that Tonia's distraction turned the dowager duchess's attention on her. The matriarch picked up the lorgnette lying beside her plate and examined Antonia. "I don't like it, girl. You don't look good. Not good at all."

"I'm sorry, Aunt Elfrida. I thought it was very clever of Isabella to put silk flowers in with the green ribbons— rather as if the ribbons were leaves." She turned her head so the green satin bows clustered over each ear would hide the thinness of her cheeks.

"I'm not referring to your hairstyle, my girl. Your eyes are too bright, and your skin is too white. I'd say you looked consumptive if I didn't know better."

Antonia froze. She felt what little color there was in her face drain away. She knew she must match the white damask tablecloth. She wanted to answer, but her mouth wouldn't move.

Charles came to her rescue. "Don't be silly, Aunt Elfrida. Tonia's a little tired, that's all. And it's little wonder with Agatha dragging us all the way down here in the midst of a January snowstorm." He turned to his wife. "I think you look splendid, Tonia. That new dress just suits you."

Tonia blinked gratefully. She knew he was referring to the luster of the pink silk that highlighted her auburn hair. Drawing attention to her dress, however, was a mistake.

The lorgnette dipped to focus on Tonia's tiny waist-line. "And how long have you been married now? Three and a half years?" Her pause was pregnant, even if Tonia wasn't. "Osbert's wife is increasing again. This will be my fourth grandson. There is no danger of the Dukedom of Aethelbert running out. Good Saxon stock. Never lets you down. Whatever may become of the house of Norville."

The hint was all that was necessary to turn Agatha treacle-sweet. "Now, Antonia, dear, don't you mind a word Aunt Elfrida says. My dear Arthur Emory is more than willing to do his duty in the succession. And we all know what a fine young man he is."

"Fine young man!" The dowager duchess's voice rose a full tone. "Arthur Emory is a nincompoop."

The dark, tapestry-hung walls and cabinets filled with silver and porcelain sparkling in the candlelight of the crystal chandelier began to spin around Tonia. She gripped the edge of the table. She must tell Charles. He must suspect the truth anyway. It would be so much better if she told him rather than make him guess or let him stumble over some evidence. She couldn't bear it if he confronted her directly. And yet how could she ever bring herself to tell him?

She raised her eyes to Danvers, and the spinning halted. She looked at the craggy features of his long face. The lines looked deep, hard. As tense as her own. She caught her breath. He knew. Somehow Charles knew.

She fled from the room.

2

Antonia's impulse was to run up the black oak staircase to her room, fling herself on the massive full-tester bed, and sob out all the ache in her heart.

But even if years of training in proper deportment had not rid her of all such behavior, she did not have the spirit for such an exhibition. She simply walked, one foot in front of the other, step by step up the stairs and down the hall, away from Charles.

Isabella had seen to it that a bright coal fire burned on the grate and all the lamps were lit in the little sitting room that was always Tonia's private parlor when they were at Aethelsham. She went to the tall, glass-fronted escritorie and drew out a sheet of her crested paper. She dipped the tip of her pen in the inkwell, then stopped.

The ink congealed on the nib. It was an excellent idea—to write the words she could not put breath to. But the words came no more easily to her fingers than they did to her lips.

If only she and Charles . . . If onlys were no help . . . and yet, if only it could have been different. But now . . . how would she tell him? And what would he say? He would divorce her, of course. He didn't have a choice.

I won't fight him, she thought. *How could I? I'd have nothing to say—after all the lies. Well, not lies exactly. Just omissions. But what are lies if not failures to tell the truth?*

A light tap at the door made her look up.

He stood framed in the doorway, his broad, perfectly tailored shoulders slightly stooped, his hands held out to her.

She couldn't meet his eyes. Those intelligent, gray eyes that always saw everything. That would see inside her if she let them.

"Tonia." He crossed the room to her. She couldn't stop him. He knelt beside the small, velvet-cushioned chair she sat on and took her in his arms. "Tonia, I'm so sorry. Agatha and Aunt Elfrida neither one ever had any tact. I know you've been upset lately, but don't let them make it worse. You are the most beautiful, the most wonderful—"

"No!" She couldn't let him go on like that. It made it so much harder.

"No. You're quite right. I'm as bad as they are with my babbling. Of course I'll be quiet. I just hope knowing how much I love you helps a little." He held her to him and drew her to her feet.

She gave in to the delicious comfort of leaning against him for a few moments, then pulled back. She couldn't let herself do this. It wasn't fair.

He loosened his hold but kept one arm around her. "Tonia, I know you haven't been sleeping well lately. Shall I sleep in the dressing room tonight?"

"No." Then, "Yes." Yes, that would be best. Start now what must be. Unless—but she wouldn't allow herself to indulge the thought. Certainly she believed in miracles. The Bible was full of them, and she believed fully. But this was the age of science.

He reached out a long arm and pulled the gold-tasseled rope on the wall by the fireplace. In a moment Isabella entered, her dark hair piled neatly atop her head, her gray dress with white collar and cuffs looking as fresh as they had that morning. "Her ladyship is tired, Isabella. See that she gets a good night of sleep."

The wide smile that always appeared when Isabella could do something for her mistress shone brightly. "Yes, yes. I will make her a nice tisane. Camomile. My mother always brewed the camomile flowers. I pick them myself when they are just right. Like my mother taught me. With just a little honey. And cream. Not milk, cream. I will be right back, my lady." She bobbed a curtsy and scurried out, such a tiny creature she barely had to open the door to make an exit.

Charles and Tonia smiled at each other as they always did at Isabella's devotion since Tonia rescued her from a bad situation three years ago and trained her in the art of being a lady's maid.

The smile broke her tension. Antonia crossed to the small sofa before the fire, and Charles sat beside her.

"My dearest." He took her hand.

She was grateful that he did not comment on the fact that it was icy.

"Are you missing Tinker?"

Tonia smiled indulgently at the thought of her little golden terrier. "I'm afraid I find it restful not to have him forever barking and jumping at my feet. Much better that he should stay home with his new family." Tinker had become the proud father of a litter of four puppies—three golden like himself, one black and curly like the doe-eyed mother.

Charles shook his head. "Amazing. The little rascal is as protective of those pups as he always was of you."

Tonia could think of nothing to say.

At last he asked, "Would it distress you to discuss this matter of Eleanor and Lansing?"

"No, not at all." She straightened. That was just the tonic she needed—anything to get her mind off her own problems.

17

"The matter does seem to have pretty well landed on my plate, and I really don't know who's right. I can't say I have too much faith in either Aunt Elfrida's or Agatha's opinions."

Tonia forced a smile and nodded.

"So I'd like to get to know this Randolph Lansing for myself. I was wondering—if you wouldn't find it too tiring—" he paused "—that is, it seems a good way to get acquainted with him."

"What does, Charles?"

"Having our portrait painted. It's something I'd very much like anyway. And he is reputed to be one of the best."

Antonia's heart sank. She could hear a future gallery guide saying, *Now the one on your left is of the sixth Viscount and Viscountess, by Randolph Lansing. That was painted just before . . . .*

"Of course I won't insist if you'd find it too fatiguing."

She could see how much he wanted this. It seemed the least she could do for him. "Don't be silly, Charles. It won't be fatiguing at all. Shall I wear my pink silk or the green velvet, do you think?"

They were deep in discussion when Isabella returned bearing the promised potion on a tray covered with a lace cloth. "Our lady will sleep well now."

Isabella's remark was a hint for Danvers to leave, but Tonia winced. *She makes me sound like a Madonna. If only she knew.* Isabella came from a large Catholic family. Tonia hated letting her down almost as much as she hated hurting Charles.

But no, nothing else could be as bad as that. He had shown again tonight how wonderful he was, how caring, how courteous, how thoughtful. It seemed that every day of their forty-five months of marriage she had made new discoveries of what a good man he was. She thought of this latest family crisis. Of course everyone would turn to

Charles. And he would handle it superbly. He always did. He always smoothed the way for all around him, taking care of everyone, seeing that all was in order.

She drank her camomile tea and surrendered to Isabella's ministrations as if she were a rag doll. Then in her smocked and embroidered white cotton nightdress and lace-edged nightcap she slipped between warmed linen sheets and closed her eyes. She forced her breathing to slow and lighten.

Isabella, presumably thinking her mistress asleep, extinguished the lamp on the table and tiptoed out to her own room in the attic.

Alone in the darkened chamber, Tonia continued to go over and over the same thoughts she had entertained for days now, ever since she had fully accepted the reality of the situation. *I shouldn't have married him. I thought it would be all right. I never meant to lie. I just didn't want to worry him.*

And then, as the camomile began to work, the fretting changed to *Please, Lord. It's not too late. I know You can still do miracles.*

Tonia opened one eye. Then the other. She couldn't believe she had slept so well. The brilliance of the light showing around the tightly drawn rose-velvet drapes told her it was well into the morning. After such a sleep one could almost hope.

Charles came in, looking equally refreshed in a soft gray morning coat that just matched his eyes. "Now all the world is waking—dawn through the dark night is breaking!" He launched into a favorite aria from *The Barber of Seville,* then interrupted himself. "Are you awake? Shall I pull the drapes?"

Antonia agreed, and he returned to his song.

> "Awake, awake my darling,
> Rise to the song I render

Come like the sun in splendor
With light to blind my eyes.
Oh dearest, oh fairest,
Oh one that I love!"

Tonia sprang from bed and stood beside him at the window. "Oh, how beautiful!" She referred equally to his slightly off-key song and to the sight out the window.

Yesterday they had traveled to Aethelsham from London in a train that belched as much soot as the sky spit sparse flakes of grayish snow. But during the night the countryside had been blanketed with a layer of sparkling, fresh white powder, which the sun now shone on.

They admired the scene before them. Then Tonia gave a small shiver, and they both looked down at her small, bare toes sticking out from under the hem of her thin cotton nightdress.

Danvers swept her up in his arms, plunked her back in the middle of the bed, and pulled the down comforter up to her neck. "I'll not have you taking a chill. How would it look for the Viscountess Danvers to have a red nose in her portrait?"

"Surely if this Lansing is all he should be as a society painter, he'll have more tact than to paint any red noses. Or worry lines, for that matter." She ran the tip of her finger along his creased forehead.

"Not worry. Hunger, my dear. I've waited to breakfast with you. Shall I tell Hardy he can serve it in here?"

"By all means," she agreed, and Charles rang the bell.

Isabella, who had apparently been waiting in the wings, bustled in with Antonia's ivory lace bed jacket. Tonia had no more than donned the garment and tucked a few errant, penny-bright curls back into her lace cap than Hardy entered, carrying both breakfast trays at once.

"And a good morning to ye both!" With golden curls falling to the collar of his green tailcoat, Danvers's rotund man looked, as always, like an angelic leprechaun. He deftly placed one tray across Antonia's knees in the big bed and drew a small table to Danvers's chair, where he deposited his master's platter of eggs and kidneys. He then turned back to the bed, whipped Antonia's napkin open for her, and poured her morning tea with milk and sugar.

When he still did not depart, Charles looked up from the toast he was spreading with golden marmalade. "Something on your mind, Hardy?"

The simple question appeared to be all Hardy was waiting for. He took his place at the foot of the bed like a lecturer in a hall. "It's making a joke you were without knowing it, m'lord. For it's what's on all minds that I've to tell you about."

He apparently took the confused looks on his hearers' faces as encouragement to continue. "And was I not telling you how fortuitous it was to be coming to Aethelsham just when there was to be a meeting of the Phrenological Society in Canterbury?"

Danvers groaned. "Oh, Hardy, surely not before breakfast?"

"Oh, I wouldn't want to be taking your time later, so I'm thinking what better chance than now that you could be feeding your minds and your bodies at once, as it were."

Charles nodded in helpless submission.

Antonia smiled, glad for any distraction.

Hardy cleared his throat. "Gladstone Simpson himself it was who addressed last night's meeting." When the name of England's leading proponent of phrenology brought no cries of recognition from his audience, Hardy continued. "Well, you see now, Gladstone Simpson was explaining how it is—just as the five senses are based on the organs of sight, smell, touch, and so on, similarly features of the personality spring from distinct organs of the brain."

"Organs of the brain?" Tonia lowered her teacup.

"You mean like those anatomical drawings we saw in Edinburgh, only all in the head?"

Hardy gave his cherubic smile. "That's it to a tee, m'lady. The brain is composed of as many particular and independent organs as there are fundamental powers of the mind. That is to say, the more developed—and consequently larger—a brain organ is, the more powerful is its corresponding mental ability."

"Nonsense, Hardy." Danvers speared a strip of bacon with his fork. "Anyone knows there are fools with big heads and geniuses with small ones."

But Antonia was intrigued. "So what are these various brain organs, Hardy?"

"Sure and I'll be forgetting some, but there's Amativeness, Combativeness, Destructiveness, Acquisitiveness —those are found to be especially strong in males. You see, the shape of the skull tells all—the heads of savages show their savagery, the heads of females show their femaleness."

Tonia gave a gurgle of laughter, her first for days. "Thank you, Hardy. You couldn't have drawn a more flattering parallel."

Hardy's blue eyes twinkled. "Ah, and sure but you're teasing me. I was meaning only that the lesser vigor in the female intellect shows in her well-developed organs of Benevolence, Veneration, Ideality, Secretiveness—"

"Hardy, you flatter my sex too much. I quite take your meaning, but I'm not certain that I care to have my character read out before I've finished my morning tea."

Antonia was amused by his lecture, but Isabella, who had been arranging her mistress's wardrobe in the adjoining dressing room, was not.

"'Lesser vigor!'" The tiny maid in crisply starched apron advanced on Hardy, holding a hat pin like a rapier. "I'll not have you be calling my lady lesser anything."

Although Hardy was not a tall man, Isabella came barely to his shoulder. But he retreated, more in capitulation to her snapping black eyes than to the threatening hat pin. "Now, now, it's no disrespect I'm meaning. It's just these gentle qualities that make the purity of the _ideal woman. If her ladyship would permit, I could be showing you." He gestured toward Tonia's head.

Isabella all but flung herself in front of Antonia. "Not a hair of my lady's head. You'll not touch one hair, you— you Irishman!"

Danvers unhurriedly finished his last bite of scrambled egg, wiped his mouth on his napkin, and deposited it on his tray. "Thank you for a most amusing breakfast, Hardy. But perhaps we could continue this matter of your scientific enthusiasm later. Lady Danvers and I will be driving up to Chatham this morning. You may see that the carriage is ready."

The servants departed with the breakfast trays, Isabella still scowling.

Charles perched on the edge of the bed, leaned across and kissed Antonia's cheek. She started to respond, then checked herself. He must have felt her hesitancy because he drew back and gazed out the window. "I believe that snow is deeper than we first thought. Perhaps we should put off going to Chatham. We can just as well go tomorrow."

"No!" Antonia sat up sharply. "Er . . . that is, no, we really shouldn't. I mean, if this artist fellow is the shabster Agatha says he is, Eleanor might really be at risk. We shouldn't put it off."

He regarded her with a furrowed brow for a moment. "Yes, perhaps you're right."

For the portrait sitting Antonia chose her green velvet gown trimmed with gold lace around the low neckline, and a tiny French hat that sat well back on her head. A billow of ostrich feather set off her wealth of copper hair, which Isabella parted in the middle and arranged in sculptured waves.

Hardy wrapped them in heavy fur robes and put a warmed brick under Tonia's feet before shutting the door on the brougham and taking his seat beside Even, the driver.

The air was cold, but a gentle sun shone on the snow from the pale blue sky as the horses trotted smartly forward.

Antonia snugged her hands deep in her fur muff. "What do you think, Charles? Could there be anything to this phrenology of Hardy's?"

"Impossible. One of these phrenologist fellows studied a cast of Burke's head—declared his bump of Destructiveness to be 'very large'—"

"Well, then?" Antonia recalled the grave robber whose activities had so influenced a murder they had once become involved in.

"Yes," Danvers continued, "but his bump of Benevolence was declared 'large' and Conscientiousness 'rather large.' While his partner Hare's best-developed organ was that of Ideality—larger than the same organ in one of our most distinguished poets, it seems."

"Mmm, yes, I see the problem." But Tonia did not want to spend any more time talking about anything connected with their honeymoon—those happy, hopeful days when it seemed they had the whole world before them.

She changed the subject. "Won't Lansing think it strange that we're going to him, rather than summoning him to Aethelsham?"

"I'd thought of that. We can say something about wanting the portrait to be a surprise for Aunt Elfrida—which it will be."

With the sound of the horses' hooves muffled by the thick snow, the carriage rolled upward to the brow of a hill that provided a view of the wide, muddy Medway. To their right was the dockyard built by Henry VIII, now choked with mastless ships. And farther around, on a hill to the east, ran the Great Lines—forts built during the Napoleonic wars. Behind these the tree-bordered street was lined with a row of tall, red-brick, terraced houses, each with a well-painted front door, well-polished brass fittings, and lace curtains at the windows.

They came to a stop before a bright yellow door that stood out sharply in the row of blacks, dark browns, and deep greens. The engraved brass nameplate declared this to be the residence of Randolph Lansing, Portraitist.

"Now have a care, m'lord." Hardy frowned as he handed them out of the carriage. "It can't be for nothing Chatham has been called the wickedest place in the world."

Tonia looked out over the pleasant, snow-covered prospect, dotted with chimneys and bridges. She laughed. "You're joking, Hardy. Perhaps the waterfront where the soldiers and sailors are stationed, but Ordnance Terrace appears the soul of respectability."

Hardy scowled more darkly and shook his head as if at the face of doom. "A place known for being as lawless as it is squalid. The number of frowsy drinking places is matched only by the number of equally frowsy brothels."

Tonia laughed again. "I'm certain you're wrong, Hardy. An acquaintance of Aunt Elfrida lives somewhere hereabouts. Aunt Elfrida would not know anyone who lived in such a place as you describe."

3

In spite of Hardy's warnings, they advanced to the door. Danvers's raps with the heavy, scrolled brass knocker were answered by a tall, slightly built young man. He had shoulder-length blond hair and a thin mustache.

"Randolph Lansing?"

The blue eyes on either side of his sharp nose narrowed. "Yes. I'm Lansing."

Danvers presented his card as he introduced himself and Lady Danvers. As he had explained to Tonia before they left the carriage, he had chosen to go to the door unannounced, rather than sending a servant ahead as would have been more usual, because he wanted to judge Lansing's reaction to being faced with Eleanor's brother.

The sensitive lips beneath the mustache curved in a sudden, welcoming smile. "Lord and Lady Danvers! I am greatly honored. Please, won't you come in?"

He started to offer his hand, then stopped, either because he saw that his hand was splattered with red paint or because he realized such an offer was Danvers's prerogative. He stepped back, holding the door open.

Tonia entered the narrow hall and stamped the snow from her high boots.

"I say, I'm most dreadfully sorry. If I'd had any idea

you were coming, I'd have let those urchins shovel my walk." He indicated two boys wielding shovels up the street. "As it was, I sent them packing. That's what I get for trying to save tuppence."

Antonia responded to Lansing's self-deprecating smile. His manner was charming. Already she could see why Eleanor was so smitten.

He led them into a pleasant room off the hall, which in other homes in the Terrace would probably be the dining room but for Lansing served as a reception area. He rang a bell that produced a stoop-shouldered, gray-haired maid. "Tea for Lord and Lady Danvers, Mrs. Gillie."

Then he looked uneasily at his crimson hands. "Ah, if you'll excuse me for just a minute. Working on some draperies with a rather broad brush, I'm afraid."

He bounded up the stairs and returned in a matter of minutes with clean hands. "Sorry. Occupational hazard. Get a bit carried away with my subjects sometimes." He smiled at them openly.

Lansing's blue eyes took on a cautious look, however, when Danvers mentioned his sister, although the artist's voice remained warm. "Indeed, Lady Eleanor does me the honor of allowing me to call her friend. I trust we shall see her at Aethelsham soon, although I quite understand the charms the city holds at this season."

The conversation fell silent.

"You have a most pleasant perspective here, Mr. Lansing," Tonia ventured.

"Yes, indeed. I'm honored that you find it so, Lady Danvers. I suppose you know that Charles Dickens once lived here."

"Here?" Tonia looked around her.

"Well, not in this house, you understand—on down the road in Number Two. Thirty years ago that was. But there's many about as remembers him. One hears stories of him stealing apples at the market stalls. And the great man hasn't forgotten us—he still sets some of his stories

27

in Chatham." Lansing indicated a current issue of *Household Words* on the table.

At last tea arrived, and Charles approached the matter of the portrait. The artist was open in his delight at being offered such a commission and was lavish in his praise of Antonia's beauty. "And in this gown, this hat, it must be, Lady Danvers. If I can capture you on canvas as first you appeared before me, radiant and sparkling against the pristine snow—ah, it would be a portrait for the Royal Academy."

He seized a pad and began making quick pencil sketches of the curve of the ostrich feather against the sweep of her hair, of her fingers holding the rose-patterned teacup, of the deep folds of her heavy velvet skirt. "Oh, yes. The texture, the line—truth and purity all the way through. If I can capture that, my lady . . ."

Tonia drew back at his choice of words, but he continued with the diffident smile that she found so appealing. "Forgive me. I know I'm babbling, but you have no idea how rare an opportunity it is for a society painter to be presented with an opportunity to reflect true beauty. It is our usual job to flatter, to pretend—I'm afraid I must say to lie. But in your case, my lady, the brush can only hope to adore."

Tonia laughed. "You must stop, sir. I shall blush until you can have no hope of finding the proper skin tone."

A few minutes later Lansing led them upstairs to his studio, where he arranged his subjects in a variety of poses before he found the one that suited him: Antonia seated by a long, French window that looked out over the snowy landscape, Danvers standing behind her to the left, to her right a low pedestal holding an exquisitely carved ivory statue of Cupid and Psyche.

Tonia ran her finger over the beautiful figures, relishing the warmth of the satiny finish, the glow that seemed to come from inside the inanimate objects. "They are lovely. They must be very valuable."

Lansing dipped his head and looked at her from under his long eyelashes, his forehead wrinkled like a naughty schoolboy's. "Alas, mere copies. But I must be thankful, for if they were rare I could not afford to keep them." He lifted his head, and his smile brightened. "So you see, all is for the best."

He set up his easel and began a new sketch. "You may talk. Just please do not move. I am working on the play of light. It is important that the shadows be as right as the highlights."

Charles took the opportunity to attempt to draw Lansing out about Eleanor. He learned little, however, beyond the fact that they had met last fall at a musical evening the dowager duchess gave in aid of the architectural committee Lansing had agreed to head for her and that he found Lady Eleanor charming.

"I fully understand your concern, Lord Danvers. I am merely a distant relative to Baron Crofthurst. Although I might hope someday to obtain a knighthood should my painting be deemed worthy—for I do aspire to more serious art than the portraiture which keeps bread on my table—" He paused and grinned with an apologetic gesture toward the sketch he was working on. "Sorry, not very clever of me to deprecate the line of work you've commissioned."

Tonia gave him an encouraging smile. "Don't worry. You can be entirely honest with us. We didn't come to be flattered, remember. I do understand what you mean about serious art though. Do you have anything you're working on in that line? What style do you like—Constable, Turner, Delacroix?"

"No . . . well, yes, of course, I like those very much. But I would prefer my own work to reflect something perhaps of Murillo. His religious works, you understand. Ah, if I could paint Madonnas as he did—the radiance, the holiness engulfing the Christ Child, reflecting in the purity of His mother—" He broke off with a shake of his head. "Forgive me. I am prone to being a bore. I don't know how

Elean . . . er . . . Lady Eleanor puts up with me. I'm sure that's what you're wondering too."

On the contrary, Antonia was delighted with him. She understood Agatha's objections less and less.

But Danvers continued his queries. "You were saying you are a nephew of Baron Crofthurst?"

"Oh, sorry, yes. That's where I went off the rails talking about art theory. I think I was about to say that I'm fully aware of how low I'm placed beneath the daughter of an earl. I want to be very straight with you on that point. My father was a younger son, you see. An excellent fellow, he did very well in the army—couldn't understand my not following his footsteps, I'm afraid." The charcoal pencil stopped in mid-air. "Excuse me, Lord Danvers, if you could just move your left foot forward. That's right, put your weight on your right leg. Oh, that's right. Perfect. You aren't getting too tired, are you?"

The pencil made little scratching noises on the paper, matching the scraping sounds of the shovelers working in the street below. Tonia looked out over the perfect, untouched covering of snow in Lansing's walled back garden and in the one next to it. A pity that a maid would soon have to make her way to the coal shed or dustbins at the back gate. What a shame to disturb such perfection with footprints.

"But you're the oldest son yourself?" Charles again brought the conversation back to Lansing's family.

"Yes, yes. You'll think me addlepated. That's the whole point I'm trying to make but keep getting side-railed. The thing is I do like your sister so awfully. I've never met anyone like her—but then I'm sure I don't have to tell you how very, very charming she is. But the problem is that I haven't a bean." He continued his monologue as he took a delicately painted silk fan off a shelf and positioned it in Tonia's hand.

"And no matter how much she doesn't seem to think such things matter, I'd never want to live on my wife's money. Not that we've actually discussed such things, you understand. So my only hopes are in my daubs of paint. And with the best of luck, it takes years to make a reputation as a painter. And even then there's not always a lot of money in it." He heaved a sigh. "There now, I've said it. Not very well, I'm afraid, but I hope you understand that I don't want to be thought a fortune hunter, and I'll perfectly understand if you forbid your sister to see me again. Though I would be absolutely crushed." He stopped and turned away. It was a moment before he could go on. "Crushed. But I would understand your position."

Antonia wanted to cry out assurances that they had no such thing in mind, but of course the decision wasn't hers.

And Charles said nothing. At last he cleared his throat. "Thank you, Lansing, I appreciate your openness. I—"

A vigorous clacking of the door knocker in the hall downstairs, followed by Mrs. Gillie's high-pitched voice, interrupted him.

And then a familiar brogue. "Now, now, and don't you be bothering to climb those stairs. I'll just pop up and announce myself to his lordship. He'll be expecting me."

A clatter of footsteps preceded Hardy's entrance. "Ah, m'lord, you'll be happy to be hearing that I located Laver Esherwood—just past Gillingham like you said. He indeed has a fine new aerostat. He was most honored that you'd heard of him. Said we should come make an ascent any time the weather's fine. He's devised a new system of valving and has a sort of wing attached to the gondola to make directing the balloon easier. Ingenious fellow."

"Fine, Hardy. I hope you told him we'd love to give it a try." Danvers's enthusiasm for his favorite hobby shone in his eyes.

"I did. And I'm happy to be telling you that I tested the matter thoroughly and Esherwood's Constructiveness

31

organ is highly developed. He's a man we can be trusting well."

Danvers gave a shout of laughter. "Hardy, don't tell me you actually felt the man's cranium!"

"And why not, m'lord? I told you, he had nothing to hide. Right here—" he turned to Lansing standing at the easel beside him and placed a hand on the side of the artist's blond head "—right here his skull was much over-developed. Obviously a man whose inventions you can trust."

Lansing did not pull away from Hardy's touch. Instead he lay his charcoal stick aside to concentrate more fully on the newcomer. "But this is fascinating. Are you telling me you can tell about a man's abilities by feeling his head?"

"That's what I'm saying. His abilities, his feelings, his morals—all exhibited by the development of the organs of his head." Hardy moved his fingertips over Lansing's cranium. "Oh, yes, you have some very well-developed organs: Amativeness, Acquisitiveness, Self-esteem . . ."

Tonia smiled. So much for Hardy's character reading. She had seldom met one of Randolph Lansing's station who seemed less acquisitive or whose self-esteem seemed more underrated. As to his amorous disposition— well, perhaps she should ask Eleanor about that.

The men moved into an animated discussion as Hardy continued his reading, and the sketching session seemed at an end. Tonia closed the beautiful fan and looked at the silver-gilt end sticks, richly engraved and encrusted with jewels like the bonding on a medieval book of hours. What an amazing ornament for Lansing to simply pluck from a shelf and place in her hands. She would have sworn the jewels were genuine.

She wandered aimlessly around the room then, look-ing at half-finished portraits of wealthy patrons, pictures of their prize animals, and paintings of their palatial country homes, most of them, she suspected, newly acquired, since the rise of the mills had generated so much new wealth in England.

She looked for the painting with the cerise draperies he had been working on when they arrived, but didn't see it. Most of his patrons seemed to prefer the somber colors they probably felt symbolized the serious position they filled in society. A large canvas against the wall depicted a woman in flowing burgundy robes, but that was not the color that had been on Lansing's hands. Besides, the paint on this canvas was dry.

Lansing's ambitions to serious art must be frustrated indeed, for there were none of the inspired religious works whose production would fulfill his deepest longings. Her heart went out to him. She knew the ache of such failure.

But then, she thought, if he did have such work in progress, he wouldn't be likely to have anything so personal open to the eyes of his society clients who were interested only in paintings that would establish their place in the elite world. Then she saw the door.

It stood in a far corner—a folding Chinese screen half covering it—and it was painted the same as the cream-colored wall. Tonia made her way slowly that direction, pausing before various paintings and sketches on the way. Behind her the men continued to be absorbed in their talk.

"Sure and I'm saying individual differences exist because different people's brains have developed differently. We all have different large and small organs, you see."

Lansing started to agree, but Danvers cut in sharply, "Errant nonsense, if not heresy. It reduces the soul of man to his brain. Such belief puts every man at the mercy—"

Holding her wide skirts so as not to brush the painted screen, Tonia ducked behind its concealing folds. She knew she had no excuse other than idle curiosity, but what might such a deliberately concealed door hide? More of the exquisite props Lansing used so casually? Some of the serious art he really cared about? The work he disdained was skillfully done. She would love to see something he approached earnestly and with enthusiasm.

Hoping the door would not creak and turn attention to her, Tonia grasped the knob, turned it, and pulled. The door was locked. She was so disappointed she must have made a small noise.

It caught Lansing's attention. "Is there something I can help you with, Lady Danvers?" The sharp edge in his voice seemed uncharacteristic.

"Oh, no." She stepped back into the main part of the studio. Thank you. I . . . um . . . was admiring this screen."

"Yes, it is nice, isn't it? Cantonese. Especially fine lacquer. A gift from a grateful client. Said I caught the likeness of his wife to perfection. Truth is, I made her look a good ten years younger and twenty pounds lighter." His voice took on a cynical note. "No matter what your nanny may have told you, honesty doesn't pay."

Danvers had obviously had enough. He flung Tonia's mantelette around her shoulders and moved toward the hall without waiting to be shown out.

The artist followed them down the stairs. "If you could return late in the week—Thursday perhaps—I shall begin the work on canvas, Lord Danvers."

A blast of cold air made Antonia shiver as Hardy opened the door. At the end of the walk she smiled as one of the industrious snow-shovelers tipped his cap to her.

The boys then waded on through untrampled, ankle-deep snow to the door of Lansing's neighbor, and the clacking of the heavy knocker sounded on the crisp air as Charles started to assist Tonia into the brougham waiting at the curb.

Her foot was on the step when a shriek behind her shattered the calm. She whirled just in time to keep from being slammed against the carriage as the boys, snow shovels abandoned, hurtled past with strangled cries and wild gestures.

34

Tonia looked to the doorway from which the boys had fled. The sight so stunned her she reeled against the brougham, able only to point at the grisly scene. Framed in the doorway stood a young woman, red hair wildly askew, maid's apron mottled with blood, reddened hands flailing, and bleeding copiously from a cut throat.

4

Danvers took one look and darted forward. He caught the maid before she swooned. "Hardy, summon a doctor! And a constable!"

He attempted to lay the woman on the parlor sofa, but she resisted. With strangled noises and frantic gestures she insisted on being carried up the blood-spattered staircase. In the front bedroom they found the reason for her insistence.

A frail old woman lay in a crumpled heap in the center of a floral Aubusson carpet. It took Antonia a second look to realize that the flowers were actually gold and purple, not the deep red the old lady's blood had stained them. And the hair, still done firmly in a tight knot on the top of her head, was actually steel gray, not the red-brown of its gory dye. One thin cheek appeared more sunken than the other, as if the bone supporting it had been crushed. The forehead was battered and the skin broken. One ear was crumpled shapelessly.

Tonia barely made it to the washbowl.

By the time her retching ceased and she had found fresh water to wash her hands and face, heavy footfalls crashed up the stairs. A constable burst into the room, slamming the door back against the wall, and stood staring, wide-eyed.

Constable Orson, he said he was. The man resembled nothing so much as a block of building granite. His stocky, square-shouldered body was topped with a square-jawed face framed by a short, square, black beard. But for all his appearance of solidity, he seemed on the verge of crumbling. He knelt before the remains of the battered woman and took one hand, which appeared little more than a bunch of twigs in his own thick, square fist.

"Ah, Catherine, my dear, and how could such a thing have happened? You who were like my very own granny to me. Who did this to you? Who could have done such a thing?"

His questions set off another round of wild gestures from the maid, whom Danvers had placed on her mistress's bed.

"Bessie—" the constable turned to her but did not drop the skeletal hand he held "—did you see who it was?"

The maid nodded and tried to speak but produced only bubbling sounds in her throat.

"Don't try to talk!" Charles commanded. He put his hand on her head to try to calm her. "Where is the doctor? Did Hardy go for one?"

Orson nodded. "Dr. Benson's got a locum in. He's just up the street. Should be here any minute."

At that Tonia heard the front door open.

"Up here, Hardy," Danvers called.

Hardy entered, escorting the interim doctor.

"Gilchrist!" Tonia had to restrain herself from rushing to the dowager duchess's young nephew Gil Morris, whose medical career they had rescued four years ago when they proved him innocent of a murder charge. She had seen him only once since—at his wedding. She had heard he had gone into practice with an established doctor in London—but all that must wait upon the desperate

needs of the maid Bessie, whose slashed throat was staining the crocheted white coverlet on which she lay.

The one useful thing Tonia had managed to do was to put water on to heat when cleaning up her own sickness. Now she brought a basin for Gil and held Bessie's head while he attended to her throat.

"Apparently her assailant was in a hurry. Lucky. If he'd sliced any deeper it would've been all over for her. Cut to the bone in the center, but the major arteries are on the side. Looks like he had a sharp knife—maybe with a short blade—but was in too much of a hurry to make sure of his job."

When Bessie—Elizabeth Law, Orson told them the maid was named—was resting as comfortably as possible, Gil turned to the dreadful sight of Catherine Bacon.

Orson dashed a tear from the corner of his eye and shook his head. "I never had a granny of my own. When I started the Ordnance Terrace beat ten years ago, Mrs. Bacon just sort of adopted me. I was a skinny young whippersnapper then, if you can imagine." He patted his well-padded front. "She invited me in every night for a cup of cocoa. Every night without fail, she did. Rain, snow, frost, it didn't matter none—there was always a cuppa cocoa at Catherine Bacon's." He turned away.

After a moment Charles asked, "Had she told you anything that might make you think she was in danger?"

Orson's square shoulders slumped. "I warned her and warned her. Just last night. Soon as I finished my chocolate, I put my cup down—great big one it was, she always kept it special for me, has strawberries and ivy all around it—I put it down and said, 'See you lock up good behind me now, Catherine.' It was Bessie here's night out, you see, and I didn't like the idea of her being alone in the house. 'Lock up good,' I said. 'You've too many valuables in this house. And you're the most valuable of all.' She always laughed when I fussed over her, but I could see she was pleased. Then I put on my helmet and went out. I never thought . . . if only I'd stayed around longer . . . but I had my beat to do. Still, if I could have . . ."

Danvers shook his head. "Nothing you could have done last night would have made any difference. Blood's a lot fresher than that. But did she lock her door, do you know?"

Orson shook his head. "It was snowing pretty hard by then. You know how that muffles sounds. Not sure I could have heard the key turn anyway. Didn't think to check. If only . . ."

"No, never mind, constable. Hardy, I think we all need some tea. And see if you can find some brandy or something to put in Orson's."

The constable shook his head. "No chance. Teetotal she was. Not a drop in the house. I'll have extra sugar though."

"And for Bessie," young Dr. Morris said from his patient's side. "Swallowing will be good for her. Then she'll probably be able to talk enough to shed some light on this."

Gil stayed with his patient. Tonia, Charles, and the constable moved to a sitting room next to Mrs. Bacon's bedroom.

Here the mantel and every table and shelf were draped with crocheted doilies or fringed, cut-velvet shawls and were covered with objects. Absently Tonia examined the grape-patterned silver candlesticks engraved with a scrolled B, the carefully arranged dried flowers in a crystal vase, the Chelsea porcelain shepherd above the fireplace. It was odd that in a room so cluttered with memorabilia there should be no family pictures.

She looked at a pair of delicate oval miniatures hanging beside the fireplace. They appeared to be a generic Georgian lord and lady, not family pieces. "Didn't Mrs. Bacon have any family?"

Just then Hardy entered with a tea tray—complete with a bottle of gin beside the flowered teapot.

39

Orson frowned. "Gin? Where did that come from?" He shook his head. "Not Mrs. Bacon."

Hardy beamed unconcernedly. "Maybe she fancied a drop on the side. My old granny did. I was thinking she might, so I just had a quick peek in the cellar." He added a generous splash to Orson's well-sugared tea. "Drink this up. You'll be needing it before you're taking a look below."

Orson paled under his black beard. "What do you mean? Not more—"

"No more bodies. No, no . . ."

Tonia's mind was still elsewhere. "About Mrs. Bacon's family," she prodded.

Orson emptied half his cup at one gulp. "No family. Never had any. Colonel Bacon was killed at Waterloo. She talked about it a lot. Never looked at another man but her dear Teddy, she always said. No other family. I think there was a quarrel."

"So what about a will then? Some of these things— the silver and porcelain look valuable." Tonia took a second look at the fine detailing on the shepherd playing his flute to a lamb. She turned it over and found the red-anchor marking she expected.

Her thoughts were interrupted by Gilchrist calling from the next room. Bessie could talk now.

As Gil thought it best not to move his patient, he had flung the besmeared coverlet over the body on the floor and propped up Bessie with a pile of pillows against the scrolled, fruitwood Empire headboard. The maid's normally ruddy complexion was as white as the bandages swathing her throat. Each rusty freckle stood out sharply across her nose and cheeks, matching the cinnamon of her thick hair, which Gil had lopsidedly pinned up to get it out of the way of his work. Her green eyes shown wide and bright as if the bandages squeezed on her neck and pushed her eyeballs forward. "It was—turrible!"

The effort of the outburst forced her back against the pillows. Her croaking voice broke on the last syllable.

"Now, Bessie." Her doctor spoke calmly. "Breathe as deeply as you can. Talk slowly and keep your voice low."

Bessie tried again. Her voice came out gravelly sounding. "Last night was me night off. I had some refreshment with me friends. She—" Bessie gestured a work-roughened hand toward the bump under the bedspread on the floor "—she were abed when I came in. So I went to bed too. Overslept a bit, I did. Always made her cranky when I did that, so I left her breakfast tray by her door and hurried out to do the marketing."

"So you didn't see your mistress this morning?" Charles asked.

"Not then I didn't. Not until . . ." She looked toward the carpet and shivered. "I got right to my work when I got back. Cleaned the grates first and laid new coal."

"But not Mrs. Bacon's?" Danvers asked.

Bessie shook her head. "I did hers yesterday. Always a special job hers was. Then I did me brasses. I was in the front parlor doing the brasses when I heard it."

"Heard what?" Danvers asked.

"A ruckus in the cellar fit to beat all. I ran right down, but I was too late. They was gone."

"Gone?" Orson asked the question this time.

Bessie tried to nod but stopped on a strangle of pain. "They'd dragged her upstairs. They must of passed through the hall while I was in the parlor. The cellar was a turrible sight. Blood everywhere."

Hardy nodded as if to encourage her. "What was I telling you? Saw it myself when I found the gin, I did."

A look from his employer quelled his ebullience.

"Well, I did."

"So I followed. I could hear them upstairs by then. And there was the blood on the floor . . ." Her head drooped to one side, and Gil gave her a few more sips of fortified tea. "I came in on 'em in here."

"Who, girl? Who did this?" Orson almost bellowed.

41

"Two dustmen. I didn't know 'em. But they was dustmen—faces and hands all sooty under the blood splatters. Neckerchiefs and hoods on the back of their caps, like you'd expect. I screamed. The nearest one—great, tall brute he was—he had a knife. He slashed at my neck. I fainted. I expect they thought I was dead."

"Lucky thing too." Orson, who had been leaning forward, intent on every word, took a large white handkerchief from his pocket and mopped his forehead.

"Next thing I knew I heard the door knocker, like the knocker on the gates of 'ell, knocking to wake the dead. Well, it woke me. Somehow I got down the stairs—it was boys wanting to shovel snow. I tried to get them to help, but they just turned tail and ran."

"Don't be too hard on the lads," Orson said. "They got to me before Hardy here did. Good boys they are. We can hope they saw the dustmen earlier. Shouldn't be too hard to find the murderers. You've been very helpful, Bessie. You're a good girl. Don't blame yourself too much. Nothing more you could have done. Nothing more any of us could have done." Orson stumbled to his feet.

"If that's all you'll need Bessie for now, I'll give her some laudanum drops so she can sleep." Gil opened his medicine bag and turned to his patient. "Then we'll see if we can find a neighbor to look in on you. You aren't afraid to stay here?"

She shook her head.

"Maybe Lansing's servant could come over," Tonia suggested.

That settled, Danvers and Hardy helped Orson with the body under the coverlet.

"I'll see her to the morgue," the constable said. "Then I want this house searched top to bottom, every nook and cranny. I'll get some help in from Rochester."

"Right," Danvers replied. "We'll make a start now if you've no objections."

42

Orson shook his large, square head. He was clearly still dazed. "Be obliged, sir. Could use the help."

In a few minutes Bessie was asleep, and Tonia and Gilchrist were alone. "Gil, I can't believe this. How did you come to show up here?"

He grinned the boyish grin that had always won her heart, even when it looked as if he might be guilty of a horrible crime. He wore his blond hair longer now and his somber black suit and tie made him look years older than when he was a medical student in Edinburgh, but he hadn't lost his shy, engaging manner. "Dr. Benson needed a locum. He knew me from when I visited Aunt Elfrida, so it seemed natural he should ask me since I know some of the area."

"And Madelyn?"

The young doctor's blue eyes sparkled, and his cheeks flushed. "Ah, she's grand. Only three more months to wait now. Her father's running the mill overtime, weaving tartan for the young laird."

Oh, yes. Tonia remembered. There was nothing the diffident Gilchrist looked less like than a highland chief, but the title would come to him one day. And then to his son. So the title was secure. That one. There would be an heir for Lochiel. "Gil, quick, before they come back—I need to talk to you."

She drew him into the sitting room where they could talk freely with no concern of waking the sleeping Bessie.

"Penthurst is the best," Gil was saying when Charles came in sometime later after completing his search of the house.

"Tonia." He strode to his wife and took both her hands in his. "What a dreadful day this has been for you. I'm so sorry this should have happened. Did Tonia tell you, Gil? She hasn't been sleeping at all well lately. Did you ask him for some powders, Tonia?"

"No. No, I didn't. We were talking of . . . other things."

Gil looked immediately concerned. "You should have

43

told me, Antonia. I'll have some made up right away and sent to you at Aethelsham."

She started to argue, then stopped. What difference did it make? Whether she slept or not, it all came down to the same thing.

On the ride back to Aethelsham, tucked cozily in the closed brougham, swaying to the rhythm of the carriage as the iron-rimmed wheels rolled over the snow-packed roads, Tonia went over it all again in her mind. She knew what she had to do, and yet how could she? It was the only possibility, and yet how could she deceive Charles? If only she could turn to him now, throw herself into his arms, and tell him all. But that could well be throwing away their last chance—if any chance remained.

She had deceived him this long, she could go on doing so for a few more weeks. Even on this deeper, far more dangerous, level of deception.

It had been her mistake to marry him, thinking everything would be all right. Now she must live with the results of her mistake. No, as comforting as it sounded, she couldn't pass it off as a simple mistake. She must live with the results of her deception.

And she must deceive him even more.

5

The next morning Charles slipped quietly out the side door of the dressing room where he had spent a restless night. Of all the foul things to have happened yesterday—involving Tonia in a brutal murder when she was so fragile herself. Of course she wouldn't admit it. The girl was all pluck. That was one of the things he had admired most about her when, five years ago, she helped him track down a murderer in the frost and mud of Norfolk. And it seemed as if his life had been spring and summer ever since.

But lately he'd been worried. He couldn't put his finger on anything specific. She was still his lovely Antonia. But there had been a withdrawal, a sense of distance between them he had never thought would develop. It was as if something so engrossed her thoughts that sometimes she would look at him as if she had forgotten he was there—or as if she didn't recognize him. Certainly he had never thought to find himself sleeping on a cot in the dressing room and Tonia alone in that big bed a few feet from him.

He moved soundlessly down the long staircase. Exactly when had it all started? Had Tonia's abstraction come first or her nervousness? Either way, of late she seemed to jump at the slightest sound. And though she was still beautiful, she was paler, drawn looking, with tiny lines around her eyes, and she was thinner. He had been doing all he could, in an unobtrusive way, to tempt her to eat more. But now with the scene of that grisly murder fresh in her mind, he was afraid she would have less appetite than ever.

Charles pushed open the door to the conservatory off the south wing of the house. He drew a small pair of scissors from his pocket and smiled at his prey. Stepping softly as if it would take flight, he approached the dowager duchess's prized yellow rose, pampered into winter bloom in this hothouse. One snip and the perfect bud was his. He held it to his nose to savor its sweetness.

"So, I've caught you, thief!" The duchess's walking stick rapped so sharply on the tiles behind him that Danvers almost mashed the bud into his nose. "Is this the way you repay my hospitality, young man, by ravaging my rose-bush? You'd be far better off upstairs at this hour doing your duty to your wife—and to the inheritance, I might remind you. I never thought a son of Norville would be so slow. There must be weak stock on your mother's side. Must have been, or she wouldn't have died off. You didn't find me turning up my toes after Osbert was born."

"Allow me to remind you, Aunt Elfrida, that Eleanor was my mother's fifth child, and that she succumbed to pneumonia, not childbirth." For once he didn't find the dowager duchess's fustian amusing.

"Ah, yes. Well, that's quite as bad. Weak lungs. I only hope Tonia—"

"That will quite do, Aunt Elfrida." He gave a stiff bow. "If you will permit me, I will return to my duty as you admonish me to do. I plucked this rose for Tonia's breakfast tray."

"Well, then, why are you standing here nitter-nattering? Go see to it, boy." She gave him a prod in the ribs with her walking stick.

Danvers waylaid Hardy in the hall outside their room

and took the linen-draped tray from him. Placing the rose, now in a crystal vase, on the tray, he rapped on the door.

"Come in, Hardy."

"Sure and it's myself wishing you the top o' the morning." No one ever looked less like a leprechaun than the tall, dark, spare Danvers, but he gave his best imitation, and the disparity gave the moment a hilarity that Tonia and he both much welcomed. He drew the curtains, then placed the tray on her knees and a kiss on her cheek.

"My love, I'm off to help poor, bumbling Constable Orson with his investigation. Pity the fellow. He should be able to spend his life in a quiet place like this with nothing more than a brisk case of egg robbing to deal with."

Tonia absently touched the velvet petals of the rose with the tip of her finger. "Charles, I've been thinking about Mrs. Bacon—"

"Now that's exactly what I don't want you to do." He plopped onto the bed beside her, slathered a piece of toast with pale-green lime marmalade, and held it out to her. "Orson and I will see to what has to be done. You stay tucked up cozy today." He looked out the window where a sharp north wind was whipping up flurries of yesterday's snow.

Antonia obediently took a bite, then put the toast aside. "Mmm, I don't know, Charles. I had thought of paying a call on Harriet Launceston. She lives quite near here. I haven't seen her since we made our come-out together. She married Squire Launceston about two years later, I think."

The glass in the north window rattled as a fresh gust of wind hurled against it.

"Don't go out, Tonia."

Her reply was muffled by a bite of egg, but he took the gentle look in her eyes as an affirmative. Not wanting to press her further, he kissed her on the forehead and left.

The door clicked shut.

Tonia took a quick swallow of tea and jumped out of bed. Not bothering to wrap a shawl around her shoulders, in spite of the drafts in the room, she hurried across the floor and knelt before the bottom drawer of a large, carved chest. She dug for several seconds beneath stacks of carefully folded underlinen. No, not under her shirts or chemises. She paused momentarily over the delicate white-on-white embroidered vests she had stitched so carefully for her wedding trousseau, then moved on. Rolled in the leg of a pair of lace-edged drawers she found it.

The roll of pound notes was distressingly small. It would be enough for today, but then she must see what could be done. She had a more than adequate income, but a lady was not accustomed to dealing in cash beyond such miscellaneous needs as tipping or an impulse to buy flowers from a street seller. Of course Charles was the soul of generosity. But asking for money would lead to questions she wasn't prepared to answer. She tucked the folded notes in her reticule.

When Isabella came in a few minutes later to help her mistress dress, Antonia was in bed, chewing thoughtfully on a crust of toast.

With visions of Tonia warm and secure at Aethelsham, Danvers determined to put his domestic concerns out of his mind and concentrate fully on helping the befuddled Orson.

"I'm sure you'll want to start by questioning Bessie again," he suggested, sitting across the desk from the constable, who had just broken his third nib in his struggle with filling in forms.

Orson swore under his breath and looked at Danvers blankly.

"It will help a great deal if we can get some idea why the dustmen set on Mrs. Bacon," Charles prodded.

Orson rubbed his stubby black beard with ink-stained fingers. "Er . . . right. Quite right."

"I rather thought I'd read your mind on the matter."
Danvers rose. "I know you won't want to waste any more
time. My man is outside with the carriage."

Lowering his head against the wind and holding to
the brim of his tall black hat, Charles led the way.

Randolph Lansing's stoop-shouldered little maid,
Mrs. Gillie, opened the door of 9 Ordnance Terrace. This
time Danvers noticed that it wasn't just that she was stooped
—one shoulder seemed actually deformed. That must make
her slow and awkward with some of her duties. It was
good of Lansing to keep her on.

Tucking a few strands of gray hair behind her ear,
she held the door wide. "Hurry in, hurry in. It's sharp cold
out there."

Danvers wondered whether her concern was for their
comfort or for guarding the respectability of Ordnance
Terrace against letting it be known that there was a policeman in the house.

As Mrs. Gillie led up the stairs, the cream-and-green
stripes of the wallpaper showed all too clearly where the
bloodstains had been scrubbed away. "Yes, that young
doctor's been and gone already. Said our Bessie was doing
fine but ought to stay in bed another day. Don't want the
bleeding to start up again, that's for sure."

"It was very kind of your employer to let you help his
neighbor," Danvers said.

"Oh, aye. I'm not to leave her for one minute, he
said. Terrible thing that happened. We have to do what we
can to help."

Bessie was sitting up in bed, her broad, freckled features, heavy arms, and rough hands looking oddly out of
place against Catherine Bacon's delicate, tatting-edged
sheets.

She lowered the penny dreadful she was reading,
but not before Danvers caught the title. *Blood in the Cellar.*
He shuddered. One would think the girl had had enough

of that in real life not to want more in the pages of a cheap thriller.

"Good morning, Bessie. Mrs. Gillie said you took a good breakfast this morning, so the constable here and I are hoping you can give us some helpful information."

"I'll do all I can. Don't know what I can tell that I haven't already, though."

Danvers took her back through yesterday's events, but she had little to add apart from a few details about the appearance of the dustmen. The tall one, apparently even taller than Danvers, had thin features with a hawklike nose and heavy eyebrows. "He might 'ave had a scar on his cheek too. Or maybe just not a good job shaving. I think it was 'im that slashed me, but I can't be sure."

"And the other one?"

"Short. Light hair, I think. I didn't get a very good look at 'im. All I remember much is his bright red neckerchief—like his throat had been slit. I remember thinking that when I felt the knife—" She broke off with a shiver, making little choking noises.

"There, there, now. Don't distress yourself." Orson reached across and patted her hand awkwardly.

"Right," Charles continued briskly. "Now what we're looking for is a motive. You said you'd never seen them before?"

Bessie shook her head, and a few strands of rust-colored hair straggled across the pillow. "No. Never. Our regular dustmen come tomorrow. They're both middling height. One's young and fat, t'other old and skinny—sort of dried like."

"So do you have any idea why the two who attacked you and Mrs. Bacon might have done so?"

Bessie shrugged. "Robbery, I guess. The old lady had lots of valuables." She gestured around the room. A carved jade goddess beside a Chinese vase on the mantel. An engraved silver dresser set in the grape pattern Mrs.

Bacon seemed to have favored. "I suppose she caught them thieving and they set on 'er."

"But in the cellar? They would hardly be thieving down there."

"I thought o' that. They must of snuck in when I brought in the coal bucket. They was waitin' in the cellar until the coast was clear. But then Mrs. B. found 'em. She probably set up a howl—she would've done—and they bashed her to keep her quiet. Voice like a banshee she had."

"Now see here, girl—" Orson sprang to the defense of his surrogate grandmother "—I'll not have that kind of talk. See that you speak well of the dead."

Bessie subsided into her pillows.

Danvers nodded. "Yes, I suppose that makes sense. But why—did you leave the door open when you went for the coal?"

"I could've done. The hod's heavy. Need both 'ands on it."

"It doesn't explain why they would drag her upstairs though. Why not just leave the body in the cellar?"

Bessie considered that one. "Maybe she wasn't dead yet, and they thought they could make her show them where her most valuable stuff was. Or maybe—"

Orson interrupted. "Nonsense. Panic. Pure panic it was. All it can be. Nothing else makes sense. Makes little enough sense at that."

Charles agreed. "But then, murder's always senseless, isn't it?" He looked about the room. "So do you think they got away with anything? Have you noticed anything missing in this room?"

Bessie looked around, but Orson spoke. "Not likely, is it, with two bodies lyin' bleeding at their feet that they'd open their swag bags and set to work?"

"Perhaps not in here," Danvers said. "But maybe downstairs. If they thought Bessie was dead, there was no reason for them to hurry off. Perhaps in the parlor. I know

Dr. Morris doesn't want you moving about yet, Bessie, but can you think of some of the most valuable ornaments—things that would be likely to catch a robber's eye? We could just have a look then."

The maid hesitated.

"It will help our investigation if the trail doesn't get cold. Please try to think."

"Well—" she bit her lower lip "—let me see. There was the pair of figures on the mantel. They was pretty. I don't know about value, but Mrs. B. liked 'em." She paused. "Oh, them carvings in the dining room. They must've been worth a penny. Mrs. B. yelled at me every time I dusted 'em. Ivory, she said they were. 'Twas all the same to me. Had to be dusted the same whether they was valuable or not. Mrs. B. wouldn't have no dust about even if she was so blind as it'd make no difference to her."

Orson bristled again. "Now see here, let's not have any complaining. It was your job to do the dusting, and I hope you did a right good job of it. Mrs. Bacon was a fine lady."

"Course she was. And I got me throat slit for 'er, didn't I? And a lot of good it did either of us."

Mrs. Gillie came in to offer the gentlemen refreshment before they left. Orson's blunt features softened. "Ah, if you could just be heating up a cup of cocoa? That is, if there's any of Mrs. Bacon's excellent chocolate powder on the shelf?"

Mrs. Gillie nodded and left the room, head jutting forward.

The men looked first in the dining room. Three carved ivory figures stood on the heavy lace runner that covered the sideboard. Two were oriental figures, the other some kind of animal with long antlers.

"Hard to tell if there's any missing, but it seems unlikely they would take some and leave these." Danvers ran his long fingers over the graceful, curving lines of the Chinese woman. He paused at the figure of the child, so skill-fully enfolded in her robes as to be almost hidden.

But in the parlor Orson said, "Here now, what's this? Didn't our Bessie say there was *two* figures?"

Danvers looked back at the notes he had made on a small pad. "She definitely said a pair." He turned to the mantel. "And there's only one here now. Figures like this were always done in pairs. The other one should be a shepherdess, probably holding flowers and with a dog at her feet. Shouldn't be hard to spot in a pawnshop. I'll get Hardy busy on it right away."

As he spoke, Hardy came up from the cellar where he had been searching for any clues they might have missed the day before. "None of 'em was so considerate as to leave a calling card behind. But you can't be expecting manners like that of dustmen, can you?" He held up a tall green bottle. "Found another of these, though. Begging your pardon, Constable—know you were right fond of her —but it does look like the old dearie enjoyed her tipple."

Orson shook his head. "Not her." He was about to say more, but Mrs. Gillie entered with a tray bearing a long-necked cocoa pot and three mugs.

Danvers hurried to take it from her gnarled hands. "Thank you, Mrs. Gillie. We'll just drink this and then see ourselves out. You have enough to do without waiting on us."

She cocked her head to look at him. "You're very kind, sir. That's very thoughtful of you."

The cocoa was a sad disappointment. Ready to revel in one last cup for auld lang syne, Orson filled his mug to the brim and drank deeply. He set the remains down with a shake of his square head. "That's not cocoa. Warm milk. That's what that is. Where's the chocolate?"

"Well, drink it up anyway, Constable. It'll fortify you against the cold."

Danvers told Hardy to return the tray to the kitchen. "Then see what Bessie can tell you about the porcelain figure that seems to be missing. I want you to ask around at the pawnbrokers. See if the figure has turned up or if anyone matching the assailants' description has been offering valuables around in the last twenty-four hours."

Tracking down the snow shovelers was almost as hard as getting a lead on the illusive dustmen. With the snow a day old now, most people had shoveled their own walks. And with the wind blowing it around like autumn leaves, people were unlikely to pay to have cleared away what would probably be blown back in a few hours.

But the lads were tenacious. A postman reported seeing two boys with snow shovels three streets over, so Danvers and Orson set out to follow that lead. They had gone less than half the way when Danvers's feet were freezing. He heartily wished he had taken the carriage and let Hardy proceed on foot.

And when they finally found the boys there was little in what they had to say that justified his chilled feet.

"No, gov'nor, we didn't see nobody like that." The older boy looked at Danvers with wide, brown eyes. He was probably twelve, although, undernourished as he was, it was hard to judge.

"Didn't see nuffing." The younger one dug the toe of his scuffed boot in a mound of snow by the side of the road.

"Coo, if we had," the first one continued, "the sight o' that there woman bleedin' at the neck woulda took it clean out of our minds."

Danvers produced a shiny copper for each boy. But even that marvelous sight did nothing to jog their memories.

He hailed a hackney, and Constable Orson knew his beat well enough to direct the cabby to a warm, dry public house, which—being the one nearest the Chatham refuse tip—was the most likely to be frequented by local dustmen. Feeling thoroughly overdressed in his tall black hat of waterproofed French silk and overcoat with a black velvet collar, Danvers took a seat in the darkest corner The Dirty Dog had to offer, allowing Orson to take the lead.

The constable knew several of the men by name, and none refused his offered half-pint of the local, but his description of the men Bessie saw drew only head shakes.

"Not round here, Constable."

"No one reg'lar."

Orson was on his third round and still making no headway. Charles was ready to suggest they call it a day. It was beginning to look as if the murderers were not from the area. Probably passing vagrants. If so, the stolen goods could show up anywhere in southeast England and the thieves never be caught.

Besides, the local ale was sour, the plate of chops he ordered were unchewable, and he missed Antonia. He thought of her sitting before the fire swathed in his favorite dusty-rose velvet afternoon dress, reading or doing needlework. Or playing the piano. Perhaps working on that new book of *leider* he had bought her for Christmas.

That's what he wanted to do—go back to Aethel-sham and have Antonia play Schumann. And he would sing. The perfect way to spend a winter afternoon. He'd been a fool to offer to help Orson just because he'd happened to be there when the body was found. Let the man muddle along on his own. Danvers had family matters to see to, and this was no business of his. He got to his feet.

The gust of wind that blew two newcomers into The Dirty Dog almost thrust Danvers back into his chair.

"Right, mates, and haven't we come on a spot of luck. Set 'em up for all in the house, landlord!" A well-built man with aristocratic features, who could easily have passed as a duke or prince had he not been dressed in the linsey-woolsey shirt and leather waistcoat of a dustman, was greeted with general cries of welcome.

"Hullo, Toff."

"Win at the horses, did you?"

"Nah, I'm not a betting man, and ye know it." He drew out a couple of pound notes and gave them to the publican. "Llewyelan and me found a fancy bit in a bin. Worth enough to treat our mates, it was."

Charles sat back in his corner, watching carefully. For the first time he noted the quiet, dark-visaged man— Welsh?—behind the effusive Toff. Two dustmen, not matching any description of Bessie's, had come on a bit of luck. Found it in a dustbin, did they? Well, that remained to be seen.

But Toff and Lewyelan were adamant about their stories. A small oval painting it was. "About so big." Toff put his thumbs and forefingers together to show size and shape. "A right little lordling he were, yellow curls and a shiny blue suit wif a lace collar."

"And you found it in a bin? Where?" Orson demanded.

"Not in a bin rightly," Llewyelan began but subsided at a sharp jab in the ribs from Toff.

"The bin were full, you see, lots of papers and such strewing about. It's all the same—property of the dustman, same as if it'd been in the bin."

Orson raised a broad hand to calm him. "Nobody's questioning your right to go bin diving, Toff. We just want to know where this particular bin was. You see, some items seem to have gone missing—"

"We didn't steal." Llewyelan's dark eyebrows flared wide. "I'm chapel. Devout. Ask anyone."

Danvers noticed the little Welshman was drinking clear cider. Undoubtedly devout chapel.

"Where was the bin?" Orson continued with greater persistence than Danvers would have given him credit for. Good. He could leave the matter in the constable's hands with a clear conscience.

The dustmen's answer was no surprise. In the alleyway behind Ordnance Terrace. Apparently near enough to Number 9 that the pseudo-dustmen could easily have dropped it and probably turned over the bin as well in their haste to flee.

It was odd that no one seemed to have seen them, but all the gardens in that quiet neighborhood had high walls and not many people had been out in the snow that morning. If Orson kept on doggedly enough he would probably get his witness in the end. Then the case could be neatly tied up, hopefully with the apprehension of the murderers.

They met Hardy back at the police station. He had had less luck than they. But then it had been a long shot. He'd had little enough to go on. When Bessie was up and about, she could make a detailed list of anything missing. When she was able to go through each room, she would know exactly.

For now, Danvers could think of nothing but getting back to the comfort of Aethelsham. He was cold, he'd accomplished nothing today, he'd had nothing to eat but a mug of weak chocolate and a plate of indigestible chops— and above all, he missed Antonia.

"Spring the horses, Hardy."

Then he retreated to a corner of the seat and pulled the lap rug up to his neck. Through all the miserable ride across the winter landscape in the deepening dusk he held to the picture of his radiant Antonia and a blazing fire at the end of his journey.

The first thing he found blazing at Aethelsham, however, was not the welcoming hearth of the dowager duchess's drawing room. Rather, it was the tempers of his oldest and youngest sisters. Eleanor had apparently come down from London and was irate to find Agatha interfering in her affairs.

"You are not my mother. You are not my guardian. You have no right to say that!" Eleanor pulled off her wine velvet hat and flung it on a table. Her black curls bounced with each step as she advanced on Agatha, who stood firmly in the center of the room.

"I am perfectly well aware that I am not your guardian. I thank Providence for the fact every day. But that does not deny me the right of forming an opinion and doing what I can to keep the family name from being besmirched by the likes of Randolph Lansing."

Eleanor looked as if she would spring at Agatha. Then she checked herself and turned sharply to stamp from the room.

She all but stamped on the foot of Charles, who was directly behind her. "Charles!" She flung herself into his arms with a sob. "Charles, make her stop! Make Aggie stop. She's being horrid, and it isn't true, not a word of it. My Randy's not like that, he isn't. He's sweet and sensitive, and he makes me laugh more than anyone I've ever met. And he's talented and from a very good family and—"

"Yes, yes." Charles wrapped his arms around her and rocked gently from side to side. "I've met your paragon. And I quite agree. He's perfectly charming. As a matter of fact, he's doing a portrait of Antonia and me."

"Oh, Charles!" She jerked up on tiptoe and flung her arms around his neck. "You're the best, kindest, smartest brother in the whole world! What would I ever do without you? So you won't stand in our way? I can tell Randy he can speak to you?"

Danvers gently unclasped her hands from behind his neck and led her to a sofa before the fireplace. "Now, Nelly, the fellow is pleasant enough and seems a capable painter. That doesn't mean I'll give him one of my favorite sisters for a wife."

Eleanor grabbed his arm. "But you'll talk to him? You won't order him off the place if he calls?"

"Of course not. After all, Aethelsham's not my place. It's Aunt Elfrida's, and I gather she's quite disposed toward him."

Eleanor clasped Danvers's arm and laid her head on his shoulder with a sigh. "You are the best of brothers."

Agatha gave a loud sniff and started from the room with her nose in the air, her back stiff.

She was halted, however, by the sharp raps of the walking stick and the sharper words of the dowager duchess. She had the butler, Soyer, and three maids in tow.

"What do you mean you haven't seen her since morning? Poppycock! The girl had duties. I won't have such dereliction." She strode to the bell pull by the fireplace and gave it repeated short jangles. "I will have them all, do you hear? I want every servant in the house here. Now."

In a few minutes the entire Aethelsham staff stood at attention in a line of descending importance from butler to backstairs scivvy. The dowager duchess rapped her walking stick, and every back—even the rigid Soyer's—straightened even more.

Her Grace of Aethelsham, the jet fringes that framed the yoke of her severe black dress glinting sharply in the light of the gas lamps, paced slowly along the line, peering at each alarmed face through her lorgnette.

"Mrs. Crompton," she addressed the ample figure of the cook, "where is Lily?"

Mrs. Crompton dipped a curtsy but did not bend her back. "I'm sure I don't know, ma'am. She had breakfast in the servants' hall same as always. She weren't there for tea, but I didn't pay that much mind. I thought she must have duties elsewhere."

The dowager duchess moved down the line. She rounded on the parlor maid. "Molly, what can you tell me about this?"

Danvers, standing between his sisters on the far side of the drawing room, whispered to Agatha. "What is it now?"

Agatha shrugged. "Domestic crisis. Seems the maid Lily has disappeared. Good riddance, I say. The girl thought too much of herself by half. Not as I would cast aspersions on the way someone else chooses to run their household, but I won't tolerate servants getting above themselves."

The dowager duchess was nearing the end of the line, having learned nothing more useful than the fact that Lily hadn't been seen since breakfast but that she had seemed excited then.

"Always kept herself to herself, she did," Susan, the upstairs maid, said with a toss of her head. "Thought she was too good to mix with the likes of us. She's probably gone off with that fancy man of hers she was always hinting about."

"That will be quite enough, Susan," Soyer reprimanded before his mistress could.

There was a stir behind the rigid line of servants as Isabella hurried in, looked about in surprise, and took a place just beyond the end of the lineup. She stood politely but not at rigid attention.

Edward, the underfootman, concluded his interrupted testimony. "I haven't seen her all day, Your Grace."

The dowager duchess glowered at thirteen-year-old Tilly, the scivvy, who had been attempting to roll down her sleeves unobtrusively and had achieved only partial success. When the full gaze of the great lady of the house was turned on her, Tilly broke into a flood of tears.

"I don't know where she is. But I wish I did. She was so pretty. She always smiled at me. She was so kind—" She broke off with a loud sniff and barely stopped herself in time to prevent the disgrace of wiping her nose on her sleeve in the best drawing room.

The dowager duchess sent Tilly from the room with a wave of her hand and turned to Isabella. "Well, what can you tell us? Where is she?"

Antonia's maid dipped her head and fidgeted with her skirt. "Oh, Your Grace, I am so sorry." She looked across the room to Danvers. "Sorry, sir. Truly I am. She said she was going calling. But now it's getting so late—and dark and cold. And another storm coming up, I'm sure."

A rap of the walking stick cut her off. *"Calling?* Have you taken leave of your senses, girl?" She peered at the maid through her lorgnette as if to see whether the girl's brains were intact. "My maid does not go calling."

"Maid?" Isabella blinked her round, dark eyes. "Oh, I thought . . . that is, you see . . . Lady Danvers . . ."

Charles covered the width of the room in three strides. "Lady Danvers! Do you mean to say my wife's gone too?"

"Right after breakfast, she . . . she . . ." Isabella broke off with a hiccup.

"And she went out alone? You let your mistress go out unattended?"

"I offered, sir. But she said she'd take one of the carriages and that the groom would be enough . . ."

Isabella chattered on, but Charles could listen to no more. He strode from the room and up the long staircase without thinking where he was going. In their room Isabella had already closed the heavy draperies against the cold night, but he flung them open and stood peering out into the blackness. The wind howled and flung a bare branch against the window.

He should be questioning the grooms. He should be organizing a party to go out and search for her. But for the moment the gloom held him immobile. The darkness that had come upon his life when Charlotte died and had lifted only when he found Antonia—all the shades of despondency that his love for Tonia and their growing faith had chased away (forever, he had thought)—all descended on him.

He should pray. Indeed, he tried, but his mind whirled with visions of runaway horses, a carriage lying smashed in a ditch, and what if those desperate men who bludgeoned Catherine Bacon to death had set upon Tonia?

6

Danvers whirled at the sound of the door opening behind him.

She stood framed in the entrance, the light from the lamp in her hand illuminating her copper hair and green velvet mantelette.

"Tonia!"

She looked so lovely, so inexpressibly dear. His relief after having thought her lost made him almost too weak to cross the room to her. He took the lamp and set it on a table so that he could fold her in his arms unhampered. "Tonia, Tonia. I was so worried." He buried his face in her hair.

At last he raised his head and pulled back to look at her. "What do you mean by going off like that?" It was the whiteness of her face against the almost fevered brightness of her eyes that brought the reaction from him. "I told you to stay in. Do you realize the whole household has been upset?" His fingers gripped her shoulders. He barely stopped himself from shaking her.

She drew away and began removing her buff doeskin gloves. "I do apologize, Charles. I've already apologized to Aunt Elfrida. It seems I misjudged. Thanington was farther than I quite realized. Then Even took a wrong turning coming home."

"'Misjudged'! 'Wrong turning'! Don't you realize you could have been killed! I thought—" He broke off. "I don't know what I thought, but, oh, Antonia, don't do that to me again."

"I am sorry to have worried you, Charles. But as you can see, I'm quite unharmed. Tomorrow we can spend the entire day together. We won't even leave our room if you wish, although I can't imagine what Aunt Elfrida would say to that." Her chuckle sounded forced, but it was calming just to hear her voice.

He ran his fingers through his tousled black hair. "I only wish I could, but I promised Aunt Elfrida I'd go to Canterbury for that nuisance architectural committee of hers."

"Oh, but that's perfect." Tonia's answer was bright— a shade too bright. "We shall spend our day together in Canterbury. I've been longing to see the cathedral. You shall give me a most thorough tour, and then I will sit in the best tea shop in town while you attend your fusty old meeting." She gave him a peck on the cheek. "And Charles, don't sleep in that drafty old dressing room tonight. It's much nicer in here."

The next morning Antonia sat before her mirror wearing her best wine-velvet visiting dress while Isabella put the finishing touches on the curls that would peep from under each side of her velvet and satin bonnet. "Now bring my jewel case, Isabella."

"Perhaps your pearl drops, my lady?" Isabella brought the red lacquer case from the top drawer of the chest and lifted the pearl-inlaid lid.

"I think the gold filigree set with garnets for this dress." Isabella started to remove the earrings from the case, but Tonia held up her hand. "No, wait, I'm not sure." She poked through the assortment of jewels offered, then

63

lifted the tray and looked deeper. "Just leave me for a minute, Isabella, while I consider. Maybe the emeralds . . ."

"My lord likes those. He always says they match your eyes," Isabella said as she turned to fold her mistress's nightdress.

Tonia quickly pulled out the bottom drawer of the chest, picked a heavy diamond-and-emerald brooch off the velvet lining, and shut the drawer before slipping the brooch into her reticule. "I've decided on the garnets, Isabella. You may put them on. Then lock the case away."

When Danvers came in wearing his black, caped cloak, Antonia was ready in her wine-velvet wrap trimmed with soft brown mink.

Yesterday's storm had passed, and the gently rolling land lay open to the temperamental winter sunshine. Drifts of snow lay banked against the brown, bare hedgerows lining the fields. Hardy drove the dowager duchess's best pair of chestnuts, which stepped lively in the crisp air, blowing puffs of white steam from their dark noses.

Tonia took Charles's arm and smiled at him. She had determined to make up for distressing him so yesterday. It had been a terrible miscalculation. She hadn't realized the return train would be so late. The thought crossed her mind that she could tell him now. She was going to have to sooner or later, and it was always easy to talk to the accompanying gentle sway of a carriage.

But she didn't really know anything for sure yet. No, it would be far better to have this one enjoyable day. If it was to be one of their last, let it be perfect. Perhaps she would tell him tonight. If she had the courage.

She leaned back against the well-padded cushions and closed her eyes. Some time later she opened them in response to his nudge.

"There it is." He pointed. "Canterbury."

Tonia stared. "Oh, it's magnificent." She spoke in a whisper, her breath caught in her throat. She hadn't been prepared for the emotional impact the great building would have on her. Towering above trees and rooftops, the central bell tower led its smaller twin towers, capped with gilded pinnacles, in a great upward hosanna to the sky. The sun glistened on the carved golden stone and traceried Gothic windows lining the long nave. Here was the seat of the faith she had been taught from birth. Here were the roots of so much of the history of England.

They drove along the High Street, the traditional pilgrims' route, and turned up Mercery Lane, an alley lined with shops and stalls that had replaced the booths selling such medieval mementos as souvenirs of pilgrimage, medallions of Saint Thomas, and bottles of healing water from Becket's Well in the cathedral crypt. Peddlers' pushcarts now offered colorful shawls and tawdry jewelry. The lane bustled with tourists and merchants as it had done ever since the Middle Ages.

Hardy slowed the carriage to enter the cathedral precincts by Christ Church Gate.

"The last major building before the Dissolution." Danvers waved toward the gate's rows of colorful arms and crenellated towers. "And one of the earliest examples of a late Gothic building, incorporating as it does Renaissance touches in its style." He shook his head. "Goodness only knows what Lansing and his 'improvers' will do to it. Probably want to put gargoyle-studded spires on the towers— and a similar scheme for the Great Harry as well, no doubt."

Antonia looked at broken stones on the pilasters flanking the entrance arches of Christ Church Gate. Time, wind, rain, and frost had taken their toll. "It would be pure vandalism to destroy such beauty. But there *is* a need for repairs."

"True restoration, yes. Returning what's been spoiled to its original beauty in keeping with the design of the creator. But I'll fight to the death to keep some sham romantic front from being foisted on Canterbury."

"Of course you're absolutely right, Charles. I can't wait to see the interior."

"Sorry, my love. Afraid that will have to wait a bit. I forgot to tell you the meeting is first. But we can spend all afternoon going over the cathedral."

"That's fine, Charles. I'll have no trouble amusing myself in the shops. Some we passed in the High Street had very colorful window displays."

Tonia scowled at his order to Hardy to "stay with Lady Danvers." It would have been much easier if she could have gone alone. She clutched her reticule in both hands. She had noted a particularly promising pawnshop just before they turned into Mercery Lane. She would have to contrive something.

Hardy left the carriage with the hostler at the inn where they had agreed to meet for lunch, and Tonia docilely permitted herself to be escorted up the street.

She spent some time in a French millinery shop, poring over an exquisite collection of fans. A small blue brisé fan with ivory sticks engraved in a floral design and embossed with gold especially took her eye. She moved on to one with sticks of pearl matrix, painted with scenes from *The Barber of Seville.* She swallowed at a lump in her throat as she recalled happier days when Charles had sung Count Almaviva's aria from Act III to her, and she had chided him for being off-key. She moved on to a fan of Chantilly lace mounted on carved ivory.

Hardy showed no sign of offering to take himself off to a public house, and after yesterday she dare not dismiss him. If anything should go wrong today, Charles might not forgive her no matter how anything else turned out. Yesterday was the first time she had seen him truly angry with her in all their marriage. In truth, his temper was short-lived, and it had all been for her welfare. But she was warned.

"Thank you, I don't think I see just what I'm looking for." She smiled, and the shopgirl returned her black velvet tray to the glass case.

Antonia turned right, working her way slowly toward her goal at Mercery Lane. A bow-windowed sweet shop had gathered a clutch of children gazing at the colorful sticks of hard candy and jars of fruit drops and lozenges. If she gave Hardy a few shillings and told him to treat the children, she might be able to snatch enough time. No, it wouldn't do to be hurried. She was uneasy enough about what she must do.

A painted teapot hanging over the next doorway announced the refreshment being served beyond its lace-curtained windows. But the next shop window brought her to a full stop so abruptly that Hardy, following patiently behind, almost ran into her.

"M'lady, sorry I am. Gazing at the cathedral I was. What a fine sight to be sure."

But she paid no attention to his ramblings. She bent to scrutinize a delicate porcelain figure surrounded by a brass Turkish smoker, a set of crystal paperweights, and a case displaying a pair of long-barreled dueling pistols. Where had she seen a figure like that recently?

Not at Aunt Elfrida's, and yet she was certain it had been since they left London. Yesterday at—no. She remembered. In the parlor of that poor murdered Mrs. Bacon.

She had thought it strange at the time that the shepherd had no matching shepherdess. And here she was.

Perhaps Mrs. Bacon had been forced to sell some of her things, but it was odd to have broken up the pair. They would have fetched far more as a set. Charles had been reluctant to talk about his investigations last night, though he had said they were following the line that the dustmen had been surprised in a robbery.

"Hardy, look." She pointed.

He bent forward, hands on knees, and knocked his derby against the windowpane. "Well, faith, and if I didn't spend all day yesterday treading the streets of Chatham looking for this very thing."

"Hardy, you go question the shopkeeper. If you think it's the right one, you'd better find a constable. I think I saw a policeman near Christ Church Gate. I'll just go on up the street and see if I spot anything in any of the other shops. I noticed another pawnbroker's at the top of the street." She moved quickly away.

When they met at the inn at the appointed hour for luncheon, Tonia's reticule was lighter but considerably thicker for the presence of a roll of banknotes. However no one would notice such a detail as Hardy regaled them with an account of his success.

"No doubt about it, m'lord. Remember the red anchor on the bottom what you told me to look for? Well, the shepherdess had the identical mark. The constable held it for evidence and sent a note off to Orson. Only trouble was the shopkeeper said his assistant had taken the piece in a couple of days ago while he was home with the croup, so he couldn't tell us anything about whoever brought it in. Signature in the book looked like a man's, but we couldn't really make out the name."

"Good, good. That's fine, Hardy. I've no doubt Orson can handle things from here."

Hardy's face fell. "You mean a fine clue like that and you don't intend to follow it up?"

"That's exactly what I mean, Hardy. Let the duly established officials do their work. That's what they're there for. I intend to devote the rest of my day to considering far more pleasant things." He smiled at Antonia.

And she agreed.

From the moment she entered the west door of the great cathedral some time later and gazed down the full length of the magnificent Perpendicular nave of golden stone pillars and arches to the high altar, she felt the weight that had been growing inside her lift. It was impossible to stand beneath those lofty, interlacing vaults and not feel one's spirit drawn upward. What a great shout of praise this whole building was.

And then, far up in the choir, the organ started. It was probably the organist's regular practice time, but Antonia felt as if God had sent angels just to sing to her. Surely this was a sign that everything would be all right.

Her hand rested on Charles's arm as they walked the length of the nave. Then they stood at the stairs leading to the choir loft and gazed at the beautiful carved-stone choir screen with its rows of angels and monarchs. Next she looked up at the lacelike fan-vaulting. Its rich red, green, and gold design work was lighted by arched windows under the Bell Harry Tower.

"I'd like to hear the bell ring."

"No, you wouldn't. Not Great Harry," Danvers replied. "He tolls only for the death of the monarch or the archbishop of Canterbury."

"Oh." Tonia went up the wide steps toward the choir, then paused and looked back the length of the nave. "It's so incredibly beautiful. Such absolute perfection must be something of a reflection of the mind of God."

"But, my dear, any person of taste can see that it's much too light, too spacious." Charles's voice was heavy with satire. "It must be darker, more melancholy."

"Charles, no—Lansing can't mean to redecorate the nave."

"'Make it a vision of God brooding over the sins of the world' is more or less what he said."

"But that's terrible. It's such a wonderful vision of *heaven:* order, symmetry, harmony—all things combining to praise the Creator. If we can't leave off brooding over sin and rejoice in God here, where can we?"

He shook his head ruefully. "I can see your sensitivities have much to be informed. But come, I'll show you where the martyrdom was."

Charles turned toward the transcept to their left and pointed to a commemorative plate on the wall. "Here.

Becket was making for the altar, but he turned back to speak to Henry's knights."

"Who thought the king had asked them to kill his archbishop." She shook her head. "Martyrdom sounds so much better than murder, doesn't it?"

"Antonia! You didn't tell me you were coming to Canterbury today," a shrill voice interrupted.

Tonia turned toward the ebullient speaker, and her heart sank. Harriet Launceston. There was no way to avoid it—she must introduce her old friend to her husband. And how many sentences would it take before Harriet gave the whole thing away?

She'd been such a fool. Why hadn't she sworn Harriet to secrecy? Though it was unlikely it would have done any good if she had. Harriet never could keep a secret.

The woman's ample form, swathed in a deeply flounced Clarendon blue dress over the widest crinoline Antonia had ever seen, swooped toward them. She held out a gloved hand to Danvers, exposing at least six rows of lace ruffles lining her pagoda sleeve.

Charles bowed over the hand as Antonia offered introductions.

Before Harriet could make any reference to her call yesterday, Tonia steered the conversation in safer directions. "And what brings you to the cathedral today?"

"Horace's sister and her two dear little boys have come all the way from Scotland on holiday. You would have met Alice yesterday if you could have stayed longer. Anyway, the lads are so anxious for educational experiences. They were much excited to see the spot where the horrid murder of Thomas Becket took place. And here we are—Hamish, Angus?"

She looked to one side, then the other, turning much like a dog trying to see its tail. "Now where did those boys get off to? They are such dears. So lively and bright. Very lively, I must say—but good lads. And such sweet companions for my Lavinia. She's such a serious child, you know. Would spend all day at her music if she could. But what would she wind up with then, I ask you, but a horrid squint? And what good is a music education if it ruins your looks?" She nudged the pink-ruffled, blonde, twelve-year-old Lavinia, who indeed squinted at them.

Harriet started back toward the nave, still talking. "Very gifted, my Lavinia. Takes after me, you know. Horace can't carry a tune in a bucket." Then she stopped. "It was very nice to meet you, Lord Danvers, very nice. Antonia and I had such a sweet chat yesterday, but then I imagine she's told you all about that. We must talk more." She turned with a swish of her skirts and bustled up the north aisle, pulling Lavinia behind her and calling, "Hamish, Angus. Don't be naughty boys for auntie. Come along now . . ."

The sound of muffled giggling from the small chapel just beyond the transept told Antonia that Harriet would be back soon—and who could tell what she might say then?

"Charles, where did you have your meeting this morning?" Antonia sought a change of topic.

"Oh, right through here. Let me show you." He led the way out a side door. "The Chapter House has a most marvelously intricate roof."

Tonia gave a sigh of relief, which she hoped Charles would interpret as delight at the perfection of the Perpendicular arches and fan tracery of the Great Cloister.

In the Chapter House she gazed upward at the complex geometrics of the barrel ceiling until her neck ached. How long could she stay hidden in here? How long would it likely take Harriet to locate her nephews, show them the place of the martyrdom, and move on? Given Harriet's garrulousness, it could take quite some time.

The sound of two pairs of small, running feet on the stones of the cloisters behind her told Tonia it was time for her to move Charles on. Quickly. "What else is there to see of the monastery?" She would have loved to go back into

71

the cathedral itself, from which organ peals could still be heard, but she felt safer in the outlying parts.

"The Norman water tower is one of the oldest structures. Most of the main part of the church had to be rebuilt following a fire four years after the murder."

"Oh, good. Let's see that."

Tonia was thankful that the cloister remained deserted during the moments they walked along its passage again.

Then Charles led along a dim walkway, explaining that this was the passage the monks would have taken from their dormitory when they made their way to the choir to pray the night offices. She thought how cold and dark it must have been. It was cold enough now. Those stones probably never got warm even in summer.

The water tower was a round stone structure standing on arched pillars with ornate Gothic windows and a steep, conical leaded roof.

"The water tower and wash place was at the center of the new water system built just before Becket's time." Danvers paused only long enough for her to admire the remarkable workmanship. "But come, you must see the shrine." He strode along another walkway back toward the church.

Tonia thought of asking to be shown the crypt instead, but his long stride was unstoppable. Their way led up some steps, then along the north aisle to Trinity Chapel, the place that for hundreds of years had been the focus of their journey for thousands of Canterbury pilgrims.

She looked across a wide, empty space of bare, polished stone. "This is it? But there's nothing here."

Danvers shook his head. "For over three hundred years it was the finest shrine in all England—perhaps in all Christendom. It drew pilgrims from all walks of life. But then, you've read your Chaucer."

Tonia walked the full circle of the chapel, trying to imagine what it must have been like in medieval times.

She imagined being part of a group of wide-eyed pilgrims, waiting until a monk drew the cover off the shrine by a system of ropes and pulleys. The crowd would have gasped, many of the devout falling to their knees at the sight of the golden casket so heavily encrusted with jewels that the gold was barely visible. All had been gifts of pilgrims— many royal, some humble—who had come seeking the intercession of Saint Thomas for their souls.

Tonia blinked. "What a pity it's all gone."

On the south side of the chapel Danvers paused before a railed tomb and pointed to a stunning gilded bronze effigy. "At least this one escaped Henry's destroyers. But I'm afraid it may not escape Lansing and Aunt Elfrida's."

"What?"

"Edward the Black Prince. This tomb dates from the fourteenth century, but it seems that it has been given to the nineteenth century to correct the great error."

"What error?" Antonia admired the perfection of detail of the golden knight in plate armor. His head rested on his lion-crested helmet, gloved hands folded in prayer, a little dog at his feet.

"But isn't it obvious? He was the Black Prince. The effigy is gold."

"Charles, you can't be serious. Lansing can't mean to deface this?"

"Oh, but he does. Forthwith. With a thick coat of black paint."

"Can't you stop him?"

"Mine was the only voice of dissent—a voice crying in the wilderness. It seems the dean has given them free rein. He's an ardent admirer of the 'True Gothic.'"

Antonia was about to commiserate when a scrabbling noise from across the chapel caught her attention.

Then, "Och, you'll nae catch me!" A small Scottish voice rang out followed by giggles.

"Now, Hamish, dear, come to auntie."

"The crypt!" Tonia grabbed Danvers's arm and propelled him out of the chapel.

"Easy, my love. I had no idea you had such a passion to see the undercroft, although it *is* one of the finest in England." He patted the hand resting on his arm.

"Oh, I do, Charles. I do. I quite love crypts. So picturesque, you know. They give one the most delicious tingles, don't you think?"

"Well, I can't say I've given the matter much thought. Although to be sure, this one must be sufficiently gloomy even for Lansing's taste." He led her down a narrow staircase.

Antonia shivered. If she had been seeking Gothic chills, this would certainly have been the place for it. The enormous vault was lit with only a few gas lanterns for the convenience of visitors who might want to see where Becket's body had lain for fifty years until it was moved to the rebuilt Trinity Chapel above. No other visitors were present, and the pale, carved stone pillars supporting the low, arched ceiling glimmered in the faint light like a winter forest in the snow.

Danvers picked up a lantern from a nearby table and held it above his head to illuminate the capital of one of the columns. An exotic, winged creature leered down at Antonia. "Such carving shows the Byzantine influence—"

But Antonia's ears caught the giggling and clumping sounds of approaching danger, and she said, "Oh, but just see what's back here," propelling him forward before he had time to set the lamp back down.

She rushed along the ambulatory with such speed she almost cannoned into one of the massive support columns. Was she trapped down here? If there was only one entrance, they would be forced to go back through the undercroft where Harriet would be waiting to babble on about yesterday, asking her compromising questions in front of Charles while those little terrors climbed the pillars or worse.

"Oh, look, a little chapel." She started to dart into a small room to her right when the wavering light from the lamp indicated an opening in the wall farther along. "No, no. Let's see this one. It looks far more . . . romantic." She could hardly say "hidden."

The only trouble with having chosen such a hideaway was that the small chapel offered little she could use as an excuse to stay concealed here. She could only hope the boys would soon tire of their new playing field. The high-pitched squeals echoing off walls and ceilings, however, gave little hint of approaching boredom.

"Hold the light here, Charles. Can you read the inscription on this memorial tablet?" She led him to the corner farthest from the doorway.

Danvers obediently peered at the ancient carving in the weak light. He traced a few letters with a finger to make sure of the Latinate letters. Then he drew back with a satisfied smile. "Well, now, isn't that interesting? This is a chapel dedicated to Saint Gabriel—he it was who directed Joseph of Arimathea to build a church in honor of the Virgin Mary in Glastonbury. Joseph, you know . . ."

Tonia was delighted that Charles continued with his lecture, but her ears were occupied with sounds from the crypt. The boys now seemed to be engaged in a game of seek-and-find. Apparently Harriet had abandoned any attempt to keep them in tow, because their antics were accompanied by no tut-tutting.

Danvers was examining a niche holding an enameled casket—perhaps the relics of St. Gabriel? "Tonia, look at this."

As she bent her head close to his in an attempt to see better, Tonia caught a glimpse of a small form slithering into the chapel. It ducked behind a sarcophagus in the curve of the east wall.

"I'll find you, Hamish, no fear." Angus's voice rang from the undercroft.

Indeed there was no doubt as to the hider behind the casket's being found. The silence of the tomb held for perhaps three seconds. Then the tiny chapel rang with the terrified shrieks of wee Hamish.

7

Hamish hurtled from behind the stone coffin, then froze in the center of the chapel, still screaming. Tonia rushed to his side. Harriet, with Lavinia in tow, bustled in behind the wide-eyed Angus.

Danvers held the lamp aloft and peered into the darkness Hamish had vacated. "It appears Aunt Elfrida is to be denied the privilege of dismissing Lily," he said.

Tonia didn't want to look but knew she would regret her cowardice later if she didn't. It took her only a glance to confirm his statement. "Done by the same person who attacked Bessie, do you think?" she asked into his ear, as Hamish still let out howls behind her, accented by wild jabbings toward the spot.

"Could be. At a glance, the slit throat looks the same."

Too late Tonia saw Harriet and Angus turn to the sarcophagus. "Don't look—" Tonia began but was drowned out by Angus's cry, which outdid his brother's.

Harriet gave a piercing shriek and collapsed on top of the coffin. Lavinia, after one nearsighted squint into the darkness, turned calmly to pat her mother's insensate hand.

"And could you be using any assistance, m'lord?" The addition of two newcomers to the chapel—Hardy and

77

a man in uniform—filled the space that already seemed full to bursting with noise.

"Hardy, I've never been happier to see anyone in my life. See to that bedlam!"

Prepared for any emergency, Hardy pulled two rock-candy sticks out of his pocket and plunged one into each open mouth. The bellows ceased, although it seemed the stone walls still reverberated. "Now then, my laddies, that's better, isn't it? A great many sleepers there are down here —at least there were at one time. You wouldn't want to be disturbing their rest, would you?"

The boys looked at him wide-eyed and sucked on their sweets.

"Right, now. Fine, developed voices like your own ought to be put to some use. Seems like I saw some village lads forming up for choir practice upstairs. Shall we go show them how those songs ought to be sung?"

Hamish nodded, and Angus made no complaint.

"You too, lassie. Come along with ye." Hardy led the three children out with a signal to Danvers that they would be above in the choir.

Antonia turned her attention to the still-prostrate Harriet. She massaged her friend's temples. Then she looked through Harriet's bag to find her vinegarette.

She held the vial of astringent scent under the woman's nose, and after a few breaths the voluminous figure stirred. She coughed and sat up, clearing the way for Danvers and the uniformed man to deal with what was behind the sarcophagus.

Constable Miller introduced himself. He had come to Canterbury to ask a few questions about the Chelsea shepherdess, he explained, but in view of what they had here, that could wait.

"Come, Harriet. You need fresh air." Tonia led her friend out.

They found seats in the presbytery between the choir and altar, where a few others waited for the children to finish choir practice—which, from the perspiring red face of the choirmaster, Tonia judged could come none too soon.

He rapped his stick sharply. "Sims, we do not stand on the kneeling rail." Three more sharp raps. "Now again from the first. The pre-Lenten concert is only two weeks away." He mopped his forehead.

The choir made a wobbly start. "Lead us back to You, O Lord, that we may be restored. Give us anew such days as we had of old . . . "

A boy in the second row pinged a stone from a small catapult, then stuck the sling back into his pocket with a wide-eyed angelic look on his round face.

The atmosphere was hardly conducive to a confidential chat, but at least Tonia could speak to Harriet alone.

If Harriet would listen to any voice but her own. "Oh, that poor woman. Whatever could have happened? My poor nerves. My poor nerves. I'll never get over the shock, I'm sure. And my poor Lavinia." She gathered the child into a smothering embrace. "So delicate, just like her mother. I've never been strong. I'm sure you remember, even when we were girls." Her ample bosom heaved up and down as she patted her palpitating heart.

"Yes, Harriet, I remember. But I've got to talk to you about yesterday."

"Oh, yes, my dear Tonia. It was so grand to see you again after all those years. And we had been so close, really bosom friends. And now here you are married to a viscount—and taking notice of the wife of a mere squire. Not but that Horace hasn't done very well by me, you understand, very well indeed. But it's most condescending of you to be so kind."

"No, no, nothing like that, Harriet. Will you just listen? Yesterday morning after I left you—"

"Yes, and much too soon you left. I'm so happy for this little chat, Antonia. Next time you simply must stay to

79

tea. I won't hear of you leaving Thanington a second time without refreshment."

"That's what I want to talk to you about, Harriet. If I could just rely on you to say nothing—"

"Why, my dear Antonia, you may rely on me implicitly. Anything you want to ask. Anything you want to say. I'm entirely at your disposal. You know I've always been a very good listener. Anyone will tell you. Now just let it all out, and don't give a thought for that poor dead woman in the crypt."

A figure moved toward them from the north aisle.

Antonia sighed and stood to meet Charles. Any chance she had of forewarning Harriet of the delicacy of her situation was lost. At least this time she had no need to invent an excuse to keep him from Harriet's wagging tongue. Indeed, she almost had to run to keep up with his long strides through the choir and down the length of the nave. The sound of the choirmaster rapping his stick and pleading for attention was the last thing she heard before the massive west door slammed behind them.

The next morning Inspector Futter of Scotland Yard arrived at Aethelsham. His hair was no less white-blond, his round cheeks no less pink, his blue eyes no less clear than when Antonia had met him seven years before. Then, he had been a mere sergeant sent out from Norwich to investigate a particularly gory murder. She could see that the years of experience had added confidence to his bearing, as the cooking of his newly acquired wife had added to his girth. But his modest smile was no less winning as he looked at Tonia from a slightly ducked head.

"Ah, thank you for inquiring, Lady Danvers. Mrs. Futter is blooming indeed. There's nothing to top the bliss of the married state, is there? But then, you'd know all about that. Fact is, there'll be a little Futter any day now—just in time for our first anniversary." His smile grew even shyer and his cheeks redder.

"Well, congratulations, man." Danvers gave him a hearty handshake. "Under the circumstances, I'm sure you don't like being away from home. With a little luck maybe you can get this matter cleared up quickly."

"That's my hope, sir. My fervent hope. Mrs. Futter's sister lives nearby in St. John's Wood, but I don't like her staying alone, and that's the truth of it."

The sound of the dowager duchess's walking stick on the parquet floor outside the morning room snapped Futter to attention. He reached out to remove a hat already entrusted to Soyer's care.

"Well, Futter—" she peered at him through her lorgnette "—I hear you've taken a wife. I hope you haven't done anything foolish."

"Thank you, Your Grace. I'm very happy."

"Happy, humph. You tell your wife she's using too much fat in her gravy. And she should use less cream in her puddings. Feeding you too high. Brides always do. Ruinous to the constitution. I told my daughter-in-law the first thing. I won't allow her to ruin Osbert."

"Yes, Your Grace. Thank you, Your Grace. If I might just have a word . . ."

"Well, of course. What do you think I'm here for?" She sat in a straight-backed chair and indicated that the men might sit as well.

"Yes, quite. Thank you, ma'am. Now—" he pulled a notepad from his uniform pocket "—now, your maid, Lily. What can you tell me about her?"

"She did her duties well enough. I wouldn't have had her if she hadn't."

"Quite. And what were her duties?"

"She was the housemaid."

"Yes. Quite. If you could be more explicit, ma'am?"

"She did what Soyer told her to do."

"Yes. I see. And what do you know of her background?"

"She had been here for two years."

"Yes. And before that?"

The dowager duchess blinked at the thought that Lily might have had a life before coming to Aethelsham. "Soyer interviewed her."

"Yes, of course, thank you. And you would say she was what you'd call a good girl?"

"Of course she was a good girl. I hope you aren't suggesting I would have a girl in my house who wasn't respectable?"

"No, no. Of course not. Forgive me. I meant did she seem to have any particular . . . friends?"

The dowager duchess drew herself up. "Followers, you mean? Certainly not. I never permit such a thing. Just what are you suggesting, young man?"

Futter scrambled to his feet. "Well, the fact is, Your Grace—" he ground the toe of his shoe into her deep Turkey carpet and cleared his throat "—that is, you see, Your Grace, she was . . . er . . . expecting."

"She was not. I would never have permitted such a thing." The authority of generations of Aethelberts swept from the room with Her Grace.

The butler was next. This morning Soyer's pouter-pigeon chest seemed more held out by the starch in his shirtfront than by pride in his position, and the shine on his bald head suggested perspiration even on a frosty morning. "Most distressing, most distressing." He wiped his forehead with a linen handkerchief and refused the chair Danvers offered. "If you don't mind, sir. I feel more comfortable standing."

"Quite as you like." Danvers nodded. "Inspector Futter is an old acquaintance of mine. You can rely on him to handle anything you tell him with discretion."

Futter asked for a description of Lily's duties.

"First thing in the morning she opened the shutters of all the lower rooms and took up the hearth rugs of the rooms to be done before breakfast."

"And which rooms would those have been yesterday?" Futter's pencil paused, waiting to note the answer.

"The breakfast room, library, and front drawing rooms."

"And her duties would be sweeping, dusting, cleaning the grates, laying the fires?"

"That's right." Soyer nodded. "Then she laid the breakfast table and brought in the tea."

"And does . . . er . . . did Lily serve breakfast?"

Now the chest swelled fully under the black coat. "I serve all meals. The housemaid assists."

"Yes, yes. Quite understood. Thank you. And yesterday morning, did you notice anything different about Lily? Anything that would give you a hint she might be planning to meet someone, for example?"

"Lily was always quick, a little high-strung. She must have been distracted because she forgot to check the dryness of the salt in the cellars. When I noted the salt for Lady Eleanor's egg was lumpy, I sent Lily to the kitchen for more. She failed to return with it on the tray, so I had to send her back again. But as to your suggestion that she might have been meeting anyone, that's entirely out of the question. I would never permit such a thing."

"Yes, but she apparently did, didn't she?"

"What do you mean?"

Futter raised a pale eyebrow. "She met her murderer, sir."

In condescension to Lord Danvers's involvement in the questioning, Soyer permitted the staff to be lined up once again in the morning room, a rare convenience for Futter, who was accustomed to conducting his interviews in spartan servants' halls. They queued up in order as they had two nights before, from Mrs. Crompton down to little Tilly.

The dowager duchess returned and surveyed them like Queen Victoria reviewing her troops. She rapped sharply for the attention that was already fully hers. "I will not have this. Do you hear me? I will not have my maids getting themselves murdered. Such behavior in any of you will result in immediate dismissal."

Futter questioned each servant individually. None had anything to offer beyond gossip, supposition, or hysteria, however. Except Susan, the upstairs maid. She was at least able to help establish the time of Lily's departure.

"When she finishes with breakfast, she's supposed to help me upstairs. She manages never to get up until the slops are emptied. I can always count on it. Soon as I have the basins emptied, dowsed with hot water, and plenty of vinegar in them, she'll come up. Not before."

"But yesterday?"

Susan shook her head. A few brown wisps appeared under her starched white cap. "Had to do the beds all myself, I did. Except Her Grace's. She likes sleeping right on a mattress, so that means the top mattress has to be taken off, then the feather bed shaken and turned. It's not possible to put the mattress back on top all alone without bunching the feather bed all up. So I rang for Tilly. It's not her place, but what could I do?" She turned pleading brown eyes on Soyer.

Soyer looked stern, but Charles spoke. "I'm sure your mistress appreciates your attention to her comfort, Susan."

Futter appeared ready to dismiss the household staff when Hardy bustled in, cheeks and nose red from the cold. He rubbed his hands together briskly. "Ah, top o' the mornin' to ye, top o' the mornin'. And would ye be having me read the bumps of any of these?" He waved a hand toward the line of servants.

Soyer brought the full prestige of his position into his reply. "I dare to hope, my good man, you do not mean to imply that any of my staff are under suspicion. I can attest that every one of them was attending fully to their duties."

84

"Lily wasn't." Few could have caught Futter's muttered reply, but Antonia smiled at him.

"I know you mean to be helpful, Hardy, but I think Inspector Futter has finished with the staff for now," Charles said.

Futter nodded, and Soyer dismissed the servants, but not before Hardy could scrutinize the head of Edward, the underfootman.

"You'd do well to watch that lad closely. A bulging forehead like his is a bad sign. And did you notice his ears—fair to being jug handles they are. Cattle stealer from Paisley had ears just like that."

"As do several members of the House of Hanover," Danvers reminded him.

But Hardy was not to be repressed. He studied the unbending Soyer, then stepped back with a satisfied air. "Typical sugarloaf. Common shape for a criminal head, bulging at the back like that. That Adams who shot his wife, perfect example of a sugarloaf. Described as 'very low type,' he was. And there was a laborer in Swansea who killed his wife's lover—"

"That will *do*, Hardy." Danvers emphasized his words by advancing on his man.

"Yes, sir. Just trying to be helpful, m'lord."

Soyer turned on his heel and walked woodenly from the room as if he had not heard a word of anything that had passed.

Hardy looked from Danvers to Futter and asked conversationally, "Did you know that there is a ten per cent greater chance of men with dark hair and eyes being criminals, while lunatics are more inclined to blond?"

"How very fortunate you are that I have gray eyes, Hardy, or I should be sorely tempted to take out my inclinations on you."

Hardy subsided. "Sorry, m'lord. Nothing personal intended, I assure you. Thing is, I've just come from Lily's reading, so I rather had my mind on the subject."

"You mean to say Constable Orson allowed you to examine the victim's body?" Futter asked.

"Oh, no, sir. Very improper that would be, I'm sure. Just her skull. He was verra grateful for my help."

"He would be." Danvers nodded. When Hardy made no reply he prodded, "Well? You may as well get it over with. What were your conclusions?"

Hardy shook his head ominously. "Her organ of Destructiveness was highly developed. Highly developed."

"Yes. Well, that's very enlightening, Hardy. Only trouble is, it seems she's the one that was destroyed, doesn't it?"

"No need to shout, sir. I had thought of that. Thing is, if she was trying to destroy something, and met someone with a larger organ of Destructiveness . . . if you take my meaning, sir?"

"Yes, Hardy. Well, it seems quite obvious that Lily was involved in something unsavory to wind up in the fix she did."

"I was wondering . . ." For the first time Tonia spoke up. "Aunt Elfrida, you haven't had any valuables go missing lately?"

"What are you suggesting?"

"I'm not suggesting anything. Just asking. You know —porcelain, silver, jewels."

"Certainly not. I would permit nothing of the sort."

When they were alone again in their room, Charles asked, "What were you thinking of when you asked Aunt Elfrida about her valuables?"

"It seems likely, doesn't it? Bessie's throat was slit. Lily's throat was slit. Mrs. Bacon seems to have been robbed. Perhaps Aunt Elfrida . . . "

"But that's impossible. There's no way dustmen could sneak into Aethelsham Hall."

"Of course not, but Lily was already in."

Danvers ran his hand through his hair as he always did when a new train of thought took him. "So you're suggesting Lily might have attempted sneaking valuables out to accomplices?"

"That's what I was thinking. But then why kill her? That rather seems to be killing the goose who laid the golden egg, doesn't it?" Tonia thought for a moment. "Unless she got greedy when she heard about the murder at Chatham and wanted more money. Maybe she even threatened to tell what she knew. She would have needed money if what Futter said about her condition was true."

Danvers nodded slowly. "Yes, that all makes good sense. I'll suggest to Futter that he look into that line."

A small clock on the mantel chimed the hour. He drew out his pocket watch and checked the time. "I had no idea it was getting so late. Shall I send a note to Lansing that we can't make it today? After all this with Lily—"

"Don't be silly, Charles. There's no reason we shouldn't keep our appointment." She rose and pulled the bell for Isabella. "I shall be ready in three-quarters of an hour. Will that suit?"

"You suit extremely, my love." He planted a kiss on her temple.

Isabella entered and began arranging her mistress's hair.

Tonia approached the afternoon with mixed feelings. She was still not certain the whole matter of a portrait was a good idea. It had been a perfect tool to get acquainted with Lansing for Eleanor's sake. But wasn't going along with this yet another deception? If it all ended as badly as she feared, wouldn't Charles be more hurt—or angry—for her having let things go so far?

Still, what was a mere portrait added to the weight of the whole scheme of things? If only . . . but no, she mustn't let herself go down that futile road again. It was far better to have the sitting today than to take a chance of having it rescheduled for the next day. That would be disastrous indeed.

A short time later Antonia was nestled in the corner of the brougham, looking out at the shop windows beyond Chatham's tree-lined High Street. Hardy, who was driving today, drew the horses to a stop behind a horse-drawn delivery van.

More to relieve the silence in the carriage than anything else—there never used to be such periods of uneasy quiet between them—Tonia started to remark idly on an ornate set of silver candlesticks in a pawnbroker's window. Then she suddenly grabbed Danvers's arm. "Look! There—beside the candlesticks. That silver perfume bottle. It's that grape pattern like Catherine Bacon's."

Danvers rapped on the panel behind the driver's seat and gestured toward the shop.

Hardy nodded. "Won't be going nowhere for some time, m'lord. Looks like he's meaning to unload the whole of his van at Wickham's Dry Goods here."

Danvers helped Tonia from the carriage, and they hurried to the window of Owen Dorset, Pawnbroker. "Remarkable." He squeezed her hand. "You have excellent eyes to have spotted that from the street."

"I was lucky. Of course, I didn't see the monogram then." She pointed to the ornate B engraved in the center of a smooth oval framed with grape clusters. And beside it was a matching powder box, too flat to have been visible from the carriage.

They were met inside the shop by a tall, unsmiling man with a fringe of gray hair. "The person who offered the grapevine silver set?" The lanky shopkeeper peered at them through a pair of spectacles perched uncertainly on his nose. "I'm not accustomed to divulging . . . that is, it isn't customary in the business . . ."

Danvers tucked a coin in the man's vest pocket. "Perhaps that will help relieve the inconvenience of consulting your books?"

"Ah, yes, quite so. For a gentleman and lady like yourselves, I'd not like to be saying no, you understand."

He shuffled around to the back of his counter where he scrutinized a heavy, black-bound ledger kept neatly in copperplate handwriting. "Ah, yes. I remember now. It was four weeks ago." He pointed a bony finger at the date. "A Mrs. Bacon it was."

"Mrs. Bacon?" Danvers said. "You mean to say the lady brought the pieces in herself?"

The pawnbroker wrinkled his forehead, making his spectacles teeter precariously. "No, no. I remember her quite well." He wagged a long finger. "It was the maid. Ruddy girl, heavy-built. Looked more of a farm girl than a housemaid, I thought."

The traffic had cleared by the time they returned to the carriage, and none too soon for Lady Danvers, intent on being taken to Bessie Law by the fastest route.

A few minutes later, Charles alighted at Ordnance Terrace and slammed the carriage door behind Antonia. "Hardy, you get on to Orson. Tell him we've found new evidence. We'll be with Bessie or on over at Lansing's."

Although her neck was still swathed in thick white bandages, and she talked with an odd, breathy, grating sound, Dr. Morris had pronounced Elizabeth Law well enough to be up and around.

"You're staying here for the time being, are you then?" Danvers asked her.

"Mrs. Bacon's man of business asked me to stay on. Said he'd see I was paid all right. Seems they can't quite make out who her property goes to. Apparently had a nephew in Cornwall, but there was some family squabble when he ran off with a married woman or something. Or maybe it was the nephew's father was disinherited. I'm sure she never talked to me about it none." She shrugged. "Anyroad, I'd as lief stay here, long as I gets paid. Fact that my mistress was murdered won't do me no good when it comes to getting a new position. Even if I did get my throat slashed trying to defend her. That's the way folks thinks, and there's no changin' them."

"Yes, Bessie, I'm sure you're right. But we've come to talk to you about a different matter." Danvers stood before a blazing coal fire in the front parlor. It appeared that Bessie had made herself quite at home in the absence of a mistress.

"Pieces of Mrs. Bacon's silver dresser set—they're in the window of a pawnshop in the High Street. The pawnbroker says you took them to him."

Tonia watched carefully for any sign of guilt on Bessie's wide, plain face, but the girl didn't blink.

"That's right. Took 'em in three or four weeks ago, not long after Christmas. Pawnbroker should be able to give you the exact date if you're interested."

"He did, as a matter of fact. But what I want to know is what you were doing pawning your mistress's belongings?"

Bessie shrugged. "She asked me to, didn't she? Wouldn't be genteel for her to take her own things to bargain with a pawnbroker. Ladies don't do that."

Tonia knew that the guilt she had looked for on Bessie's face was written large on her own. No, ladies didn't. Ladies should not find themselves in situations where they were desperate for large quantities of cash. Situations they could not speak of to their husbands.

But Danvers was not looking at his wife. He took a step closer to the maid. "But why would Mrs. Bacon do that? She had money in the bank. Your mistress was very comfortably fixed."

Bessie shrugged again. "I don't know nothing about 'er accounts. Always paid me on time, she did. Not over-generous with her Christmas tips, but there you are."

"Bessie, I'd advise you to think very carefully about your answers. That silver was Belgian." He picked up a companion piece from a table and turned it over. He pointed to the silversmith's mark, complete with date. "See, this came from Brussels in 1815. If I'm correct in my guess,

Colonel Bacon bought it for her just before Waterloo. In that case it was the last thing she would have parted with."

Bessie shrugged her broad shoulders a third time. "Don't know, I'm sure. She must have forgotten. She was gettin' awful foggy. Ask anybody. Batty half the time."

They were nearly out the door when the maid added, "Did that Constable Orson tell you he found the dustman? One of 'em at least."

"What?" So much had been happening lately that Tonia had forgotten about Orson's search.

"Where?" Charles asked.

"Picked him up drunk down by the river, I think. Anyroad, I feel a mite safer now, I can tell you."

Tonia took Charles's arm as they walked over to Lansing's. "Well, that's something. It looks as though Orson may have it all solved soon. If he can just find the other one now."

But Danvers was thoughtful. "Yes, maybe. But if that fellow was drunk by the river yesterday afternoon, he wasn't in Canterbury slitting Lily's throat."

Tonia turned wide eyes on Danvers. "Then who did?"

8

Lansing had already heard the news. "Yes, a relief to all of us to have the fellow apprehended. Just hope they get his partner soon. Dreadful thing to have happen practically on one's own doorstep. Not a good thing for business, I can tell you. I would have to move if the gentry started fearing for their lives coming to my studio."

Tonia removed her gloves. "But surely they don't connect you with that horrid affair?" She picked up the exquisite silk fan before taking her place in the chair where Lansing had posed her on her previous visit.

"No, no. Not personally, of course. But the neighborhood bears a certain stigma. Those blasted—excuse me, my lady—er . . . those nosey broadsheets *would* have to give the address. Carriages have been driving up and down the street ever since. All the tone we acquired from Dickens having lived here will wash off once word of scandal gets around."

Lansing set a framed canvas on an easel and adjusted its position slightly. But before he began work, he picked up a sketch pad. "Just let me show you these."

He quickly flipped through several pages of rough drawings showing a "restored" Canterbury Cathedral. "What do you think? Much deeper spirituality, don't you agree? More truly a reflection of Christian attitudes."

Danvers drew himself up. "Since you ask, I'll tell you what I think. I think it's a desecration. You appreciate beautiful things. You're obviously a man of sensitivity and taste—" he gestured to the fan Tonia was holding "—how could you possibly propose doing this to the mother church of the English faith?"

The artist's thin mustache quivered. "Most people of elevated taste consider the true Gothic the highest expression of man's devotion, reflecting as it does the spirit of medieval Christendom."

Danvers set his jaw in a look that told Tonia he would say no more on the subject. For the moment. The silence in the room grew loud before Lansing turned back to the portrait and made a show of busying himself.

Today there were no more charcoal pencils. The artist picked up an oval palette and began blending colors. In a short time he was laying bold strokes on the canvas.

When he had worked for some time, there was the noise of an arrival, and Mrs. Gillie led Constable Orson upstairs.

"I've been next door talking to Bessie about that pawnshop business. Very clever of you to spot those items, Lady Danvers."

Lansing peered over the top of his canvas. "What's this? I hadn't heard anything about a pawnshop."

Orson explained, then concluded with a shake of his head. "I suppose Bessie's story makes sense. The dear ol' granny was well into her eighties—stands to reason she'd forget a detail here and there."

"But you didn't notice any signs of senility when you had cocoa with her?" Danvers asked.

"Course I never questioned her closely about anything. But she for sure never forgot *me*—or how to make the world's best hot chocolate." He ducked his massive head.

93

Tonia thought he might have wiped a tear from his eye, but she couldn't be certain.

"So you're satisfied you have the murderer, are you?" Danvers asked.

"No doubt about it that I can see." Orson stuck his thumbs in his brass-buttoned jacket and leaned back in his chair. "Soon as I can convince him to tell me where to find his partner, we'll have it done up all right and tight."

"But what do you make of the Canterbury business?" Charles asked. "Your dustman couldn't likely have done that if he spent all day yesterday in Chatham."

"What Canterbury business?" Lansing asked.

Orson told him about the murdered maid.

"I suppose you saw her around Aethelsham when you called on Eleanor," Danvers added.

Lansing paused, his brush poised in mid-air. "Lily, you say? What did she look like?"

Antonia described Lily's soft brown curls, round blue eyes, and full pink lips.

Lansing nodded. "Yes, I remember. Served at dinner sometimes. Pretty little thing. Always thought I'd like to paint her. Put a lace mantilla on her and do her Spanish style—have to darken the hair, but the mouth was right. Too late now. Pity."

"And what do you think about the Chelsea shepherdess?" Tonia continued to Orson.

The constable rubbed his stubby black beard. "Right fond of that pair Mrs. B. was. They'd been her mother's or somebody's. She must of been farther gone than anybody had any idea of, or she'd never have sold that."

"I thought the theory was that she was robbed," Lansing said.

Orson was quiet for a moment, then he shook a plump finger at his listeners. "Now here's a theory for you. Maybe those there dustmen saw her—or rather Bessie—hawking the valuables, so they figured there was more in the house for the pickings. That would explain why they chose that house to burgle."

Tonia nodded. "It's true—the whole terrace looks pretty much the same from the outside. Why this one?"

Orson continued, "But the murderers wouldn't dare unload their stuff in Chatham, so they took it on to a bigger town where there's lots of tourist trade and less danger of being asked questions they wouldn't want to answer." He slapped his knee and got to his feet. "Well, guess that just about does it. I'll just get on next door and question Bessie about the shepherdess, but I doubt she can add anything. All nice and tidy now."

"Except one thing," Danvers reminded him.

Orson paused in his progress toward the door. "What's that?"

"Who killed Lily. And why?"

Orson screwed his face into a puzzled frown and went out shaking his head.

Lansing picked up the palette he had laid aside while all were concentrating on the constable. "If you could move just a little closer to Lady Danvers, my lord."

Danvers moved.

"Perhaps your left hand just resting on her shoulder? Ah, perfect. Now don't move."

Charles's hand felt warm and reassuring. Tonia smiled as the comfort of his touch spread along her arm. She would have leaned farther back against him if propriety allowed. As it was, she sat very still and tried to discipline her mind to think about Orson's visit.

If Bessie was telling the truth—if Mrs. Bacon *had* asked her to pawn the silver (and Tonia had her doubts)— that still left the porcelain unaccounted for. But if the dustmen had stolen and pawned the shepherdess—and perhaps other pieces not yet discovered—they must have been robbing Mrs. Bacon for some time before the murder. Yet apparently neither maid nor mistress had noticed any sign of an intruder or anything missing.

She went over and over the questions in her mind but got nowhere. She longed to talk to Charles. Perhaps he could make sense of it all.

"There." Lansing put his brushes aside and picked up a rag to wipe his fingers. "I fancy that's enough for today. You must be tired of sitting. We've made quite good progress, I think." He stepped back to study his canvas.

Tonia and Danvers came around to view it. A lump rose in Tonia's throat. The lady on the canvas sat there as naturally as she had been sitting, a few feet across the room. Light from the snowy window fell on her hands and face, emphasizing her leaning back against the tall, handsome man behind her.

And there he stood, lifelike on the canvas, stalwart and comforting with his hand on her shoulder. The features were only lightly sketched in, and yet the expression on his face, glancing down at her—did he truly look like that? Was his caring so apparent for another to read?

"We look very . . . companionable," was all she could say.

"Yes, I flatter myself that I've captured you very well." Lansing cocked his head to one side, then picked up a brush to add another dab of shadowing to the right side of the canvas. "I can work on the fabric and background this week. Our next sitting I'll work on the faces. If all goes well, one or two more sittings should be sufficient."

Antonia hurried down the stairs and out the door, anxious to talk about all the puzzles on her mind. She barely waited for the door to click shut behind her. "Charles, do you think the dustmen had been robbing Mrs. Bacon for some time?"

Danvers placed his tall silk hat on his head. "It seems unlikely. Thieves wouldn't just take a piece here and there and run the risk of having to come back again."

"But the shepherdess was stolen some time before the murder."

"Yes, I'd thought of that. Of course, it's possible they made one successful haul of all they could comfortably carry, then returned for more later. But it's not the usual pattern."

She nodded. "And it seems strange that nothing was missed. Even if Mrs. Bacon was as dotty as Bessie says, you'd think Bessie herself would have noticed anything missing when she dusted."

He handed her into the carriage Hardy had waiting for them. "Shall we stop at the jail and talk to Orson's dustman?"

They found Futter in a back room attempting to interview the suspect. It was impossible to tell whether the inspector or his subject was the more frustrated.

The man sat on a cot positioned against the wall. *"Soy Miguel."* The small, swarthy man gestured to himself with grimy hands. *"Miguel. Soy Miguel."*

"Now see here, man, it's no good taking on like this. We'll get the truth from you. I just want you to tell me where you were on Monday, and where your partner is. Now that's not too hard, is it?"

"¿Cómo?"

Futter turned to Lord and Lady Danvers, shaking his head in exasperation. "A good ten minutes I've been here, and that's all I've got—gibberish. Can't get a word of sense out of him. He must be Greek or Italian or—see if you can do any better."

Danvers started forward, but Antonia laid a hand on his arm. *"¿Qué dice usted?"*

A broad smile broke across the man's suntanned face, revealing surprisingly white teeth. *"Soy Miguel. Estoy Barcelona."* A string of rapid, highly inflected words followed. He jumped up and reached for Tonia's shoulders. His kisses would have landed on each of her cheeks if she hadn't stepped back.

The flow of words continued until she held up a hand and shook her head emphatically. "No, no, no. No more. I don't understand. Er . . . *no comprendo.*"

The eager face fell, and Tonia was aghast to see the bright black eyes fill with tears.

"Lo siento," she murmured, shaking her head. *"Lo siento."*

The prisoner slumped, his shoulders so drooped that his hands almost reached the floor between his knees.

"What was that all about?" Danvers asked.

"His name is Miguel. I think he's from Barcelona. But I didn't get anything else. Unfortunately, I only know a few phrases of Spanish. The poor man thought I spoke his language. It must have been like a lifeline snapping to find out I don't." She turned back to the dejected figure on the cot. *"Lo siento mucho.* I'm truly sorry," she repeated.

"You're amazing, Tonia. I didn't know you knew any Spanish," Danvers said.

"I've just picked up a few phrases from Isabella. Her mother was Spanish, you know."

"What's this? Spanish, you say?" Orson bustled in. "Is that what's the matter with the fellow? I couldn't make out whether he was drunk or an idiot."

"Strange," Danvers said. "Bessie didn't mention her assailants being foreign. You'd think she would have heard them say something."

"Right," Futter agreed. "Especially since they wouldn't have had any worry about anyone understanding anything they said."

"Orson—" Tonia studied the constable "—you haven't told anyone about your suspect being foreign, have you?"

Orson shrugged. "Couldn't have, could I? Wasn't sure myself."

Danvers took up her meaning. "Good, then be sure you don't." He turned back to Tonia. "We can come back tomorrow with Isabella. She can question him for us, and we'll get to the bottom of this."

"Er . . . tomorrow?" Antonia twisted her hands together under the cover of her cloak. "Well, I had an appointment with my dressmaker, but of course Isabella could come with you." She brightened. "Yes, that's a very good idea, my love. Isabella would do perfectly." She smiled.

How fortunate. She had been wondering what she would tell Isabella. Her maid was so devoted and protective that Tonia knew she wouldn't be able to slip off for the day many more times without alarming her. And then, in her concern, Isabella would be certain to run to Charles. "Yes, tomorrow would be quite perfect."

Hardy held the carriage door for his lord and lady, but instead of closing it behind Danvers he cleared his throat. "Begging your pardon, I am, sir. But there's a matter of some delicacy I'd be liking to speak to you about. I was wondering if I . . . that is, if you wouldn't mind . . ."

Danvers smiled and picked up his hat from the seat across from him. "By all means, Hardy. Even can see to the driving. Sit here and speak up."

"Thank you, m'lord." Hardy settled himself on the seat as the brougham rolled down the cobbled street. "The thing is now, I was wondering if you'd noticed that Orson seemed too quick by half to settle for the first tramp he could pick up. So that set me to wondering, that is . . . you don't suppose, do you . . ."

"Hardy, what are you suggesting?" Tonia asked.

"Well, it seems that by his own admission Orson had free entrance to the old lady's house. He'd have plenty of chances to look out for the good pieces—she'd probably even tell him which ones were really special."

"Hardy, I don't really think—" Danvers began.

"Now, if you'll just be giving me a listen, sir. Can't you be picturing Orson sitting before the fire with his feet on the fender, sipping his chocolate just as if he owned the place, maybe even thinking what he could do with it all if he did own it. And the old lady going on about some fine piece of silver or carved ivory. Just might be enough to set

99

a man to thinking. So just say our Catherine Bacon leaves the room for a few minutes—maybe he asks for a refill on his cocoa, like—see?"

"And when she returns she doesn't notice the fact that her silver gilt candlestick is gone or that Orson has a strange bulge in the pocket of his uniform?" Danvers shook his head.

But Tonia was thoughtful. "Maybe he was cleverer than that. Maybe he slipped in somehow later—his rounds took him by there regularly, he said. And after all, who would suspect a policeman?"

"Tonia, you don't actually think Orson would bludgeon a frail, little old woman to death, do you?"

Tonia sighed. "No, of course I don't. And if he had, Bessie surely would have recognized him, even disguised as a dustman."

"And," Danvers continued, "it's less than likely Orson would conspire with dustmen if he had been robbing."

"Of course the robbery and murder could have been quite separate things. The porcelain being in that shop in Canterbury a week or so before the murder indicates that," she suggested.

But Charles shook his head. "Then we're left without a motive for the murder. No, it has to be the robbers who murdered Catherine Bacon."

"But then, why Lily?"

"Dash it, nothing makes sense." Danvers hit his fist against his armrest.

"Er . . . umph." Hardy cleared his throat. "If I might just . . . that is, I do have another line of evidence."

"Evidence?" Danvers sat forward. "Well, let's have it, man."

Hardy drew a notebook from his pocket. "When we were in Canterbury I took the liberty of calling on Gladstone Simpson. I knew you wouldn't mind, m'lord, seeing as how you weren't needing my services at the moment."

"Yes, yes, get on with it. Gladstone who?"

"Simpson, sir. Remember? He and his sister Grace are the most noted phrenologists in all the east of England."

Danvers groaned and sank back in his seat.

The late February afternoon light was beginning to wane, but it was sufficient for Hardy to read his notes. "You see, sir. The average size of criminals' heads is probably about the same as that of ordinary people's heads."

"Surprise, surprise," Danvers muttered.

Hardy was unperturbed. "But you see, sir, the thing is, among criminals both small and large heads are found in greater proportion—the same is true of the insane, by the way—but for our purposes the thing to note is that thieves more frequently have small heads. Large heads are usually found among murderers."

"And so if we have a thief that commits murder, where does that leave us?"

That bit of logic made Hardy blink but did not stop his flow of information. "Now, I'm sure you will have noticed the police constable's large, square head. Especially his jawline. This is what phrenologists call 'prognathism.' With careful measurement of many convicted criminals it's been shown that a large jaw is a prominent characteristic of criminals, especially of criminals guilty of offenses of violence. And you'll be agreeing, I'm sure, from your own experience that the lower jaw is more massive in the inferior than in the higher human races. And even among our own race, it's to be noted that the lower social classes have larger jaws than the higher orders."

"Really, Hardy, this is too much," Danvers objected.

Tonia was thoughtful. "Surely you overstate, Hardy. But it is undeniable that Orson does have a remarkably large head and a square jawline."

"And large, heavy features." Hardy pressed his advantage. "In fifty murderers, as compared with fifty recruits, the researchers found larger facial development. And then, among thieves there is a marked exaggeration of the orbital arches and frontal sinuses."

"I've read that study," Danvers waved it aside. "Such development was also found in individuals living in the country—a lifestyle which invites energetic respiratory systems."

Tonia barely restrained herself from putting a hand to her forehead. Was it only her guilt that made her think her companions were both staring at her own somewhat underdeveloped lower brow?

Thankfully, Hardy turned a page in his notebook and carried on. "Now, m'lord, if you'll just be listening a moment longer. Among cranial anomalies which have been found with special frequency in criminals may be noted small bones in the lambdoid suture which have ossified separately—a keel-shaped head due to the premature union of the sagittal suture, and especially plagiocephaly, an asymmetry of the two sides of the skull.

"Now if I could just examine Orson we might learn something very interesting. You see, the thing is—all these anomalies may be found with undue frequency not only in criminals but also in the subjects of other forms of degeneracy."

He snapped his notebook closed and leaned back with a satisfied air.

"It won't do, Hardy. It really won't. And I won't have you exposing Lady Danvers to such anti-Christian heresy."

"No, m'lord. No, no." Hardy crossed himself with each denial. "I'll be swearing it on the grave of my sainted grandmother. I meant no respect to the Holy Church or to Saint Patrick or to—"

Danvers held up a hand. "Save that for Father O'Callahan. But I'll have none of a philosophy that says we're the victims of the way our skulls develop. What about the moral element? Criminality—the desire to do evil—is born in the heart of man, not in the shape of his head."

Hardy subsided against the seat cushions and looked up at his master through lowered eyes. Then he let his notebook fall to the floor.

"And what, I ask you," Danvers asked, "of the repentant criminal who comes to our Lord for forgiveness and a clean heart? Do you suggest that our Lord then changes the shape of his head as well?"

Still downcast, Hardy brushed his blond curls away from his forehead, exposing his decreasing brow.

Danvers picked up the dropped notes and thumbed through them. "Ah, I thought so." He read, "Receding foreheads, very commonly observed among criminals, have always been regarded as evidence of low mental and moral organization." Then, taking pity on his man's crestfallen state, he continued, "But it must be taken into consideration as well that many men of marked intellectual power have had receding foreheads."

Hardy looked up with an abashed grin.

The rest of the journey was accomplished in peace and quiet.

But when Even pulled under the carriage porch of Aethelsham, another rolled out ahead of them, having just disgorged its passenger. Danvers groaned. "Stormy weather ahead, I fear. Only bad news could bring Agatha down from London at this time of night."

Hoping to miss the worst of it, Tonia and Charles took their time making their appearance in the dowager duchess's drawing room. But they misjudged. It seemed they arrived precisely at the moment to take the storm at full flood.

Eleanor was prostrate on the rose-velvet fainting couch, weeping noisily into a handkerchief too heavy with lace and embroidery to be of any practical value. "I won't, I won't. You can't make me," she wailed.

Agatha stood in the center of the room, hands on hips. "I most certainly can. I don't know what our father was about, leaving you in Charles's custody. But I shall deal with this matter if I have to have our brother declared incompetent on grounds of insanity."

Danvers bowed before his elder sister and kissed her mischievously on the cheek. "And which side of the issue do you wish me to give testimony on?"

"You must be insane, Charles. That's the kindest thing I can think of. Insane or incompetent. I really cannot bring myself to think you are uncaring. You who have always put duty to family and family loyalty above all else. A month ago I would have sworn to anyone that there was nothing you wouldn't do to keep the title of Norville unsullied. And yet here you are—doing nothing."

Danvers made his bow to the dowager duchess, who sat like Juno quite apart from the fray. Then he turned back to Agatha. "I know I shall regret this, but perhaps you would care to inform me of the nature of my latest malfeasance."

"While you, sir, have been off consorting with the enemy—I can put no kinder construction on it—I have been about the work you should have done weeks ago when first I informed you of this brouhaha."

"You refer, I take it, to the fact that Antonia and I are having our portrait painted by one who has asked permission to address our sister."

"What else could I be referring to?"

"The fact that I have taken for valet a man with a receding forehead?" Fortunately the remark, delivered under his breath, apparently failed to reach Agatha's ears.

"I, sir, have been to Somerset House. And I have learned all. It is just as I suspected. Randolph Lansing is a fraud."

A loud sob from Eleanor was the only response to Agatha's announcement. Tonia crossed to her young sister-in-law's side and slipped her a more useful, plain cotton handkerchief.

"Sailing under quite false colors. There is no Randolph Lansing connected in any way to Baron Crofthurst. Made it all up, it seems." She gazed around the room with a satisfied air.

Eleanor dabbed her eyes and sat up. "No. It's Fowler."

"*Fowler?* Who's Fowler?" Agatha snapped.

"Randolph is. His name is Randolph Fowler. Lansing was his mother's name. He took it to honor her memory. He loved her most dreadfully. That's what made it so awful for him that his great-aunt disinherited the family when Randolph's father married his mother. She was an actress, you see. Randolph must have inherited his artistic talent from her."

"Ha! Disinherited. I'm not surprised. What did I tell you? A fraud and a fortune hunter." Agatha lifted her chin in triumph. "Now what do you have to say to that, brother?"

Danvers crossed his legs and leaned against the white marble mantel. "Only that you should have asked me. I could have saved you a beastly lot of trouble, Aggie."

"Asked you? You mean you knew? You couldn't have."

"Yes, I could, quite easily. Lansing told me. He was very straightforward with it all when he asked permission to call on Eleanor."

"He *told* you? And you still permitted him to call?"

"Of course. He seems like a decent fellow. And an excellent portraitist."

Eleanor gave a loud sniff from the sanctuary of Tonia's arms and cast a wavery smile at him.

"Only thing I have against him is his taste in architecture. I'll admit that's almost enough for me to forbid him calling."

A wail broke anew from Eleanor.

"There, there, he's only teasing." Tonia smoothed the girl's tangled hair back from her forehead. "Don't, Charles."

Hardy cleared his throat and bowed from the doorway. "If you'll be allowing me to speak."

Danvers waved a hand permissively. "Why not? You're not likely to make matters any worse."

"Very good, sir. It's just that I'd like to observe to Lady Agatha that the gentleman in question has a most superior cranial development. You will recall that I gave him a most detailed reading, and it's rare indeed, even among the highest classes. You'll pardon my saying this, I'm sure, m'lord—" he bowed to Danvers "—but Mr. Lansing has a phrenological symmetry found only in the most sensitive of artists."

"If you'd said architects I'd have throttled you, Hardy. As it is, you may be dismissed."

Agatha took a deep breath as if she were about to burst forth in a Wagnerian aria. Fortunately she was cut off by three raps of the dowager duchess's walking stick.

"That's quite enough of that. All of you. In case it had escaped your memory, this is my drawing room, not a cattle market. Go to your bed, girl." She dispatched Eleanor. "And you sit down." She rounded on Agatha, who backed her way to a small bench against the wall. "I have matters of importance to discuss with my grandnephew."

Danvers blanched but was punctilious in his bow. "At your service, Aunt Elfrida."

"Of course you are. You're my nephew. We always do our duty. Saxon blood."

"Well, there was Ethelred the Unready . . ."

Tonia almost laughed. She had no idea Charles was capable of looking so like a naughty schoolboy as he did when the dowager duchess rapped her walking stick at him.

"Ethelred was not in our line. If he had been, the history of England might be a great deal different. You will not find our ancestors unready for anything. That is what I told the committee."

"Er . . ."

"Pay attention, boy. Canon Dettra has taken to his bed with an attack of hives. I told the committee they need have no worry. You would do it."

"Dettra? I don't remember a Canon Dettra on the architectural committee. But Aunt Elfrida, no matter what you told them, I will have no part in it. I realize it's too late to save the effigy of the Black Prince, but I will not approve

106

those horrendous sketches Lansing showed me. Nor will I approve any scheme to pad Saint Augustine's chair in red velvet, to reconstruct the shrine of Saint Thomas, or to have Madame Tussad set up wax figures of the murder of Thomas à Becket."

The dowager duchess peered at him with an unblinking scowl. At last she let her lorgnette fall with a snap. "February is quite the wrong month for sunstroke, but I can think of no other explanation as I will not tolerate insanity in the family. What you would want with wax figures of Thomas à Becket I can't imagine. The music has nothing to do with the martyrdom."

"Music?"

"Certainly. What did you think I was talking about? I clearly told you Canon Dettra is unwell. He will be unable to lead the chorus for the pre-Lenten concert. You will take his place."

When Danvers turned aside to attend to a demand from Agatha, Tonia spoke to the dowager duchess. "Aunt Elfrida, you can't be serious. Not Charles. Have you ever heard him sing?"

"Precisely, my dear. That's why he'll be perfect. The Charity Choristers are so unspeakable that only someone totally tone deaf could stand to direct them. I'm sure that's what caused poor Canon Dettra's hives. He has a very fine ear."

9

F igaro, Figaro, Feeegaro-o-o!"

Danvers, a brush in the palm of each hand, vigorously attacked his perennially unruly hair while serenading his image in the mirror.

In the next room Tonia staunchly took her fingers from her ears before entering her husband's dressing room. "You're in fine voice, my love." She kissed him lightly on one cheek between swings of the brushes.

Charles stopped and cleared his throat. "Yes, I am rather, aren't I? Good thing too. With rehearsal tomorrow night I don't have overlong to prepare." He ran a quick scale. "Do, re, mi—"

"Er . . . your duties as choirmaster won't entail your singing a solo at the concert, will they?"

"I wouldn't think so. Pity, though, isn't it?"

"Yes, love." She just managed to keep a note of relief out of her dutiful reply.

"I'll admit it, Tonia, it is nice to have my talent appreciated. I must say I never could understand why you and Hardy always seemed to discourage my singing. Here, it seems I'm known even in Canterbury."

Tonia bit her lip. "Yes, odd, isn't it?"

"Well, a prophet not without honor except in his own country, and all that." He laid the brushes aside and began to work on his black satin necktie while attacking Count Alamviva's Act I serenade con spirito.

When the song came to an end Tonia said weakly, "The concert is certain to be memorable, my love."

Danvers stood, crossed the room to her, and grasped both her hands. "Are you absolutely certain you can't come with me today?"

Tonia hoped the flicker of alarm she felt didn't show in her eyes. "No. No, Charles. If I'm to have my new gown in time for your debut as charity choirmaster of Canterbury Cathedral, I mustn't miss this fitting."

"Yes, of course. Pity, though, that I promised Futter I'd go to Chatham today, or I could go with you."

Tonia caught her breath and paled. "Oh, no. Don't give it a thought, Charles. It would spoil the surprise. I hadn't meant to say as much as I have."

He laughed. "But you've not said a thing. And we've never kept secrets from each other, have we?"

How on earth did the conversation get here? This was decidedly tricky ground. Was Charles probing? Did he suspect something? She forced a smile. "Well, there was that matter of your father's at Loch Leven that you wouldn't tell me about."

"True. And then, when it all came out, you were so understanding, and I saw what an idiot I'd been not to tell you. But we learned then, didn't we? No more secrets. I think that's one of the best things about marriage—absolute trust in another person." Still holding her hands, he looked at her across the space of three heartbeats. "Tonia, I do love you so very much."

She looked up at him, her eyes brimming. Then he bent to kiss her, and she leaned against him.

When they drew apart he asked, "You're sure you don't mind my taking Isabella? You won't need her for the fitting?"

"Madame d'Arbley is quite competent to stick pins in me without my maid. Isabella is very excited about meeting someone from Spain."

Just then Isabella appeared, wearing her gray traveling cloak. Danvers picked up his hat and gloves and ushered her out.

As soon as the door was shut, Antonia heaved a sigh and turned to extract from her bottom drawer the money she had raised by pawning her brooch.

Danvers and Futter sat on oak chairs beside Orson's desk. Isabella, her round black eyes snapping, sat on a padded horsehair settee along one wall. Orson brought in his prisoner. "Miss Isabella, I thank you for helping us out here. Rather awkward spot we seem to be in—not being able to understand the fellow's confession. This here's Miguel. But don't you be afraid none, my girl, for all that he's an horrid murderer. We'll keep 'im restrained." He held up Miguel's hands to exhibit his handcuffs.

Then Orson cleared his throat and yelled at the prisoner. "Now don't you try nothing funny with this young woman here. You tell her the truth, or we'll string you up." He blinked, then added under his breath, "Course you'll get strung up for telling the truth too."

Isabella smiled at Miguel. *"¿Comó está usted?"*

The result was startling. Miguel fell to his knees and clasped his manacled hands as if in prayer. *"Oh, señorita, yo hajo nada. Nada..."* A furious flood of tearful words followed as Miguel inched toward her on his knees.

The best Danvers could tell was that the Spaniard was protesting that he had done nothing.

Orson clasped Miguel by the collar to halt his progress across the floor. "That'll do now, my fellow. Ask 'im where is he from."

Isabella obeyed, and a lengthy, emotional story poured from the prisoner, accompanied by gestures only slightly hampered by the handcuffs.

110

"He is a sailor. From the *Barcelona,*" Isabella explained at last.

"Cor, you mean he's with the Armada?" Orson rubbed his forehead with a copious pocket handkerchief.

Danvers raised an eyebrow. "That's all right. I believe we defeated them quite a number of years ago."

Orson stuffed the handkerchief back in his pocket. "Still, can't be too careful. These foreigners never change their ways." He looked at Isabella. "Well, girl, what else does he have to say for himself?"

"He say he was having a drink with some other sailors the night they docked. He had too much to drink and lost his way to the dockyard. When he woke up in the morning, his purse was gone, and he had terrible headache—and then you arrest him. He does not understand why. If it is for not paying for his drinks, if he can be taken back to the *Barcelona* he can borrow some money from a friend. If he is arrested for jumping ship, he begs to be returned to his captain. He will be flogged, but it would be much worth it that he could sail to Spain once more. He has a mother and seven brothers and five sisters in Madrid. His mother will be so sorrowful. It will break her heart if he does not return. He—"

"Yes, yes. That's enough," Orson cut in with a wave of his beefy hand. "What's all this then? Does he expect us to believe such an unlikely story? Ask him what he did with the rest of the stuff he stole." He dug in a desk drawer for several moments, scattering papers every direction. "Ah, here it is. Bessie gave me a list. Ask him about these here. A jade figure—goddesslike; an ivory statue . . ." He thrust the list at Isabella. "Here, see what kind of a tale he can make out of that. And remind him there's no use lying. The shopkeepers will recognize him."

Danvers raised his eyebrow once again. "I'm sure they would, Orson. But have you considered how a man who speaks no English could manage to pawn valuable art objects?"

111

"He had a partner, didn't he? Thank you for reminding me, my lord. Ask him about his partner, my girl."

Isabella nodded, and for a few moments the station room was filled with their lyrical, sibilant exchange. At last Isabella shook her head. "He does not know 'partner.' He has many friends in the crew of the *Barcelona*. I ask him, do any of them speak English? He say only the captain."

"Aha! There it is then!" Orson slapped his knee in triumph.

"Well, I've heard enough." Futter got to his feet. "I think I'll just nip along to the dockyard and have a word with this captain . . . er . . . what did he say his name is?"

"Reyas. Captain Reyas," Isabella supplied.

"Yes. Right. Orson, continue to hold your prisoner for a few more hours, but see that he has a good lunch." Futter picked up his hat.

"Hold him!" Orson's wide jaw stuck out even more squarely. "I should think so. You won't find Constable Orson letting loose of a prime murder suspect."

Danvers turned to Isabella. "I would like to have Hardy take you back to Aethelsham, but you may be needed later. Will you be quite comfortable here?"

"Oh, but yes. Miguel say the food is terrible. If I can find garlic at the market I will make him *sopa de ajo*. I pour in the well-beaten egg the last minute and simmer, oh, so gently, so it never curdles." She kissed the tips of her fingers.

"Here now, I'll not have you stinking up my kitchen, girl. What does he mean the food's terrible? Sausage and beans I gave him for breakfast—same as I had myself. You can't ask better than that, now, can you?"

"Save us some of your soup, Isabella. We're sure to be hungry when we get back." Danvers accompanied Futter out the door and told Hardy to instruct the coachman to drive them to the docks.

The wide waters of the Medway looked sullen and brown under the dull winter sky. Crows, gulls, and herons called and dipped to their feeding among the marshes left by the ebbing river.

Danvers tried to imagine how it must have appeared to the Romans, who built one of their first forts just up the river at Rochester and plied the Medway with their galleys. He didn't have much success conjuring up a fleet of flat, oar-powered vessels in the face of the tall masts of Her Majesty's Royal Navy filling the docks.

He had better success recalling the lessons of a history master who had gone into great detail to reconstruct in his boys' minds the battle on the banks of the Medway when Emperor Claudius overpowered the native Celts. "He came himself and used elephants, you know."

Futter's pale blue eyes blinked. "Pardon me, my lord. I don't think I quite follow you."

Danvers laughed. "No, sorry. Just reliving a history lesson. Right around here, it was—probably on the other side of the river." He gestured across the uninviting expanse. "The Celtic chieftains were doing quite well against the Romans—valiant charioteers, the Celts were. The Romans were having a lot of trouble getting across the river. Then the German auxiliaries just plunged right in and swam across—in leather armor and everything."

Futter looked at the water and shivered. "Swimming that muck, can you credit it?"

"But the real defeat came when the emperor arrived to see to the final victory. He brought elephants with him, and their scent spooked the Celts' horses."

Futter laughed. "Fine story that." He shook his head. "Elephants. What a faradiddle."

"No, no, it's history."

Futter laughed until he had to wipe his eyes. "Pardon me for saying it, my lord, but your teacher was having you on. Everyone knows there's no elephants in England— saving the zoo in London, I suppose."

"Well, of course not. Claudius took them back with him. As well as taking the Celtic king, Caractacus."

Futter stopped laughing. "Oh, him. Why didn't you say so? Course I know Caractacus—he's the one what made that speech we had to learn at school about how he was of noble birth just like Caesar—with men and horses, arms and wealth, and that if Caesar would let him live he would survive in history as one example of Roman clemency."

Futter sat up and looked out of the carriage with more interest. "So this is where all that started, is it?"

Since their carriage bore the Dowager Duchess of Aethelbert's arms, they were waved through the main gate of the naval yard. But inside, the confusion of men, supplies, and barracks of one of the chief naval stations in Great Britain was daunting. The yard rang with pile-driving, sluice-driving, and the incessant din of blacksmiths, carpenters, and mills as the work of shipbuilding, oar-making, and rope-making went on amid the smell of timber shavings, turpentine, and tar.

They abandoned the carriage and proceeded on foot, asking several likely looking passers-by about the *Barcelona*. At last they found a young lieutenant who directed them along to the top of the yard. At nearly the last dock they found the Spanish vessel. Its crew was working industriously tarring ropes, swabbing the deck, and scraping barnacles from the wooden hull to get the vessel seaworthy for the return journey to Spain.

After several inquiries, accompanied by vigorous head-nodding and arm-waving, Captain Reyas came forward. His thick black beard covered much of the gold braid on the front of his uniform.

"*Si, si.* Miguel is my man. A good man. I do not understand why he jump ship. He was a very good man."

Danvers explained as clearly as he could what had happened.

The captain shook his head. "When did you say this terrible thing happened?"

114

"The morning of January twenty-nine," Futter answered.

The captain shook his head, more firmly this time. "No. Is not possible. We were not in port yet. Terrible storm was in the channel two nights before. We were blown against rocks. Making for London, we were, but we taking on too much water. Your Royal Navy, they let us dock here to make repairs. No crew left the ship until the next day."

Futter looked up from the notes he had been making. "Well, thank you, Captain. That seems to about take care of it. We'll get your man back to you—sure and you can give him a good stiff lecture about the evils of overindulgence."

"He's probably figured that out for himself by now," Danvers said. "I wonder if any of your men could tell us where Miguel drank that night?"

Several sailors in heavy canvas pants and striped jerseys with colorful scarves around their necks were working on the deck nearby. The captain questioned them, then returned, pointing to the west. "That way, a few streets beyond the docks. The *Tres*—how do you say—*Carillons?*"

Danvers considered. "The Three Bells?"

Captain Reyes nodded vigorously. "Three Bells, yes. Carlos, he is not sure, but he think perhaps that was such a name. There was a picture over the door of . . ." He gestured with his hands.

"Bell buoys. Yes, thank you."

They drove back along Dock Road and turned up Church Hill. The streets were clogged with marine stores, stalls selling chestnuts and flatfish, and—outnumbering all others—old clothesmen: outfitters, tailors, army and navy accoutrement makers. Beyond that, a block off Medway Street, a row of public houses lined the waterfront. The third one along indeed displayed a signboard painted with white bell buoys riding stiff-looking waves.

115

"Er . . . m'lord, you'll be pardoning me for mentioning it, but the time is getting on a bit, and that is . . . with the fresh air and all . . ."

"Are you trying to tell me you're hungry, Hardy?"

"Oh, it's not myself that I'm thinking of, m'lord. But Even here is a fine fellow, very good with the horses he is—"

"Never mind." Danvers put some coins into his man's hand. "If the menu runs to steak and kidney pies, see that you get good hot ones."

Danvers and Futter approached the publican, standing in white apron behind the bar, polishing glasses. He wrinkled his bald forehead at their questions, making the ends of his drooping mustache wave. "Spanish, you say? We don't get much foreign trade here. Mostly good, honest English limeys." He held out a glass. "Can I offer you gentlemen some refreshment?"

Both men declined. Futter described Miguel in his heavy, dark blue coat. "Most likely some of his mates would have been wearing striped jerseys—wide, blue and white." He indicated horizontal stripes across his chest.

"Oh, that lot. Spanish, were they? Didn't take no note of how they talked. Busy we were that night. Gets a bit lively in here sometimes. Yeah, they had a few rounds. Didn't cause no trouble. Didn't notice your bloke in particular though."

Danvers considered suggesting they might question some of the staff, although it seemed unlikely they would learn much. It was clear Miguel couldn't have robbed or murdered anyone in Chatham while the *Barcelona* was still in the Medway estuary, limping along with a hole in her hull. But a whole new line of questioning occurred to him when Hardy appeared at his shoulder carrying two steaming pies.

"Guess who's at the table over there by the window, m'lord." He nodded across the smoky room toward a large round table where two women and three men sat drinking and laughing loudly.

Danvers stared at the broad back and straggly rust-colored hair of the woman who sat with her face turned away from him. "Unless I am much mistaken that is Elizabeth Law."

"Sure and it is. Spotted her before she saw me, so I just kept my head down, so to speak, while I got my pies. Thought you'd like to know with her unawares."

"Good, good, Hardy. You and coachman enjoy your pies. You've earned them." He turned back to the landlord. "The woman there with her back to us. Do you recognize her?"

The publican nodded. "Of course. That's our Bessie. One of my regulars."

"She comes here often then?"

"Always on her nights off—and maybe more when she could sneak in between times. Terrible harridan her mistress was. For all she gave right generous to charities, they say. Course, speak well of the dead and all that. But truth is truth, I say. You fellows maybe heard about that? Pair of dustmen, they say. Battered the old woman to death, stole every stick of furniture in her house, and slit our Bessie's throat. Lucky to be alive, that girl is. I give her a pint of my best when she came back, I did—to celebrate the fact she still had a gullet to pour it down."

"Er . . . yes. I quite take your meaning." Danvers rather wished he hadn't. "But Bessie—she comes here every week, you say."

The publican patted his ample, round stomach as a sign of satisfaction. "More now. But then every night's her night off now, isn't it?"

Futter picked up the questioning. "Yes, quite so. But if you could just think back a few days. The night of January twenty-eight. Was Bessie here then?"

"That the same night you were asking about that Spanish lot?"

Futter shook his head. "No. No, that should have been two nights before the Spaniards came."

The drooping mustache wobbled from side to side as the landlord considered. He seemed to be giving his full attention to wiping an already thoroughly polished glass. Then he brightened. "Yes. I do remember. That was the night there was a fair scuffle—some limeys arguing over a girl, it seems."

"Not Bessie?" Futter asked.

"No, no, little blond with the brightest red lips—suppose it was paint, but still . . . No, I remember Bessie Law was here then because I no more than got that lot settled than Bessie started arguing with some fellow she was drinking with."

"One of those at the table now?" Futter asked.

"No, some fellow I never seen before. Nice looking chap—refined like. Didn't sound too refined when he started threatening Bessie though. Not but what she couldn't have defended herself all right. Bigger than him, our Bessie. Anyway, I told her she'd had enough to drink. Sent her home, I did. Knew her employer didn't like her coming in drunk—heard Bessie say so often enough. So I sent her along. Wouldn't do either of us any good if she got dismissed, would it? But then that awful thing happened. Suppose it would of been better for Bessie if she hadn't been there. Still, she were lucky."

"Thank you, landlord, you've been most helpful." Danvers placed a coin on the counter.

"Thank you, sir. Any time. You know where The Three Bells is to be found."

They moved away, Danvers explaining his idea to Futter. Futter nodded and approached Bessie's table. A few moments later he returned, escorting a flushed Bessie Law on his arm. "You keeping those 'orrid murderers locked up tight, are you, gov'nor? Good riddance to 'em, I say. People got to know they can't go about bashing unsuspecting little old ladies in the head."

"True enough, Bessie. That's true enough." Danvers held open the door of The Three Bells. A gust of wind made the sign creak on its hinges over his head. "Thing is, we've only got the one, and he denies it."

"Well, he would, wouldn't he?" Bessie looked around with a brilliant smile as she saw the elegant carriage she was to ride in. "Cor, I never been in nothing so fine as this before."

"Well, just get right in and make yourself comfortable, my girl," Futter said. "Sure, it won't take you a moment to tell us if we've got the right man. We appreciate your cooperation."

At the police station Danvers had a quick, quiet word with Orson, who turned to the back room to arrange matters. When Futter escorted Bessie in, Miguel sat at a small table that had been cleared of dishes, even though the scent of garlic still hung in the air. The room was dark, but three gaslights had been turned up high, making patchy golden pools around the room. Miguel sat with his head down, toying with the cutlery still on the table.

"Now, just take your time, Miss Law," Futter said. "We want to be very sure about this."

Elizabeth Law took one step inside the room and stood stock still.

Miguel looked up.

Bessie pierced the air with her scream. She clutched her throat with both hands and began backing toward a corner. "It's him! It's him! Take that knife away from him afore he slashes us all."

"You're very sure, Bessie? You couldn't be mistaken?"

"Course I'm sure. Ask him where his partner is. Ask him about the stuff they pawned at Greenwood's."

"How would you know about that?" Futter asked.

"Just remembered. I heard 'em talkin'. With me layin' on the floor bleedin' to death—dead already, they thought, no doubt. Two bleedin' corpses in the room and cool as a

119

cucumber them discussin' how much they'd get for Mrs. Bacon's jade rings at Greenwood's."

"You heard them talking?"

"That's right, just afore I passed out. That's why I didn't remember it none sooner. Must of been the shock of seein' him that brought it back like."

"Isabella, ask Miguel what he has to say about Bessie's charge," Danvers instructed the tiny maid sitting quietly beside the door.

She spoke a few quiet, rapid sentences in Spanish.

Miguel answered with a flood of vehement speech and gesticulations that even the least linguistically inclined could tell were ardent denials.

Bessie leaned forward, her eyes growing wide. "Here now, what's he sayin'? That's not proper speech."

"You don't understand that, Bessie?"

"Course not. How could I?"

"That's what we want to know," Danvers said. "Because it's the only language Miguel speaks."

"Well. Er . . . well, maybe I made a mistake." Bessie looked around wildly like a cornered animal. "It's too dark in here. I couldn't see proper. I made a mistake."

"Yes, indeed you did, Bessie," Danvers said. "Only thing I'm trying to figure out is just what that mistake was."

10

The next morning in the breakfast room, the dowager duchess balanced a thin, crisp slice of toast on the edge of her plate.

"I'm not at all surprised to hear that you're mixed up in another horrid murder, Charles. As a matter of fact, it is precisely what I would expect from one so attached to debased architectural forms as you are. That my own nephew could fail to pursue the elevation of the pure Gothic is simply shocking to me. Shocking."

Danvers grinned at her, his intelligent gray eyes sparkling. "One thing I will admit, Aunt Elfrida, is that the movement is certainly well-named."

"Of course it is, my boy. That's my whole point. Architecture reflects the state of the society by which it is built. Monuments of architecture are in fact nothing but the aesthetic expression of social, political, and religious institutions. The society of the Middle Ages was good. Therefore Gothic architecture is good."

Danvers handed his empty coffee cup to Edward, standing behind him. "I'm afraid that wasn't quite my reference, Aunt Elfrida."

"Then whatever can you mean?"

"I refer to the fact that the Goths, after all, were barbarians. The Goths were not builders but destroyers. And that is exactly what anyone who attempts to deface the perfection of Canterbury Cathedral will be—a destroyer. The clean lines of the Perpendicular—"

"Twaddle. No less an authority than Horace Walpole expressed himself as shocked—dismayed—at the nudity of Canterbury. Completely lacking the dramatic, sentimental gloom one expects of abbeys and cathedrals." She paused to take a sip from her brocade-patterned cup. "And no less an authority than Augustus Pugin, son of the author of *Specimens of Gothic Architecture*—"

"Ah, yes. Forgive my interruption, Aunt Elfrida, but you will be happy to know that I have been reading Pugin's book. Concisely titled, it is something like *Contrasts: A Parallel Between the Noble Edifices of the Fourteenth and Fifteenth Centuries and Similar Buildings of the Present Day; Shewing the Present Decay of Taste*." He paused for breath. "Titles aside, I must say that the principles he laid down for the Gothic revival are sound. The Gothic was true because it was the result of an honest use of materials in which structure was exposed and function demonstrated."

"There! Exactly. What did I tell you? Now get about it and give your cooperation to my committee. And I expect a substantial monetary subscription as well, you understand."

Danvers accepted his refilled cup from the underfootman. "If you will forgive me, Aunt Elfrida—which I know you won't, but I intend to continue anyway—I must point out that everything I've heard proposed by Lansing and his demolitionists runs precisely counter to Pugin's principles."

"Don't be absurd, Charles."

"It is the basis of Pugin's philosophy that every feature of a building should be essential to its proper functioning and construction, and every feature of this construction should be frankly expressed. Architecture must be judged by the highest standards of morality and integrity."

"Precisely. In other words the building must be Gothic if it is to rise to the highest standard. Ruskin says that the Gothic style is supreme for its truth to nature and moral force. Surely you wouldn't go so far as to refute Ruskin?"

Danvers held up a hand. "Aunt Elfrida, I wouldn't think of it. And with *The Stones of Venice* on every bookshelf of taste in England I have no doubt that the country will now be dotted with Italianate buildings. If that is what people want, let them build them, I say."

"Well, then—"

"Let them build as an expression of the ideals of this age. Don't let's tear down what other ages have done—in many cases far better than we can ever match. Let us not cover honest Early English churches with fake Italian."

"Charles, I despair of you. I fear you are quite past redemption, but I shall make one last attempt to rescue you. Go to Ramsgate. Pugin's church and home there are his masterpieces. View them with as open a mind as you are capable of. Then read the notes he left on all his work. If that leaves you unmoved, I shall abandon all hope for you."

"And allow me to resign from the committee? I accept. Edward, send my man to me. I shall send Hardy ahead to request permission to peruse the man's papers. His family maintains them, I assume."

"There will be no need, dear boy."

"Surely, Aunt Elfrida, you don't suggest I drop in unannounced?"

"Certainly not. I sent a note yesterday."

Still shaking his head, Charles stood as the dowager duchess rose and made a triumphant exit. He glanced at the half-eaten meal still on his plate. The sausages were cold, the bacon limp.

In their room Antonia was just finishing her own breakfast.

123

Danvers caught his breath and smiled at the sight of his wife wearing the peach-silk and ivory-lace dressing gown that she had worn on their honeymoon. Her undressed auburn hair was spreading around her shoulders. "Tonia, you look delicious. It isn't fair. I had hoped to spend the day with you. Now I find I must hare across the length of Kent."

"What is it, Charles?"

"I've just spent the better part of an hour having Aunt Elfrida's theories hammered over my head. And as if spoiling my breakfast wasn't enough, I now find I must continue by poring over old documents in Ramsgate."

"Ramsgate!"

Danvers was caught by what seemed a note of alarm in her voice. Then he realized how silly that notion was. She was surprised. That was all.

Yet her eyes and voice both held caution as she asked. "Whatever could you need to go to Ramsgate for, Charles?" It seemed that she held her breath for his answer.

"That is where Augustus Welby Northmore Pugin built his finest monuments to true Gothic architecture. Afraid I rather played into Aunt Elfrida's hands on this one—started quoting his principles to her, so then I couldn't very well refuse to study his work."

"Will he be there?"

"No, no. Died about three years ago, I think. The deuce of it is that with choir practice in Canterbury later this afternoon I won't be able to return all day, and I had so hoped we might have a really pleasant day together . . ."

He left the invitation hanging. He did not want to push her, and this was hardly the season for visiting seaside resorts. But he did so want to give Tonia a nice outing. She had been so withdrawn and introspective lately. Perhaps if he encouraged her just a little . . .

"No, Charles, I—"

"No dissembling now, Tonia. I know you too well

124

not to realize that all this murder and robbery business is bothering you more than you'll admit."

"Oh, that." She looked confused.

"Yes, just that. We shall try to make up for it with a fine day together. What do you say?"

"Of course, Charles. I'd be delighted to go with you. Pull the bell for Isabella. I'll make a quick toilette."

Far quicker than he had any right to expect, she was before him, radiant in a gold-and-brown visiting suit trimmed with ball fringe. He put her fur-edged cloak around her shoulders and gave her a small hug.

When they stepped out of doors, Danvers surveyed the clear sky over their heads. "What a pity. If this matter had arisen earlier, I could have sent Hardy to Laver Esherwood to arrange an aerostat for us. It would have made a jolly diversion for you."

Antonia drew the folds of her cloak about her. "Never mind, Charles. The train carriage will be quite drafty enough."

On the drive to Canterbury where they would take the train to Ramsgate, she seemed unusually thoughtful.

"You aren't worrying about anything, are you, my love? I know our last visit to Canterbury didn't have a very happy ending, but I'm sure Futter will have the whole matter wrapped up in a few days."

"What? Oh, Lily, you mean?" She shook her bonneted head. "Poor girl, I'm afraid I'd quite forgotten about her. No, no. I was thinking of something quite different." She reached over and took his hand. "I was thinking how good you are to go chasing about the country without regard to your own wishes, just to keep Aunt Elfrida happy."

Danvers laughed. "I fear that's an overstatement. I'm not sure Aunt Elfrida is ever happy. I think it is only being unhappy that makes her happy. But yes, one must do one's duty and all that."

"That's what I meant, Charles. There really isn't anything you wouldn't do out of family loyalty, is there?"

He felt the pressure of her hand increase on his. "Short of murdering anyone, you mean, of course." Then he turned serious. "I can think of only one thing I would put ahead of duty to my family, and that's duty to my God."

Tonia nodded, and they remained silent until they were settled on the train. Then he drew a slim, calf-bound volume from his traveling case. After a few moments of reading, he held out a carefully detailed sketch for Antonia to see. "There—that is Lichfield Cathedral's west front. What would you think of something similar for Canterbury?"

"Charles! You can't be serious." She frowned. Row after row of indistinguishable figures appeared to be stuck on the cathedral front in a maze of pointed arches and something resembling children's pinwheels. "It would be horrid. It's—it's all wrong. It wouldn't suit Canterbury at all."

"That, my love, is the crux of the matter. Lansing, on whose every word the dean hangs, is convinced it would be perfect. Pugin, fellow of taste that he was, saw the matter in quite a different light.

"After a visit to Lichfield, he wrote to a friend"—Charles read aloud—"'[Imagine] my horror and astonishment on perceiving the West Front to have been restored with brown cement, cracked in every direction, with heads worked on with the trowel, devoid of all expression or feeling, a mixture of all styles. My surprise, however, ceased on the verger's informing me that the whole church was improved and beautified by the late Mr. Wyatt—that monster of architectural depravity.'"

He closed the book.

"Pity Pugin is dead, or he might have addressed the committee for you. But Charles, you don't deny that there are parts that need restoring. Christ Church Gate is very nearly crumbling."

"That's just it. If only I could make them understand." Danvers waved his book as a preacher in a pulpit might wave his Bible. "Restoration means to fix, to mend, to redeem—to make new. If a man goes to our Lord to have his heart restored from sin, God does not make him into a monkey. He makes him into the finest man he is capable of being—restores him to the original vision of his Creator."

"Charles, that's beautiful."

"And it should be the same for a building—especially a church. Certainly there must be repair—refurbishing— but our goal must be to enhance the original vision of the creator! Forgive me, my dear. I will bore on, it seems."

"No, Charles. I'm not at all bored." She gripped his arm. "You are quite right to fight to preserve the work of the builders."

They were still in agreement when they arrived in Ramsgate. They took a walk along the chalk cliff above the harbor, then viewed the elegant Gothic St. Augustine's Church. "It is very fine. I can see why it is considered Pugin's monument," Antonia said.

"Yes, it is just right. It is exactly as its creator meant it to be—an honest expression of his vision based on years of study to understand the principles with which he worked. I have no argument with the concept of Gothic architecture in itself. It's just that destroying . . ." He paused. "Oh, never mind. You've heard it all before. And very patient you are too, my love."

They walked on a short distance and stood before a yellow brick building. "Here is Pugin's home. It seems I am supposed to call in and inspect some musty volumes of architectural theory."

Tonia laughed. "Dear Charles, what could any volume possibly teach you? You've been talking like the most learned Oxford don all morning."

He turned the corners of his mouth down ruefully. "Sorry. I do that when I feel strongly about something, don't I?"

"I'm afraid you do, my love. It's one of your most endearing qualities. But for the moment I am feeling rather strongly about my desire for luncheon. If I remember correctly, the London Hotel is just along the High Street." She started to turn, then became suddenly quiet, biting her lip.

The walk was bordered by a sturdy iron fence, newly erected to protect the cliff edge. Danvers took her arm and led the way. "You're quite right. It's the corner of High and King Streets. My father dined there before embarking for Waterloo, if I remember correctly. But I didn't think you'd ever been here before."

Her trill of laughter sounded forced. "Oh, didn't I mention it? Well, it's little wonder. I was quite young."

"It must have been a lovely place to holiday as a child. I love the seashore. Did you stay long?"

"Oh . . . well, yes. Rather, I guess. Children don't really notice time, do they? Oh, Charles, let's walk faster. What a lovely view of the harbor. The lighthouse is so picturesque, don't you think?"

She tried to increase their pace, but Charles held back. "Odd, though, your parents choosing Ramsgate rather than Margate. Margate is so much more fashionable."

"I . . . I believe some friend of my father's advised him that Ramsgate is more sheltered. Therefore the breezes are just as fresh but gentler."

"And I wonder that you came all this way and yet didn't stop in Canterbury to see the cathedral."

Again Tonia's laughter carried a strained note. "Papa must have been in one of his utilitarian phases. I remember he was most intent that . . . that we not lose a moment of breathing sea air." She paused for a deep breath. "It is marvelous, isn't it?"

Danvers likewise breathed deeply. "Very restorative."

The hotel dining room offered tables in long window alcoves overlooking the harbor and the system of stone piers that almost completely enclosed Ramsgate's port. The masts of a score of sailing vessels rocked gently at anchor, while two steam-powered ships, tall smokestacks billowing, chugged toward the open channel past the lighthouse that marked the harbor entrance.

Between the potted palms along the wall behind them hung oil paintings depicting scenes of Ramsgate: Pugin's St. Augustine Church, the Church of St. George the Martyr, the enormous Conyngham House for the open-air treatment of consumption, a summer beach in front of tall white cliffs, the sand lined with red-and-white-striped bathing machines, each a little room for conveying one modestly into the water.

A white-jacketed waiter interrupted their contemplation to present them with large white menus ornamented with exquisite scrollwork and gold tassels.

Danvers ran down the rather usual bill of fare, offering boiled whiting, broiled whiting, and whiting au gratin; veal pie, mutton pie, rabbit pie; and roast sirloin of beef, roast ribs of beef, and beefsteak, rolled, roasted, or stuffed. He was just about to select the latter to accompany his whiting au gratin and boiled vegetables when a most unusual item caught his eye. "Tonia, did you see this? They offer fresh goat's milk and boiled seaweed. How very singular. You don't suppose their chef's Chinese, do you?"

"I shouldn't think it likely. French, I expect."

Danvers gave their orders. He couldn't help feeling that his goal of giving Antonia an enjoyable holiday had gone a bit awry somewhere, although he couldn't put his finger on it. Certainly they had had pleasant conversation, the weather was far better than he could have hoped, and Tonia seemed determinedly cheerful. That was it, wasn't it? Where was the natural, relaxed camaraderie he so cherished? Why would his Antonia have to force herself to be a charming companion?

A number of possibilities presented themselves. She was worried about the murder, even though she denied it. She wasn't feeling well, although she professed to be in the top of health. He had done something to offend her, although he couldn't imagine what. Looking up, he caught her unaware, brow furrowed, lower lip tucked in tightly at the corners. This air of worried control, he now realized, had hung around her for days. Since they'd come to Canterbury perhaps?

He searched his mind for reasons. Only dark, completely unacceptable possibilities came to him. He would entertain no such thoughts.

Fortunately the sun broke through just then, streaking the white-framed windows beside them with beams of gold. "I believe it might be almost warm in the sunshine. Perhaps you would like to stroll about the piers after lunch? I've seen quite enough of Pugin's work to satisfy Aunt Elfrida. You must have memories of favorite places where you played as a child that it would amuse you to revisit?"

Tonia shrugged. Or was it a shiver? "I was very young. And I wasn't allowed to run about much. My nurse was very strict."

"Yes, of course. But did you bathe?"

Antonia looked up from her boiled salad: beetroot, celery, potato, and boiled brussels sprouts sliced and dressed with a rich sauce of cream, eggs, and mustard. The dish was undoubtedly much tastier than boiled seaweed, but she had eaten little of it.

Charles frowned. Antonia had always had such a healthy appetite.

"Oh, yes. Most regularly. I remember enjoying the hot baths at Clarence's. But sea bathing was a bit of an ordeal. Very strict about it, Miss Gordon was. A cold sponge bath first thing upon rising, then a five- or ten-minute walk before breakfast. A very light breakfast. Bathe in the sea two hours after breakfast. Keep moving about while in the water. Stay in the water no more than ten minutes, rub down well, and dress. We always walked very slowly back up the hill. I remember being starved by then, but the rules were a cup of cocoa and a tiny biscuit. Then a nap."

"Doesn't sound much of a holiday for a child." He

grinned. "I can imagine you were very active. Must have given Miss Gordon a run for her money."

"I think I would have liked to, but there was no disobeying our Miss Gordon." Tonia paused for a long time, obviously struggling to make a decision. At last she took a deep breath and looked up with a determined glint in her eye. "Charles, I have to apologize to you. I've been putting this off, but . . . everything I've said is perfectly true . . . it's just that—"

The waiter appeared at her elbow to clear away the charlotte russe and present them with a selection of tangy cheeses. Danvers made his choice off-handedly, wishing the man anywhere but here. What did Antonia mean? What had she been about to say?

At last the fellow was gone. "You were saying— about everything being perfectly true, but—" he prodded.

Tonia nibbled the edge of a water biscuit. He could plainly see she was rethinking her earlier decision about whatever it was she was about to tell him.

At last she nodded. "Yes, I was here . . . you see, that is . . ." She stopped as the host ushered a couple to a table three alcoves beyond them. *"Charles!"* She tugged on his sleeve, and whatever she had been about to divulge was gone. "Look. Over there, just beyond that palm."

His neck would not crane far enough to see, so he turned in his chair. Then he stared. "That's Eleanor! What can she be doing here? And is that—"

"Yes, that's Lansing. I spotted him first. Charles, this really is too bad. I've seen nothing objectionable in him, but Eleanor is only nineteen—and dining alone with a man in a hotel. It won't do."

"No, it certainly won't. I gave him permission to call on her, not to ruin her reputation by going about in public unchaperoned." Danvers got to his feet. "You'll excuse me for a moment, my dear." He did not wait for her reply but strode the length of the dining room, moving between

131

round tables draped in stiff white linen, half-hidden by luxuriant potted palms.

"Eleanor, I would like to know what is the meaning of this?"

"Why, Charles, I didn't expect to see you here." His sister smiled up at him, her long, dark lashes drooping over her eyes.

"Obviously not. But that hardly explains matters, does it? What have you to say for yourself, Lansing?"

Randolph Lansing came to his feet. "Why, I came to study Pugin's work. Your sister most graciously agreed to accompany me. I am giving her luncheon. Much similar, if I may assume, to your own schedule. I have made some excellent notes on some of Pugin's sketches—"

"Pugin can go to blazes and his notes with him. You presume too much, sir. What is proper for Lady Danvers and myself has no bearing on what you may do with my sister. For the first time I believe I understand Agatha's objection."

A gasp broke from Eleanor. "But Charles, this is a perfectly respectable—"

"Not for an unmarried, unchaperoned woman, Eleanor. You will come with me now."

"But Charles, I'm hungry."

"That is unfortunate. Perhaps Tonia will escort you to a tea shop in Canterbury while I have my choristers' rehearsal. If not, I can only hope the hunger pangs will serve to recall to you a sense of propriety. You are the daughter of the Earl of Norville. You will not behave like a guttersnipe." He held her chair for her to rise.

Then Danvers turned to the man still standing quietly. "We will speak no more of this, Lansing. The matter is closed. But you are to see my sister only in proper company. And most would consider me far too liberal in granting that privilege."

Lansing's features were rigid as he bowed.

"Eleanor is returning with us, Tonia."

132

He helped his wife with her chair. The day had been a disaster. Why did Eleanor have to show up just at the moment Tonia was about to confide in him? Now there would be no chance of it. The best he could hope for was a successful rehearsal and a quick return home.

They were on the train to Canterbury when Tonia, whose efforts to bring Eleanor out of her sullens had met with little success, said, "Charles, why don't you show Eleanor the sketches in your architecture book? I'm sure they would amuse her much more than this dull, brown scenery. How a county as beautiful as Kent can look so dismal in February is quite amazing."

Danvers doubted that his book would add much to any attempt to raise his sister's spirits, but he could think of nothing better. He opened the little volume and began pointing out various cathedrals.

Much to his surprise, Eleanor did show an interest. "Why, yes, that's St. Alban's. Randolph said there is much talk of restoring it."

"Not St. Alban's surely! It's one of the oldest and most perfect Norman naves in the country." In his agitation he snatched the book away.

There was a tearing sound, and a corner of St. Alban's Cathedral fluttered to the floor.

"Oh, I'm so sorry, Charles. Truly I am. My bracelet caught—" Eleanor gasped, blushed, and covered her mouth with one hand and her bracelet with the other, all in two seconds' time.

Tonia caught Eleanor's left wrist and examined the piece of jewelry circling it. "Why, Nelly, what a charming bracelet!"

Twelve individually set jewels resembling miniature brooches were linked by gold chains. Tonia pushed each one along its slide as she admired it—an exquisitely carved cameo, a gold star set with a sapphire, an ornate fleur de lis set with a pearl, a filigree gold rose . . .

133

"I'm very fond of slide bracelets." Antonia touched the crescent moon set with diamonds, which ended the string, and dropped Eleanor's hand. "I quite believe this is the loveliest one I've ever seen. Be very careful with it. It must have been frightfully expensive."

"No. Well, that is, I don't really know. I . . . er . . ."

Now it was Danvers's turn to grip his sister's wrist. "Nelly, what about the bracelet? Where did you get it?"

"It was a gift from . . . from a friend."

"Lansing, you mean. Did he give this to you?"

Eleanor hung her head. "Yes, Randolph gave it to me. It was very precious to him because it had belonged to his mother."

Eleanor drew back as Charles's heavy eyebrows loomed forward and his craggy features darkened formidably. "Agatha is right. The man is an encroaching puppy. I'll not have it. This is most improper. What can he have been thinking of? You may not keep the bracelet, Eleanor."

Eleanor nodded miserably and sniffed loudly but did not cry. When she fumbled to undo the clasp, however, her eyes were so clouded with tears that she could not see what she was doing.

"Here, let me help, Nelly," Tonia said gently.

Eleanor obediently held out her wrist.

Tonia undid the clasp and slipped the bracelet into her reticule. "There, now, we'll say no more about it for the present."

Danvers nodded at the sharp look his wife gave him. Antonia was clearly rebuking him for being so harsh with his sister, undoubtedly accusing him of putting duty and family respectability ahead of the feelings of others again.

But he wasn't, he argued silently. He was protecting his sister against what was looking more all the time like a grave mistake. One that was in many ways his fault. Eleanor had become seriously involved because he had been slow to see the danger.

"Yes, Nelly, don't cry. Tonia's quite right. We'll think no more about it."

Easy enough to say, he reflected. He knew he must think about it a great deal more. How could everything be going so wrong? His whole desire for the day had been to cheer Antonia up. Instead, apparently he had inadvertently unearthed some unhappy childhood memories, memories she hadn't even been able to talk to him about. And now he had involved her in Eleanor's unhappiness.

Dear Nelly, his favorite sister. Nineteen was too young to have one's heart broken. And yet, what could he do?

11

At least when the train pulled into Canterbury, it became easier to follow Charles's directive to think of something else. "Here, Nelly—" Tonia slipped her sister-in-law a lace-edged handkerchief "—we'll see what we can do now to have a lovely time in this charming town."

She studied Eleanor, trying to decide on the best course of action to cheer up the girl. It was pleasant to have another's happiness and concerns to think about. She had had quite enough worrying about her own. Eleanor's tenuous grip on her emotions did not make it appear she would be feeling up to eating or shopping quite yet. "Perhaps we'll just go along with Charles for a bit and see how he gets on with his choir before setting out on our own, shall we?"

Eleanor nodded.

Tonia leaned toward her sister-in-law's ear. "If we don't have to listen too carefully, it might make for some amusement."

Eleanor smiled.

Tonia felt a small triumph. The smile was wobbly, but she was making progress. And raising Eleanor's spirits would help raise her own too.

Danvers hailed a hackney in front of the station to take them to the cathedral, and in a few minutes they were seated quite comfortably on the wooden chairs between choir and altar, where the clergy sat for services. That is, Tonia and Eleanor were seated. They seemed to be the only ones in the entire expanse of the great cathedral who were sitting at ease.

Certainly Danvers was not sitting. He appeared to be going in ten directions at once in a frenzied attempt to gather his twenty-some choirboys into their seats. Herding chickens into a coop would surely have been an easier job.

The situation was exacerbated by the fact that the train had arrived several minutes behind schedule, so that the boys had all arrived before their choirmaster. In the absence of authority, they had immediately dispersed. The cathedral offered too many opportunities for exploring. No nine-to-twelve-year-old boy could be expected to sit still in the face of such temptation.

Tonia was uncertain, but she had the impression of an impish face peering over the high railing that shielded the choir from the south aisle. Surely that wasn't possible. She was relieved that none of the boys actually went so far as to attempt climbing the pillars or walking the railing around Trinity Chapel. But there was no mistaking the impropriety of the grubby urchin who mounted the spiral stairs to the pulpit or the two shaggy heads that surveyed the length of the apse from behind the archbishop's chair. Each neck rested on a curve of the chairback as if in the bottom half of a pillory.

For every three Danvers managed to corral and herd onto one of the red-cushioned benches behind the choir music racks, it seemed that two escaped out the other end into the nave.

Tonia knew she should be assisting him, but the effort to control her giggles required all her energy. She

137

turned to suggest that Eleanor might want to help and saw that the girl was shaking with silent laughter.

"Oh, Tonia. I had some puppies once—a litter of seven. They kept wandering off from their mother. Every time I'd take one back to her, two more would meander off." She stopped to wipe her eyes. "They're just like puppies."

If Tonia had been seeking entertainment to raise their spirits, she could have done no better.

Poor Charles. Just that morning, with pride in his newly recognized musical ability and a missionary's zeal to do a good work, he had explained to her that this was no ordinary choir—not at all the regular set of choirboys who sang all year in Canterbury Cathedral and doubtless could have executed the "Restoration Contanta" leaderless should they be required to. No, these were a special lot—boys off the street brought together once a year to perform for the pre-Lenten service.

"They must be so grateful, poor wretches. It's a splendid chance for them, you see. If any excel, this is their chance to be offered an opening in the cathedral school. I can't tell you how honored I feel to have a hand in such an exemplary work."

Dear Charles. She shook her head. Would his idealism carry him through his first rehearsal? It was little wonder Canon Dettra had come down with an attack of hives. She only hoped Charles would suffer nothing worse.

"Come, we really must see what we can do to help." Tonia rose and smoothed her skirt over her crinoline. "I'll take the north aisle."

She had moved no more than three or four steps when a cheery voice rang out from the far end of the choir.

"And a fine day to be singing an anthem to our Creator, is it not? I thought I'd just look in a bit early, m'lord, in case you could be using a hand. But it seems you have everything under control." Hardy's cherubic face beamed as he marched forward. A squirming choirboy all but dangled from each hand.

"Thank you, Hardy. Very nearly under control, as you say. Perhaps just one or two more spaces to fill. If you could just . . . uh . . ." Danvers gestured toward the half-filled choir rows.

"Ah, certainly, m'lord. I take your meaning." Hardy turned and addressed the boys in the tone he would have used on a laundry maid who had the effrontery to put too much starch in my lord's shirts.

When Danvers returned with three from the organ loft, Hardy had the boys singing a heartfelt version of "Londonderry Air."

"Not quite cathedral music, I'm thinking, sir, but it'll do to warm their voices up a bit."

"Thank you, Hardy." Danvers wiped his forehead. "Now—" he rapped his music stand with a baton "—all of you, stay put. We will take the aria and chorus, 'I Will Restore Them.'"

He waved his baton to the organist in the loft above. After the peals of the prelude, he flung both arms forward for a powerful opening phrase.

Nothing happened.

"Come, come now." He rapped for attention. "You've had several practices with Canon Dettra. Surely you know this one."

A mop-headed blond in the second row raised a hand, remarkably well-behaved now that the business had actually begun. "That's a solor, me lord. Higgins's solor. He ain't here."

"Sam were here earlier, gov." A tall, skinny lad flung brown hair out of his eyes and looked upward as if hoping to see the straggler among the vaulted arches.

"Very well, we shall proceed. *I* will sing the solo. Be prepared to come in on the chorus." Again Danvers signaled the organist. He took a deep breath. "I will restore to you all the land that belonged to your grandfathers. I will restore the temple of the Lord . . ."

139

Tonia grabbed Eleanor's hand. It would be disastrous to Charles's new-won discipline if they burst out laughing. And she could feel Eleanor shaking. They escaped into the north aisle.

"Perhaps we should see if we can locate the truant Higgins," Tonia suggested. "Odd he wouldn't show up when the music started. Surely he would recognize his solo."

Behind them the clear, light voices of the choir sang —surprisingly melodiously— "So builded they the temple of the Lord. Masons and carpenters restoreth they the temple. Workers in iron and bronze repaireth the temple."

Then Danvers's solo voice, carrying no less strongly for being off-key, thundered forth. "Who authorized you to rebuild this temple and restore this structure?"

Tonia increased the urgency of her search as the question was repeated three times, each building in fervor.

The choir responded, "The Lord our God, it is He who directeth us. The Lord our God and no other. He only hath authority to touch this, His holy house . . ."

As Tonia approached the choir transept, a movement in the underportion of Archbishop Chichele's tomb caught her eye. A most unusual monument, Chichele's tomb exhibited a splendid effigy of the fifteenth-century archbishop in golden miter and flowing robes. But underneath, visible through trefoil arches, was a skeletal likeness, stripped of its earthly glory, to signify the ephemerality of worldly power and riches.

Now, however, the archbishop's bony legs were covered with a plump, quite lively figure.

Tonia squatted down, an action that made her crinoline puff out in all directions, and looked into the most lavishly freckled face she had ever seen. "Sam Higgins, I assume?"

The mop of red hair nodded, but the round blue eyes looked frightened.

"Come now, you mustn't be afraid. Can't you hear they're singing your song? You don't want to lose your solo, do you?"

This time the red hair wagged from side to side, and the blue eyes grew wider.

"Well, come on then." Tonia reached for the hand thrust in Higgins's pocket to help pull him out of his cramped position. To her surprise, he pulled farther back, then worked himself out of the awkward spot using only his left hand. The right stayed firmly in place.

"Just a minute, young man." She caught him by the collar of his tweed jacket. "What have we got here? It won't do to take knives or noisemakers or anything like that to choir practice." She gave his right arm a sharp jerk. The hand came out of the pocket with the sound of ripping.

Tonia gasped. It was nothing mischievous or destructive, as she had expected; on the contrary, Higgins's hand was empty. But on his middle finger was a most charming ring.

"Nelly, look at this." She summoned her companion, who had been searching farther along the aisle.

Now it was Eleanor who gasped. "But—it's just the same . . ."

Tonia nodded. "Identical design, I should think." She dug in her reticule and pulled out Eleanor's slide bracelet. The ring on the boy's finger was a match to the pearl-studded fleur de lis segment.

"Where did you get this?" She didn't shake her small captive, but she gripped his arm securely enough to let him know she meant business.

"I didn't steal it. I wouldn't do that. But it was so pretty. And whoever dropped it down there, it must of been a long time ago—it's all so dark and musty. I didn't mean to be stealing."

To Tonia's amazement, Higgins burst into sobs interspersed with a high-pitched wail. Now she did shake

141

him. "Stop that. Do you mean to say that you found this ring just now?"

A loud sniff of the freckled nose and a nodding of the russet head followed.

"And where did you find it?"

"Down there—where it's all dark and spooky. In a little room."

Tonia grasped the beringed hand. "Show me."

She was sure she knew where they were going, and she had no desire to enter again the tiny crypt chapel, which had been far from empty the last time she saw it. But she must know.

Higgins led her straight to it. "We didn't mean no harm, but we got here early, before the choirmaster, so we thought we might as well have a bit of a look-see. Only my mates were too scared to come in here. They said it was where they put dead people, and it might be haunted."

"But you weren't afraid?"

The shoulders squared under the tweed jacket. "Course not. I'm not afraid of anything."

"I think you were afraid of having the ring taken from you. I think you were afraid to go to choir practice."

The shoulders shrugged on each side of a drooping head.

Tonia led the way back upstairs to better air and better light. "Well, it appears you were quite right, Higgins. You really can't keep this until we learn more about it—who owned it, how they lost it, that sort of thing." The head drooped lower.

"But there might well be a reward for your being so clever as to find it and so honest as to return it.

Higgins brightened considerably. "Yes, ma'am, but I can't give it back."

"I'm afraid you must."

"Well, you see, the thing is—it's stuck."

Tonia looked again at the hand she grasped. It was remarkably fine-boned under its plumpness. But the ring

142

was quite definitely stuck. "We need soap." She looked at Eleanor, but the girl shook her head. *There must be a public washroom somewhere,* she thought. What had Charles said about a washroom when they were here before?

Then she remembered. Not a public washroom, but the monks' lavatorium. In the Norman water tower—fitted with copper basins—and hopefully with linen towels and lanolin soap. She looked around. It was on this side of the cathedral, she was sure. If only she could get her bearings. Oh, yes, down this walkway.

Higgins's lower lip was thoroughly chewed by the time the ring had undergone repeated soapings, tuggings, and twistings, but at last it slid over the knuckle without actually taking a layer of skin with it. Tonia slipped the ring into her reticule, and they started back toward the choir from which wavering strains reached them.

"Restore to us the joy of Your salvation, and grant to us a willing spirit. Now restore us!" The recitative rang overhead in the arcading of the transept.

Just before they crossed the aisle to the choir area, Tonia stopped. "You're very brave, Higgins. Does no one else know you're a girl?"

The child's jaw dropped. For a moment denial flashed in the blue eyes. Then surrender. "Name's Sarah, but I like Sam better. They wouldn't let me sing if they knew. Expect some of my mates know—they just sort of forget like." She shrugged.

Tonia nodded. "Right. Well, you're very lucky, Sam, because I seem to have a very bad memory as well. Now get in there and behave yourself."

12

Restore us, O God; make Your face shine upon us, that we may be saved. Restore us, O God . . ."

The choir rang behind Tonia and Eleanor as they retreated down the long nave under its forest of giant, arching stone trees.

They found a tea parlor in the High Street and ordered lavishly. Tonia took pity on Eleanor, who had been denied her lunch, and waited until the girl had finished her third thick slice of fruitcake and started on the compote of marzipans shaped like fanciful birds, fruits, and flowers. Then she refilled both of their cups and said firmly, "Now, Nelly, we really must talk about Randolph."

The apprehension in the girl's eyes frightened Antonia.

"What do you mean, talk about Randolph? You know him."

"Don't be silly, Nelly. You know perfectly well what I mean. I know him very little, and I know even less of your feelings." She set down her teacup and took Eleanor's hand across the table. "Listen to me, Eleanor. If Randolph Lansing has behaved dishonorably toward you—"

The girl gasped and withdrew her hand. "No! That is—" She dropped her head, and the glossy black curls on each side of her face covered her pale cheeks. "Not in the way you mean. It's just that . . ." The voice trailed off to a muted sniff.

"Nelly, whatever it is, you must let Charles deal with it. You mustn't be afraid. You know there is nothing Charles wouldn't do for his family."

Eleanor dabbed at her eyes. "I know. Charles is the best of brothers—that's what's so awful. I feel I've betrayed him—let the whole family down."

Tonia braced herself to hear the worst. The Earl of Norville's family would not be the first or the last great family to endure scandal. But she did hate to think of more bad news for Charles—on top of what she would soon have to impart to him.

"You see—" Nelly took a quick gulp of tea "—we weren't just having lunch at the hotel today."

"Do you mean to be telling me that you were eloping?"

Eleanor looked at her through tear-blurred eyes and shook her head slowly.

"Then I can only assume you are trying to tell me that you had agreed to go there with Randolph for an . . . an assignation."

Now the tears brimmed over and ran silently down the smooth, white cheeks. "Oh, Tonia, I'm so miserable. He says he loves me desperately—and yet sometimes he treats me as if I'm not there."

"And so you thought that agreeing to an illicit tryst would get his attention?"

Eleanor sighed. "I'm not sure what I thought. It's just that I do love him so terribly, and I know he loves me. But he's in some sort of trouble—that is, he was. Something to do with money. He said it's all settled now and things will be different. He said he knew he hadn't been as attentive as he should be and begged me to allow him to show me how much he really cared." She paused for a wavery breath. "Oh, Tonia, he was so charming. I told him I thought he had . . . had found someone else. But he said see what a silly goose I was and gave me that bracelet. He wouldn't

145

have given me his mother's bracelet if there were another woman in his life, would he?"

Tonia agreed that didn't seem likely. "But, Nelly—at the hotel . . ."

Eleanor shook her head. "No, no, nothing happened. Truly. We had just arrived. Well, Randolph had signed in . . . oh, Tonia, I'm so ashamed. If you hadn't seen us . . . but what now? Will he ever speak to me again? Will Charles allow him to? Must you tell Charles what I've just told you?"

Those were good questions indeed, and Antonia didn't know the answer to any of them. But the rapid closing in of the winter evening outside the cozy tea shop told her it was time to get back to the cathedral.

She squeezed Eleanor's hand. "Try not to worry, Nelly. I won't say anything to Charles just yet, and we'll pray that it all works out for the best. We do care terribly for your happiness, you know."

Eleanor gave her a wobbly smile. "I know you do. That's what makes the thought that I almost let you down so terrible."

"Well, just thank God that you didn't, and we'll carry on from here."

Tonia paid for their tea and asked the shopkeeper to hail them a cab as it was now too dark and cold to walk. The lamplighter, duly leaning his ladder against each tall, black pole and clambering up to light the gas chimney, had done his job the length of the High Street, and thin swirls of fog hung around every patch of illumination as the hackney rolled up the street.

Rehearsal was just ending when they arrived back at the cathedral.

"That was good work, boys." Danvers beamed at his wiggly crew. "Higgins, you have an outstanding voice. We shall have to see about getting you recommended for the cathedral school."

The ragtag group pulled on caps and mittens, twisted knitted scarves around their necks, and went out in much better order than they had come in. Some even left singing—a few on key. They must have been listening to the organ rather than to the choirmaster, Tonia thought.

She grimaced as Charles came up, singing. "'I will restore them! sayeth the Lord our God.' Ah, wonderful music, wonderful!" He turned as if he would stay and sing more, but Tonia took his arm firmly.

"Charles, we shall be frightfully late for dinner. Aunt Elfrida will not be amused."

Hardy urged the coachman to his best pace and held a pole lantern out near the horses' heads to illumine the road in addition to the lanterns hanging on each side of the carriage. But the going was slow. It was, indeed, well past Aethelsham's established dinner hour when they arrived.

Aunt Elfrida was sitting stiffly at the head of the long Jacobean table in her dark-paneled dining room when Antonia looked in. The dowager duchess was not eating. She was merely sitting, surveying the table set with gleaming china, silver, and crystal. Now she picked up her lorgnette and surveyed Antonia as if a stranger had walked in. "It is my habit to come to the table at seven o'clock. I see no reason why I should change my schedule just because others are unreliable."

"Aunt Elfrida, I'm most dreadfully sorry. I am afraid Charles's choir rehearsal did run a bit overtime. But you would have been very proud of the results he got. It will be a splendid concert." When the dowager duchess did not respond, Tonia hurried on. "I'll just go change. I'll be as quick as I can."

"You may tell my nephew and niece we will dispense with the formality of a complete toilette. You may remove your bonnet and wash. I will receive you at my table in your afternoon dress."

Tonia curtsied. "Thank you, Your Grace. You are too considerate." She fled up the stairs to make the best job of it in the least time possible. The day had been filled with far too many tensions as it was. They did not need a stressful dinner to top it off. Unfortunately the removal of her bonnet revealed locks hopelessly mussed from a day of travel.

"Quick, Isabella, do something. I mustn't keep Aunt Elfrida waiting longer, but I can hardly appear at her table like this."

"Not to worry, my lady." Isabella picked up a pearl-handled brush. With a few deft strokes she swept Antonia's straggling hair into a loose torsade at the back of her neck and enclosed it in a shimmering gold net set with pearls and brilliants.

"Isabella, you're a genius."

The maid bobbed her head in acknowledgment, but Tonia thought she looked worried. She sighed inwardly—she really didn't have time for anything else, but she couldn't be heartless. "What is it, Isabella? Is anything wrong?"

"No, no. I think not too much wrong, my lady. But the Inspector Futter, he has been here all day. He questioned me so closely. You do not suppose he thinks I know anything of Lily's death, do you?"

"I'm sure he doesn't, Isabella. It's just his job to question everyone carefully—in case you saw something of importance that you didn't even realize mattered."

"Oh, I see." She shuddered. "I will be so glad when it is all settled. I do not like to think of one from this house . . ."

"Yes, I know, Isabella. None of us do. I'll have a word with Futter after dinner if he's still here. Maybe I can learn something that will reassure you."

"Thank you, my lady." Isabella put a single drop of perfume on a lace handkerchief and handed it to Tonia as she went out the door.

Indeed Futter was still there, and Charles was talking to him in the hall. Her husband had miraculously managed to change to a formal tailcoat and bow tie, but apparently Hardy had not been given adequate time to subdue his master's hair.

"My love, we must go directly in."

She took his arm just as he returned an object to the policeman. The light from the gas lamp in a wall bracket caught the tiny diamonds forming a crescent moon on a golden ring band. "Oh." She would have reached for it, but there was no need. She knew it was another to match the bracelet Lansing had given Eleanor—his mother's, he had said.

"Where did you get that?" Her tone was edged with fatigue and worry.

"Pawnbroker in Chatham, ma'am." Futter launched into his story. "Did the pawnshops at Chatham again. Found this at Greenwood's—"

Tonia cut him off with a wave of her hand. "Yes. Sorry, but there really isn't time to go into it right now. Could you possibly have something to eat in the kitchen, and we could talk later? I am sorry to ask you to stay so late—"

The inspector's broad smile stopped her apology. "Ah, that Mrs. Crompton is a fair hand with the pastry. It'd be no hardship at all to take a meal of her making—not having Mrs. Futter's cooking to sustain me here."

Eleanor joined them, hastily tied pink ribbons holding her still-bouncing curls in place.

Tonia shook her head. It wasn't fair that the girl could look so fresh after all that chasing about in the damp sea air. Then she rebuked herself for begrudging anything to a poor girl who seemed headed for certain heartbreak.

Between making polite murmurs to the dowager duchess's tirade regarding the sanctity of the dinner hour among members of polite society, and attending to her tasty cauliflower and almond soup, Tonia thought about the ring Futter had recovered. It had to be part of the unique set.

Lansing had made no secret of being short of money. So had he pawned his mother's jewelry? If he was that desperate, it seemed odd he hadn't pawned the entire set. Was there more yet? Perhaps a ring to match each segment of the bracelet?

She ate the portion of fricasseed sole with mushrooms that Edward set in front of her without giving a thought to the excellent dish. If only she could make some sense out of all this or, failing that, put it out of her mind and cheer Eleanor. At least Charles was doing his part. He remained unfailingly polite to Aunt Elfrida and complimented his sister on her appearance.

At least the dowager duchess switched topics as the next course was set. "I am most gratified to hear that you made a good work of it with the choir, Charles. I have decided to send out my card for a few select friends to make up a party for the concert. Considering the theme of the work you are performing, it will be a most appropriate occasion to reveal the plans for the restoration work. As soon as I heard what the program was to be, I knew it was most providential. I trust your excursion to Ramsgate was sufficiently instructive to elevate your sadly deficient taste, Charles?"

By the time the meal made its way to its stately conclusion, Tonia's head was aching abominably. Already the day had entailed enough activity for three normal days. And the perplexing matter of Futter's ring remained. She thought of excusing herself. No one would question her fatigue after such a day. But she knew the evidence she held was important and her questions were vital, although she could offer no answers. The sooner they were asked, the more quickly solutions might be found.

Danvers asked Hardy to invite Inspector Futter to join them in the library. A coal fire burned on the grate, and softly shaded lamps made the room glow. Tonia was thankful for the gentle lighting as she massaged her throbbing head.

"Tonia, it's abominably late. Why don't you go on up? I'll talk to Futter."

But she staunchly refused Charles's solicitous offer.

The inspector was quick to accept the chair his host offered him. "I don't remember when I've had such a confusing case. Seems the trails go off in every direction over half of Kent, then just sort of peter out. We've been working on the theory that Mrs. Bacon and Lily were done in by the same hand—the wounding being so similar and all—thought for a while it might even be the same knife. Then we found a bloody butcher knife at Mrs. Bacon's that they apparently grabbed to see to Bessie."

He stopped and shook his pale head, which looked almost white in the firelight. "Sorry, know I'm going on a bit. Getting late it is. Point of all that is, we're trying to find a link between Mrs. Bacon and Lily. There just doesn't seem to be any. Catherine Bacon was noted for her charity work but had nothing to do with housemaids, it seems."

"I think I know of a link."

Danvers and Futter stared at Antonia.

"Only trouble is, the link just seems more confusing than ever. That ring you showed us, Inspector. How did you identify it as being connected with the case? Was it on Bessie's list of missing objects?"

"Not at first, but she thought she remembered it when I showed it to her. She said the old lady had lots of jewelry—she wasn't sure."

"So why did you single it out?"

"Thing is, Greenwood the pawnbroker described Bessie to a hair."

"*Bessie* pawned that ring?" Now Tonia was more confused than ever. What could Bessie have been doing with Lansing's mother's ring? Another woman, Eleanor had said—but Bessie Law in that role was unthinkable. And how could the third piece of the set have shown up in Canterbury Cathedral in the room where Lily was found? Bessie had said the dustmen mentioned Greenwood's. Did

151

that mean Lansing had been robbed as well as Mrs. Bacon? If so, why hadn't he reported a theft? Why, why, why?

"Well, Charles, I have some more confusion for you." She opened her reticule and reached for Eleanor's bracelet. An edge of delicate lace from her handkerchief caught in the chain linking the medallions. When she pulled out the bracelet, the handkerchief tumbled out as well, bringing with it several other items from the small, beaded bag.

Futter scrambled to retrieve the coins that fell to the hearth rug while Tonia dug in the folds of her voluminous skirt for the matching ring.

At last they were all on the table—the bracelet and both rings.

Futter bent close as Antonia demonstrated the workings of the slide bracelet and pointed out how the rings were a perfect match. He moved the sparkling blue star along the chain, then pushed at the fanned wings of a tiny golden housefly with a black pearl body.

"Ah, that's a fine thing, that is. Mrs. Futter would right like that, she would. I don't suppose such a thing would be within my reach." His blush showed in the firelight.

Tonia smiled. It seemed incongruous to her that such a gentle soul had chosen to be a policeman. "I'm afraid this one would be very expensive. You see, the stones are quite genuine, and the gold ornaments beautifully handcrafted."

Futter's hopeful face fell.

"But there are others of this design—quite pretty ones—that should be perfectly reasonable."

It was not until Tonia was drifting off to sleep that night that her mind sifted to the surface something she had only half-noticed while she talked to Futter—Charles poking at a small white rectangle with the toe of his highly polished shoe. An object that had fallen from her reticule along with the handkerchief, coins, ring, and bracelet.

152

Then she saw him again, in slow motion, bending over, picking up the card, sticking it in his pocket.

Did he look at it? If so, it could have been no more than a glance. Had he looked at it carefully since?

With an icy certainty she knew what Charles had picked up. How could she have been so careless? Why, oh, why had she ever kept such a thing in her purse?

13

Charles saw Futter out, assuring the inspector he would see him on Monday in Chatham after their portrait sitting. Then he walked back into the library to turn out the gaslights. If he hadn't stumbled over a corner of the red-and-black Persian hearth rug, he might have forgotten about the object he had picked up from it earlier. Now he pulled it out and examined it.

As he had thought, it was a train ticket. A ticket to take the holder from Canterbury to Tunbridge Wells. Yesterday. The day he had asked Tonia to dine with him in Canterbury and she had said she was visiting her dressmaker—newly arrived in Canterbury from Paris, highly recommended. A new gown for the charity choristers' concert, she had said.

He cast back carefully in his mind. No, he was absolutely certain Tonia had not said anything about going to Tunbridge Wells.

Danvers groped his way to the straight, wooden chair beside the writing table. The small pale rectangle he held loomed so large it was as if it were the only thing in the room. His fingers holding it went so cold they were numb.

A dozen excuses crowded his mind. Litter. Tonia had picked it up somewhere, and there was no dustbin

154

available. She was holding it for a friend—Eleanor? Harriet? She had stumbled across evidence in the investigation she hadn't told him about yet.

He even tried to convince himself that the ticket had not fallen from Tonia's bag at all. It had been there before they came in. It had been Futter's. But the rigorous honesty with which he approached everything required him to recall distinctly this ticket tumbling from the depths of his wife's reticule. The wife who had never lied to him.

He tried again on the line that it was somebody else's ticket. Harriet's name brought with it a warmth of hope. He wanted to believe it was hers. That made sense. Harriet lived near Canterbury. Tonia had visited her there. For some reason Tonia had put Harriet's ticket to Tunbridge Wells in her reticule—just as she had Eleanor's bracelet.

And yet fear pricked the back of his mind. It didn't really make sense. It was much more likely that the ticket was Tonia's, retained to present at the exit barrier, then forgotten when—as so often happened—there was no agent on duty to collect the used tickets.

All the evasions, the withheld confidences of the past days, came back to him. Was it possible . . . no, not Tonia. She was the truest person he knew. He would not doubt her. Next to his own salvation there was nothing he believed in more firmly than his wife. His relationship with her was second only to his relationship with God.

A sudden void filled him, an ache of homesickness for her. He wanted to go to her, to lie beside her under the thick goose-down comforter of the giant tester bed, to hold her in his arms.

He threw the ticket on the dying embers, watched the edges turn brown and disintegrate. Then he turned and hurried upstairs.

The next morning and the morning after as well, he woke with Tonia, warm and soft, curled against him. He

155

rolled on his side and circled her with his arms. With his chin he nudged her thick, sweet-smelling hair out of the way and began kissing her neck. She made a small sound in her sleep and turned her head toward him. He kissed her cheek.

Then stopped. The kiss tasted salty. He looked and saw the hairlike trail of dried tears down her cheeks. Why had Antonia been crying in her sleep? Whatever it was, he longed to kiss her troubles away. If only she would talk to him. Surely there wasn't anything they couldn't cope with together.

He buried his face in her tangle of hair and breathed a prayer for her.

Danvers was startled to an upright position by an energetic, jolly warbling from the hall. Then Hardy burst into the room after a most perfunctory knock, bearing two lavishly filled breakfast trays and rendering a remarkable imitation of a lark to the accompaniment of a tiny mechanical bird perched in a golden cage on one of the trays.

He deposited his burdens on the table and turned with equal energy to pull the rose-velvet drapes. "And top of the mornin' to you, m'lord. Ah, and if it isn't the finest morning you could ever ask to encounter in the fair month of February."

The mechanical bird's song died, its wings stilled, and the little feathered head drooped. Hardy wound it up again with a golden key. Cheery notes trilled from its tiny beak.

Danvers was about to send his man out with a flea in his ear, but Tonia, now thoroughly awake, gave a cry of delight and held out her hand for the music box. "Hardy, it's charming! Where did you ever come by such a delightful thing?"

He placed it in her hand with a flourish. "Soyer, ma'am. He was turning out Lily's room. As she doesn't seem to have had any family, the disposition was up to him. He was very pleased when I told him as how I'd been

156

thinking that I should just be working harder to give better service to my lord and lady. There's not many as has such a fine place as I have—"

"That's very admirable, Hardy. Lady Danvers and I much appreciate your care for us—but if you could just see it clear to apply your excellent intentions elsewhere . . ."

"Oh, yes. I quite take your meaning, m'lord." Hardy backed toward the dressing room, bowing all the way—not a simple maneuver for one of his solid girth.

A scraping of hangers, a rumpling of clothes, a scrabbling of shoes and accessories sounded from the adjoining room. In a few minutes Hardy reappeared in the doorway, his arms piled almost to his eyes with objects from his lord's wardrobe. "I'll just be nipping downstairs with these, m'lord. A little brushing here, a spot of polish there, a bit of pressing everywhere—nothing but the best. Don't you be giving it a thought. Nothing's too much work."

Danvers surveyed the stack in his man's arms. "Just be sure you've left me something to wear today. And don't tumble down the stairs."

"Not to worry, m'lord. Not a bit. All will have my best attention." He went out whistling with the mechanical lark Tonia still held.

With the closing of the door, Antonia burst into laughter. "Was that our often morose, always slapdash Hardy? What could have gotten into him?"

Danvers shook his head. "Whatever it is, I hope it wears off soon. I think I liked him better morose and slapdash. I'd far prefer a loose button on my coat to being wakened by a steam engine every morning."

Tonia got out of bed. The ruffle-edged collar of her white cotton gown framed her face. Deep ruffles at the wrists of the full sleeves encircled the delicate hands holding the musical toy. The thought crossed Charles's mind that she looked paler than usual. Her porcelain skin seemed to have an almost transparent look.

157

A terrible fear suddenly gripped him. A roaring in his ears blotted out the sound of the chirping lark. He was forced to lean back on the pillows for a moment. Tunbridge Wells. One of the most famous spas in England. Renowned for its miraculous cures of all manner of diseases. Tonia standing in the pale morning sunlight looking as ethereal as an angel in her full white gown . . .

"Tonia." He was beside her in a single bound, gripping her hands so hard he almost knocked the bird to the floor. "Tonia. Are you sick? Tonia, you must tell me . . ."

She gave a trill of laughter that sounded as mechanical as the bird's song. "Why, Charles, whatever made you say that?"

"You—you look so pale, so delicate, so—so angelic." He would not let himself say "ghostlike."

She stood on tiptoe and kissed his cheek. "Silly boy. I always look pale in white. Do you mean to tell me you have never noticed it before? How like a man."

He shook his head. "You're certain. Absolutely certain you aren't ill?"

Again the sharp laugh that sounded so little like Antonia. "I haven't been sick since I was a child." She turned to lift the cover from her breakfast tray. Her next words were spoken so softly he almost missed them. He puzzled for a moment, but he was quite certain she had said, "A very light case. No complications."

He pulled his red-and-black brocade dressing gown on over his nightshirt and tied the fringed belt. Part of him would have liked to question Tonia directly about that ticket, but he could think of no questions that wouldn't sound like accusations. Finally he remarked, "Well, this should be our last sitting with Lansing today. And a good thing too. Don't think I could abide much more time in that fellow's company." He took a sip of steaming coffee. "Pity, though, that your new French gown couldn't have been immortalized by his fashionable brush."

158

"New gown?" Tonia blinked at him across the table. This morning her green eyes looked like pools darkened by muddy water, not at all the glassy depths that he usually felt he could look clear through. "I thought you liked my green velvet."

"I do. Very much, my dear. I simply thought that as you were going to all the work to have a gown fashioned by a former dressmaker to the empress, it might be nice—"

"No, no. It wouldn't be the right feeling at all for the portrait. Besides—"

Danvers was trying to form another question when a vigorous rattling at the door told them they were to be disturbed again. This time Hardy entered with a scuttle of coal in one hand and a pair of long-handled tongs in the other.

"What is this, Hardy?" Danvers frowned at him. "Laying the fireplaces is the chambermaid's job. If you've upset Aunt Elfrida's household schedule, she'll not thank you. And I won't be responsible, I can tell you that."

"No, no. Not a thing to worry about. Just lending a wee bit of a hand where I can. After all, what are we here for if it's not to help our fellow creatures, regardless of their station? Wee Tilly has a cold this morning, so I told her—"

"*You* told her? And since when is it your place to be telling things to Soyer's staff?"

"Ah, now, don't you be worrying. Just a wee bit of help-out, and then I'll be having all your coats pressed and brushed so quick you won't even know they've been out of your wardrobe."

"I am not worried about my coats, Hardy. I'm worried about the running of Aunt Elfrida's household. What with Futter spending most of the day questioning them yesterday—"

"Hardy," Tonia interrupted, "did Soyer have any idea where Lily got this music box? It's a lovely thing. Far too valuable for a housemaid to have owned."

"I thought so meself. I asked Soyer, but he didn't know. Don't think he much appreciated the question—like his not knowing was a reflection on his running of his staff. Or as if I was implying behavior on Lily's part that he shouldn't have been putting up with. Course that is what it came to, isn't it? Her getting murdered doesn't reflect well on him."

"The bird, Hardy," Tonia prodded.

"Oh, yes." He shook down the grate with an enormous rattling of cast iron and shifting of coal dust. "Susan, the upstairs maid, said it was a gift from an admirer but Lily wouldn't tell nothing more than that. Very secretive she was. Not popular among the staff was Lily. Seemed to think she was better than the other girls."

Tonia held up a hand to stop his flow. "Thank you, Hardy. You may ring Isabella for me. We're going in to Chatham today, you know."

Hardy attacked the bell pull with such a flourish he almost yanked it from the wall, then bowed himself from the room, nearly tripping over the half-empty hod of coal.

Danvers shook his head. "Whatever this phase is, I'll be glad when it passes. And so will the rest of the servants' hall, I've no doubt. I can just imagine Mrs. Crompton when he insists on helping with one of her sauces."

"Oh, don't waste time worrying about Mrs. Crompton. As handy as she is with a rolling pin, she should have no trouble defending her kitchen from Hardy's helpfulness."

Danvers relaxed in the joy of laughing with Tonia. And the fears of the past days faded as the brougham rattled over the rutted roads to Chatham. When the spring thaws came, these roads would be impassable. He hoped all the mysteries and family crises would have been settled by then.

It had never been his choice to spend the winter in the country. And he was missing the London opera season. He gave brief thought to what they might be performing in Covent Garden now. Then he forced his mind back to the discussion that had brought them to the outskirts of Chatham.

"So has Orson found a replacement suspect since he had to let Miguel go?" Tonia asked.

Charles shook his head. "Futter said he's interviewed every dustman in Chatham, Rochester, and Gillingham. If it was someone from farther away than that, or someone merely disguised as dustmen, there seems little hope of tracing them."

"How do they explain Bessie's muffed identification of Miguel?"

Danvers shrugged. "Either it was someone who happened to look a lot like him or sheer hysteria on her part."

Tonia nodded. "Possible, under the circumstances, I'm sure. But Bessie doesn't seem the hysterical type. And the Spanish—"

"I agree. Seems like their best leads for now are the burgled items. If only they could get a consistent description from a pawnbroker . . ."

"Or," Tonia mused, "solve Lily's murder. I don't suppose they've found anyone at the cathedral who saw anything?"

"No. Futter's put the Canterbury constabulary onto that but with no results. Thing that has them all the most puzzled, it seems, is trying to link the two murders."

Tonia wrinkled her forehead thoughtfully. "Other than the fact that Bessie and Lily were both maids and both wound up with their throats slit, the girls don't seem enough alike to have continued a friendship even if they had been in service somewhere together in the past—and I suppose there's been no evidence of anything like that?"

Charles shook his head. "Not that I know of. Although I don't know what's been done to follow that line of questioning. Lily doesn't seem to have had any friends even at Aethelsham. Bessie is quite a gregarious creature, judging from what I saw of her at The Three Bells."

"Did you question any of her friends there?"

161

Danvers lifted his right eyebrow. "No, I never thought of it at the time. What an interesting idea, my love. Perhaps you'd care for a pint of the best after our sitting—thirsty work that is."

Tonia laughed, "Er . . . I think not, Charles. Beside my dislike of bitter there's the fact that I would be even more conspicuous in such a place than you would be. Why not send Hardy?"

"Excellent. An outlet for his newfound vigor. I was rather fearing he might insist on rearranging Lansing's paints or dusting canvases."

Tonia, her voluminous skirts carefully arranged, sat on the gilt chair before the studio window once again. It seemed impossible so much could have happened, so much could have changed, in the short time since she first sat here. The landscape before her that had been soft and pearlescent with new-fallen snow on the day of their first posing was now drab, winter brown. Mounds of snow lay piled against bare tree trunks, its former whiteness almost black with the soot of the innumerable coal fires in Ordnance Terrace.

She nervously fluttered the fan. The first day it had seemed exquisite, something from the boudoir of a lady of quality of the previous century. In today's harsher light it looked tawdry, overornamented.

And she wasn't at all sure about this pose. Charles's hand on her shoulder, which had felt so warm and comforting, now felt stiff and cold. This portrait had not been a good idea. She should have stood by her first impulse and refused. They had undertaken the venture as an excuse to learn more about the artist for Eleanor's sake. Well, they had learned plenty about him. There was no need to continue the ruse.

She really must think of some excuse to move around a bit. If she had to sit here another minute she was sure she would scream. Charles increased the pressure of his hand on her shoulder, as if he sensed that she would take flight and was holding her down.

Thinking of him made her settle back into her chair. What about the ticket she was sure he had found? He had said nothing about it—unless his remark about her new gown had been an attempt to learn something. How stupid of her to have almost forgotten the French gown.

She could only hope Hardy had emptied his master's pockets and she had escaped detection. Certainly Charles had been the very soul of kindness itself all day Sunday and this morning—but then, he always was.

She was shifting again, wondering how much longer she would have to sit, when the sound of the doorbell grated. A moment later Mrs. Gillie ushered Futter upstairs.

"Seems I've come too early. Sorry about that. I didn't mean to interrupt." He twisted his derby around in his hands.

"Will that be enough for you to finish, Lansing?" Danvers's voice indicated that only an affirmative answer would be acceptable.

The artist too seemed to be feeling the strain of the situation. He agreed with unflattering alacrity. "Oh, yes. Certainly. Quite enough. A specialty of mine—not many artists can complete a portrait after only three sittings. Trained myself to do it to accommodate busy patrons." He pulled a large white handkerchief from a side pocket and mopped his forehead, although the room was far from overheated.

Futter looked relieved. "Thank you, sir. You see, the thing is, we've discovered a rather curious situation in the alley outside the garden walls. Rather looks like some of the gates have been tampered with."

"My garden gate?" Lansing tossed the handkerchief aside.

"I'm afraid so, sir. I'm sure you can see the implications when a robbery is under investigation. I was wondering—that is, you haven't reported anything missing . . ."

163

Lansing frowned. "No, haven't got anything worth stealing. Still, don't take kindly to the idea that someone could be making free of my garden." He removed his smock and pulled an old coat off a peg by the door. "Can you show me what you mean?"

"Thank you, sir. I was just hoping you'd take a look at it with us."

Danvers turned to Antonia. "I'd rather like to see too. But it's awfully cold and messy out there. Do you mind—"

"Of course not, Charles. Off you go to play in the garden. I'll be quite fine here on my own."

"Shall I ask Mrs. Gillie to send up some tea?"

"No. No. I'm quite fine." She all but pushed him out the studio door.

One other line of contemplation had amused her during her period of enforced sitting—that locked door behind the screen. If the locked closet contained, as she suspected, art of real worth that Lansing was too shy to exhibit to a critical public, perhaps she and Charles could be of help establishing him. After all, Charles knew some influential people.

And that would settle Agatha's complaints. The least she could do for Eleanor's future happiness was to take a look—not to mention satisfying her own curiosity, of course. As long as she was alone in the studio, she would just see what she could do with a hairpin.

She heard the downstairs door slam shut as if a gust of wind had wrenched it from its closer's hand. She listened to be sure Mrs. Gillie seemed to be occupied. Then she pulled an extra-heavy hairpin from her carefully arranged coil and attempted bending the wires in an approximation of a skeleton key.

She worked fast, afraid that at any moment she would hear the downstairs door open again. The wire kept slipping from her fingers. If only she had a pair of pliers. If she'd had any idea such an opportunity would occur, she could even have brought a ring of keys from Aethelsham.

With the assortment of cupboards they had there, something would surely fit.

At last she held up the bent hairpin and shook her head. *Looks more like a dog's hind leg than a key,* she thought. But she hurried across the floor, remembering to step lightly so that Mrs. Gillie wouldn't hear, ducked behind the screen, and inserted her 'key' in the lock. It turned easily.

Too easily. She removed the wire, now bent like a corkscrew. She tossed it away. On the off-chance that the door might not be locked today, she gave the knob a twist. It was locked.

She returned to survey the room. If only there were a desk or small chest with drawers that would be likely to hold keys. One table covered with a collection of paint pots offered a small drawer, but it contained only dustballs.

She considered the problem. It was unlikely that Mrs. Gillie would have the key to whatever Lansing seemed to be hiding in his studio. So where would he be likely to put it?

She turned slowly, looking for pots one might keep a key under, pegs one might hang a key on. Pegs. She went back to the peg where Lansing's smock now hung. The smock with two deep pockets on each side.

Sure enough, the second pocket she put her hand into produced a key. She glanced out the window overlooking the back garden. The men were just leaving Lansing's garden and walking toward Mrs. Bacon's. There would still be time.

The key turned silently. Holding her breath, Antonia swung the door open, trying to imagine what she would find. Her disappointment was immense. But what else would an artist keep in a studio closet but paintings and props?

The light was dim in this far corner, and the door was sheltered by the oriental screen. But Tonia wanted to see the paintings. These must be the serious works Lansing had spoken of. She had gone off him as a suitor for Eleanor, but that did not mean he wasn't a good artist. She would like to view what he considered his best work—so good he chose to lock it away from prying eyes.

All was still quiet downstairs. She struck a light to the lamp sitting on a small table and carried it to the closet. Yes. Religious paintings, he had said. The first one was a Madonna. A beautiful young woman, perhaps about the age Mary had been—soft, brown hair and round, glistening eyes; full, pink lips pursed in awe and surprise, just as Mary's must have been when the angel appeared to her. And with just a hint of fear in the eyes too. Lansing had caught it perfectly. The long, white throat showing beneath her blue drape, her hands folded in prayer.

She turned to another painting, then drew back with a gasp, almost dropping the lamp. As a reflex she turned to see if anyone was looking over her shoulder. No wonder Lansing had locked this one away. Mrs. Gillie would undoubtedly give notice if she had any notion there was such a thing in the house.

This must have been the painting he was working on when they first rang his bell and he answered with red paint on his hands, for the background was a glowing crimson. And the subject . . .

It was the same model. But this was not a religious painting. The girl, her long hair loose around her shoulders, was holding the fan Tonia had held a few minutes earlier. She wore a ring on each finger—rings of a matching set. The set Tonia had suspected had been made to go with the slide bracelet. And that was all she wore.

166

14

The downstairs door slammed. Tonia jumped. She leaped out of the closet and closed the door as footsteps started up the stairs. In her hurry she fumbled with the key. It wouldn't turn.

"Excuse me, sir, if I could just have a word—" Mrs. Gillie's voice interrupted the footsteps.

Tonia turned the key with sweating fingers and had just managed to slip it back into the smock pocket when Lansing entered. He stared at the lighted lamp in her hand.

Tonia placed it on a table with a flourish and smiled. "I hope you don't mind. I was just admiring your paintings." She turned to a rather eclectic landscape on the nearest easel. It looked as if the trees had been borrowed from Constable, the sky from Ruisdale, the rustic peasants from Breughel. "It's really quite lovely."

Without replying, Lansing held her cloak for her. "Hardy has returned with your carriage." He moved to the studio door to usher her out. "I'll send a note when the portrait is finished."

Danvers and Futter joined her in the carriage a moment later. She wanted to tell Charles about what she had seen—but there was no possibility of her discussing such a thing in front of the inspector.

They drove back to the station so that Hardy could report to all of them at once.

"One of the group we saw Bessie drinking with that day was there again—Mamie, her name is. Seems she spends a lot of time at The Three Bells. No better than she should be, that one isn't, I'd be guessing. She was glad enough to talk for the price of a pint. Seems she knows a Rose, a Violet, and a Daisy, but no Lily. And she couldn't recall Bessie ever mentioning anyone of that name."

Danvers sighed. "Well, it seemed a long shot. Thank you for trying, Hardy."

"But that's not quite all, m'lord. Like I said, Mamie was quite happy to talk. Seems our Bessie was something of a moaner. Didn't think much of her Mrs. Bacon—said she was always giving money to charities, then was too tightfisted to pay a decent wage. And there she was with a houseful of treasures that she never even bothered to look at—just made work for Bessie to dust."

Danvers shrugged. "Sounds like the typical servant's complaint—too much work for too little pay."

Hardy nodded. "That's what I was thinking, m'lord. You spend as much time in servants' halls as I do—you soon enough hear it all. Not as I've ever heard such in your lordship's household," he added quickly. "But the thing is, it seems that Bessie always had enough of the ready. The night before the murder she apparently left deep in her cups—that could explain why she was so slow to hear any disturbance in the house."

"Yes, I'd wondered about that." Danvers nodded. "And why she was so far behind on her work that morning. A bad hangover would explain it."

Just then the tinkle of the bell hanging over the door announced the entrance of Constable Orson. He tossed his helmet at a hat-tree and huffed and puffed his way across the room to hold his red hands out to the fire. "Cold as blazes it is out there . . . er . . . pardon me, ma'am." He nodded to Antonia.

"I asked Constable Orson to do another round of the pawnshops," Futter explained. "Did you learn anything new, Constable?"

He shook his massive, square head. "Just more confirmation of what we've suspected for some time—seems Elizabeth Law pawned a lot of her mistress's valuables."

"Well, she admitted that, didn't she?" Tonia observed.

Orson turned his back to the fire now. "Question is, how much did Mrs. Bacon know about it? I've no doubt Bessie pawned the stuff all right. But I'd be willing to stake my badge on it that she didn't pawn it all for her mistress. At a minimum I'd wager she didn't give Mrs. Bacon all the proceeds of the transaction."

Futter ran his fingers through his pale hair. "Proving that will be very difficult. Do we have any way of telling how much of the stuff on Bessie's list was stolen by the murderer and how much she pinched herself?"

"But why would she report something she had pawned as stolen? Wouldn't that be drawing attention to her own theft?" Tonia asked.

"She may have thought it was a chance to cover her crime—maybe didn't think about the pawnbrokers identifying her," Futter speculated.

At that moment their consideration of the case was interrupted by a clattering of cups on saucers as Hardy cheerfully bustled in from the back room with a tray of tea and a tin of biscuits.

"Knew you'd all be wanting a bit of elevenses—and past that as it is now. So I just said, 'Hardy, stir yourself for these fine people.' I'd be more than happy to grill you a sausage or a nice rasher of bacon, but your cupboard's a bit bare back there, Constable."

Danvers accepted his cup, prepared exactly as he liked it. "Thank you, Hardy. I'm sure we all appreciate your newfound energy."

"Oh, thank you, sir. Like I was saying, nothing's too much work. Nothing at all. Just say the word."

"Yes, Hardy. I shan't forget."

There was momentary quiet while all sipped their tea.

Finally Antonia spoke into the lull. "I've been wondering—what about a will? Did Mrs. Bacon leave a will?"

Orson shook his head. "We haven't been able to find one. But then we haven't looked too hard. Just a routine search of the house for evidence. Seeing as no relatives have come forward, didn't seem too much use."

"What are you getting at, Tonia?" Danvers asked.

"Well, I was thinking that a will might make mention of Mrs. Bacon's most valuable articles. It would serve as a sort of check on Bessie."

He rose to his feet in one rapid, fluid motion. "Hardy, I think Miss Elizabeth Law should be the recipient of your vigorous good will. Knowing how fond she is of the libations offered at The Three Bells, why don't you just take her out for a treat. Meantime we'll see if we can uncover anything that might have been overlooked at Mrs. Bacon's." He offered his arm to Tonia. "That was excellent thinking, my love."

They waited at the end of the street until Hardy and Bessie exited Number 9. Then Charles suggested that he and Tonia search the ground and first floors while Futter and Orson took the upper rooms.

Tonia began in the kitchen. It was a mess. Whatever Mrs. Bacon had required of her maid, it certainly was not being carried out now. She drew back from the unwashed fine china plates piled in the sink with congealed food sticking to them. She examined the contents of the cupboards and ice box. Nothing but the very best labels filled the shelves. Chunks of Double Gloucester and Stilton cheese sat on a marble board under a crystal cover. The lid was half off an ornamented tin of chocolate creams.

170

However tightfisted Mrs. Bacon might have been, it seemed that her maid was stinting herself on nothing now. Mrs. B. must have left a most satisfactory amount in the housekeeping funds to provide for such elaborate marketing. Tonia looked longingly at the cheese and barely resisted helping herself to the chocolates.

Finding nothing else of interest in the kitchen, she went to see how Charles was doing in the study. She found him sitting at a small, rolltop desk, which presented a maze of cubbyholes and small drawers at its back. Papers protruded from every opening, were piled lopsidedly on the desktop, and littered much of the leaf-patterned carpet.

"Charles, what a shocking mess you've been making! Didn't your nanny teach you to pick up after yourself?"

Danvers rumpled his hair, which was looking even more disordered than Mrs. Bacon's papers. "I didn't do this. I've been trying to put it in some sort of order."

"How? With an eggbeater?"

He grinned and shook his head. "Apparently our Bessie's thoughts have been working along the same lines as ours. She's done a pretty thorough search here for a will—or something."

"Do you think she found what she was looking for?"

"There's no telling. But it seems unlikely—you'd think she would have made some attempt to clean up if she were finished."

"Is there any value in going through all this? If there *was* a will or anything else of importance, surely she would have found it."

Danvers pulled a drawer entirely out and reached into the small, black cavern. "Not unusual for these desks to have secret compartments—for love letters and the like —but I haven't found any such thing here."

"If Mrs. Bacon did make a will or a list of her valuables, it should be here. It doesn't look like she ever got rid of any scrap of paper." Tonia let a shopkeeper's bill fall back onto a pile. It was marked paid and dated three years earlier.

"With everything having been gone through, it's difficult to tell how meticulous Mrs. Bacon was, but it rather appears that she was the careful sort who wouldn't have been likely to die without making a will."

"Or who would have let her maid cheat her with the pawnbrokers?"

Danvers nodded. "I thought of that. And nowhere in here have I been able to find any pawn slips or any notice of the sale of any such items."

He drew out another drawer, and Tonia turned to examine a shelf of books. Mrs. Bacon wouldn't have been the first to have kept her will tucked between the covers of the family Bible or a copy of Shakespeare.

A few minutes later a triumphant shout from upstairs called Tonia and Danvers up four flights of narrow, dark stairs to the attic.

Futter stood in the middle of what was undoubtedly Bessie Law's bedroom. The mattress was hanging off the iron bedstead, and the rumpled bedclothes were bunched about his feet.

Orson was waving both hands, one full of pawn tickets apparently, the other of bank notes. "Under the mattress they was."

"So. Seems Bessie Law had a very nice game going here," Danvers said.

Tonia grabbed his arm. "Charles, the nonexistent dustmen—could they have been pawnbrokers who had seen the quality of the things Bessie brought in, purportedly from her mistress, and saw a chance to get some valuables without paying pawn fees?"

Futter turned from the exultant Orson. "Excellent idea, my lady. We'll follow up on it."

Then Tonia noticed Charles was still holding the paper he had been perusing when Orson's shout brought them running up the stairs. "What's that, Charles? Did you find something?"

"Yes, I rather think I have. But not the will." He held out a sheet of heavily embossed paper signed with an imposing signature. "A letter from Mrs. Bacon's solicitor, discussing the bequest of her estate."

"Jedadiah Dalrymple, Manor Road," she read.

Orson nodded. "Just off the High Street, that would be."

As Hardy had not yet returned from his assignment at The Three Bells, Danvers hailed a cab to take Antonia and himself to the office of Mr. Jedadiah Dalrymple, Esquire, while the policemen finished their work in Ordnance Terrace.

Jedadiah Dalrymple seemed to be assembled of various-length sticks—long, thin ones for his arms and legs; an equally thin, if somewhat shorter one, for his neck; and short, pointy twigs for his nose and chin. His stiff white collar stood out some distance from his throat, and the arms and legs of his black suit flapped with his jerky movements.

"Mrs. Bacon, Mrs. Catherine Bacon? Certainly she was our client. As was her husband, the colonel. So melancholy that such a thing could have happened to a valued client."

He crossed the narrow, dark hall and yanked open the door to his inner sanctum. Floor to ceiling, the walls were lined with shelves of heavy, leather-bound books. Stacks of additional volumes filled every corner and leaned drunkenly against the black oak desk.

With a single, rapid movement he cleared an armful of files off a horsehair-covered chair and offered Antonia a seat, all the time shaking his head and talking in a raspy, dry voice. "A dear woman, such a dear woman, to have come to such a mournful end. Makes us all think." He gave a final tic of his head, flipped the tails of his coat aside, and sat behind the desk. "Makes us all think."

173

"Yes." Danvers jumped into the pause. "We've been thinking about Mrs. Bacon quite a bit of late."

"We are all hoping to hear that the perpetrators of this heinous crime have been apprehended. May I hope that you have come to bring me such news?" Jedadiah Dalrymple's little dark eyes glistened, but his features showed no evidence of an inclination to hopefulness.

"Not yet. We are hoping you may be able to help us."

Dalrymple put his pencil-like fingertips together under his chin, exposing several inches of wrist bone beyond his shirt cuffs. "I would be most honored to be of service. Most honored. The firm of Dalrymple, Dalrymple, and Dalrymple has served the Bacon family for many decades. It would be our honor to continue service beyond the grave. Of course, that is what we are attempting in the execution of her will."

The head twitch returned. "But sadly, we have had little success thus far. I can assure you, though, every effort is being made. My father will tell you he has never yet failed in the execution of a client's will. It would be a melancholy matter if dear Mrs. Bacon were to be the first."

"Your *father?*" Tonia's mind boggled at the thought that this skeletal creature could have a living parent.

"Oh, yes, didn't I explain? My father, Mr. Hezekiah Dalrymple, Esquire, was the late Colonel Bacon's man of business. But Father, while still very active, has slowed down a bit of late years. So I've taken part of the load by giving a hand with some of his clients. Ah, Father—"

An apparition entered the office, and the younger Dalrymple jerked to his feet to assist his senior to a chair by the fireplace.

The father, it appeared, had been built from the same bundle of sticks as the son—except that time had warped and bent them. Hezekiah Dalrymple stooped low over his black, gnarled walking stick. A fringe of long white hair and a bushy gray beard covered most of his too-

174

large collar. Tonia was glad when the door was securely closed behind him so as to reduce risk of his being blown off-course by a gust of wind.

"These people are friends of Mrs. Bacon, Father." Jedadiah bent over and spoke loudly.

"Eh? Bacon? No, thank you, boy. Had my breakfast hours ago. Don't hold with these newfangled hours. Make people soft. You should get up earlier, boy." He jabbed his walking stick at the spindly Jedadiah. "Keep that flab off you."

"No, Father. Mrs. Catherine Bacon—these are her friends." This time Jedadiah shouted and handed his father a brass, bell-shaped listening device.

"No need to yell, boy. And I don't need that thing. Still have my own hair and my own teeth too." The ancient man had a surprisingly young grin, which displayed a full set of teeth.

"What can you tell us about Catherine Bacon's will?" Danvers's voice was just below a yell. He gave three reflexive head jerks before stopping himself. Jedadiah Dalrymple didn't appear to notice, but it was all Tonia could do to keep from giggling.

"Oh, why didn't you say so?" Hezekiah waved his ear horn toward Danvers. "You that Cornhusk fellow, are you? What took you so long? Don't usually find relations so slow to claim their rights, I can tell you. Vultures to the kill they usually are. You don't look like a vulture, I'll give you that."

"No, no, Father. This isn't the nephew—and his name's Raddison, not Cornhusk. This is Lord and Lady Danvers. They're friends—"

"I'll thank you not to interrupt, boy. Never did learn respect for your elders, did you? Raddison, you say you are? Thought the family name was Cornhusk. Glad to have the matter cleared up." He gestured to his son. "Well, boy, get on with it—read him out the will. Make the boy happy.

Good news it is for you. Good news you'll be happy to know."

Jedadiah Dalrymple showed his perplexity by an increased jerking of his head.

"It would be most satisfactory if you could just inform me of the terms of the document," Charles suggested.

Jedadiah twitched his agreement. "It's a very simple testamentary instrument. The bulk of Mrs. Bacon's estate was to go to her nephew, a Mr. Raddison. It seems there had been . . . uh . . . certain disagreements in the family. She was anxious to restore the relationship. We have set inquiries in motion, but unfortunately . . ." He spread his bony fingers.

"And if you fail to locate this nephew?" Danvers asked.

"The contingent heir is a Constable Matthew Orson."

Tonia raised her brows but asked levelly, "Were there any specific bequests?"

Jedadiah looked at the parchment he had drawn out of a stack of papers on his desk. After repeated squintings he dug in several pockets, both on the outside and inside of his coat. Finally he extracted a pince-nez from his vest and clipped it to the end of his nose. "Yes." He repeated his squint, turned the document around, and adjusted the glasses. "Ah, yes. That's better. Now, she makes no special mention as to disposition of the objects, but she mentions a Georgian silk fan from Spain, a pair of Chelsea figures, and a set of jewelry—bracelet and rings—as especially wanting them to stay in the family."

Tonia felt her heart thump. "The jewelry. Does she describe it? Perhaps refer to it as a slide bracelet? Gold, set with precious stones?"

"Why, yes. Remarkable. That's it to a tee." An extrastrong twitch toppled the glasses from his nose.

Charles and Antonia rose and began thanking him. "You've been most helpful. Can't really thank you enough."

176

Hezekiah teetered to his feet as well, leaning heavily on his stick. "Make them sign, boy. Make Cornhusker sign. Got to do it all proper. Dalrymple, Dalrymple, and Dalrymple can always be relied on to get it right."

The deep shadows of the late winter afternoon fell across the countryside as the carriage trundled back toward Aethelsham. Tonia, wrapped in two woolen travel rugs and her feet propped on bricks that were almost too hot, provided by the solicitous Hardy, puzzled over the events of the day.

"So there doesn't seem to be any doubt about it—the items were all Mrs. Bacon's, and they were definitely not pawned with her approval."

"Yes, but we're still left with proving who made off with them."

"Well, it seems certain that Bessie had her hand in the pie. She had extra, ready cash. The pawnbrokers identified her. And she had the pawn tickets in her room." Tonia ticked off the facts on her fingers.

Danvers reached out for her gloved hand. He held her fingertips against his lips briefly. "Yes, but there weren't tickets for all the missing items, and some of the pawnbrokers thought the objects were pawned by a man. I wish to goodness these pawnbrokers would pay more attention to their customers."

"Perhaps in their line of work it's best not to. But it's hard to see how Bessie could have been the one to pawn the items in Canterbury."

"So that brings us back to our murderers."

"The elusive dustmen?" Tonia shook her head. "If I hadn't been there myself—hadn't seen all that blood—I'm not sure I'd believe in their existence."

"Well, there's no doubting the fact that someone—or ones—battered Mrs. Bacon to death and slit Bessie's throat. And Lily's too for that matter. But I certainly have my doubts about the dustmen theory."

They rode on a bit, swaying to the motion of the carriage. A wheel caught the edge of a deep rut and threw Antonia against him. When the carriage righted itself, she stayed snuggled close. "Charles, you don't think there's anything to the idea that Orson could have done it, do you?"

"Well, he would have had the opportunity—for stealing and even for planting the tickets in Bessie's room if it comes to that . . ."

Tonia nodded, rubbing her cheek against his shoulder. "I know. That's what I was thinking. And now that we know he was Mrs. Bacon's contingent heir, I suppose that could be considered a motive for murder."

"It could be. But I don't like the idea any better than you do."

"If only we could refuse to suspect people we like and simply blame the ones we don't." She attempted a laugh, but it came out as more of a sigh. "How could we ever have liked Randolph Lansing?"

"Or not realized that he had an excellent opportunity for robbery, living right next door to the burgled home?"

"Well, of course the police found the trick latches on the connecting gates only yesterday. But someone trained in art like Lansing would certainly have been quicker to recognize the value of Mrs. Bacon's property than dustmen would have. From the very first I wondered about some of his props—like that fan I've been holding. If ladies made bets, I'd be willing to wager my best fan that the one he's been painting in my hands is the one mentioned in Mrs. Bacon's will."

Now Tonia sat upright, her words coming faster. "And the jewelry—his mother's, he told Eleanor. I don't doubt for a minute that's the jewelry she so especially wanted to stay in her family."

"I expect you're right. But without a better description there would be no proving it."

Tonia leaned back, deflated. Then she jolted upright again. "Charles! I almost forgot to tell you. While you were looking at those garden gates, I did a bit of snooping in that locked closet of Lansing's."

"Tonia—" His arm came around her protectively.

"Don't be silly, Charles. I was very careful. Anyway, it was full of paintings. I only saw a couple of them, but one was—" She felt her face grow hot. "Oh, Charles, all that pale skin reclining against deep red velvet . . . I . . . I believe voluptuous is the word . . ." She cleared her throat. "But the thing is, the model was wearing that bracelet Randolph gave Eleanor."

"*What!*" Danvers all but came off the carriage seat. "You don't mean to say he painted Eleanor! He dared to paint my sister in—in a state of undress! I'll—I'll—"

"No, Charles, no!" She grabbed his arm with both hands and shook him until she had his attention. "No, Charles. Listen. Not Eleanor—some model." She tried to remember. The shock of the woman's undraped condition had blurred all thought of her features. "No. She had softer hair than Nelly's, but she was older. And more—more earthy. And yet she did seem vaguely familiar, now that I think about it." She paused. "The point was the jewelry—and the fan. I suppose it's just vaguely possible Mrs. Bacon might have loaned them to him."

Danvers settled back against the seat and pulled Tonia into his arms. "My love, you have the most charitable mind. I almost think you could make excuses for Lucifer himself."

She leaned against him and closed her eyes. She didn't want to have to make excuses for anyone. Especially not for herself. And tomorrow she must go again. An uncomfortable trip with all those train changes. It would be so pleasant to skip it just this once. For a moment she dozed off, then jerked awake as the carriage lurched. No, she couldn't quit.

Tomorrow she must go again. He had been most insistent. Absolutely essential, he said, or he wouldn't be responsible. She had made the commitment. And she had some money left from pawning her jewels. She must make every effort. Then when the worst came, she would at least have had the satisfaction of having done all she could.

15

Danvers thought he had forestalled their being inundated with Hardy's solicitude the next morning by telling his man that they would breakfast downstairs. He had reckoned without Hardy's assiduity, however. Danvers had the strongest suspicion that his man was waiting outside the door, listening for the sound of his master's feet touching the floor, for Charles was still groping for his second slipper when the door burst open and Hardy arrived at his side holding a freshly pressed dressing gown.

The valet then bustled ahead of the master into the dressing room and closed the sash, which, judging from the temperature of the room, had been raised some time before.

"What are you playing at, Hardy? It's like ice in here."

"Ah, but m'lord, there's a fine fire on the grate, and all your body linen well warmed, as you'll soon appreciate. The *Gentleman's Magazine* recommends the procedure as most healthful."

With a groan Danvers submitted to his man's ministrations. He had to face a meeting of the architectural restoration committee today. He could not use all his energy arguing with Hardy. "Far be it from me to dispute the health-giving qualities of fresh air, but surely allowing icicles to form on the drapes is a bit excessive."

He lowered himself gingerly onto a stone-cold chair to be swathed in Hardy's steaming towels, preparatory to shaving. "What is that *smell*, Hardy?"

"Ah, and a fine, fresh scent, is it not? Lavender and frisia, m'lord, freshly ground and added to your shaving cream."

"*Gentlemen's Magazine* again, no doubt." Danvers determined to breathe shallowly until the worst of it had aired out.

"Highly recommended it is, sir. And a new polish for your boots I've made up too. Pounded logwood chips boiled with red French wine and strained." The recitation continued as he stropped the Wilkinson steel razor to a fine edge. "Then eight ounces each of pounded gum arabic and lump sugar, one ounce of green copperas and three ounces of brandy . . ."

"Merciful heavens, Hardy. I intend to wear my boots, not eat them."

By the time Hardy had Danvers shined, brushed, and polished to within an inch of his life, Tonia was emerging from Isabella's ministrations in a plum-and-black-striped silk gown.

Charles kissed her on the cheek. "Charming, my dear, charming. Might I hope I'm to have the pleasure of your company in Canterbury today?"

"Oh. Er . . . certainly, Charles. If you are to be going in soon after breakfast."

He offered his arm to escort her downstairs. "Another dressmaker's appointment is it? And then we could meet for a late luncheon or tea?" He felt her hand tighten on his arm.

"I think not, Charles. I don't want to rush Madame D'Arbley. And then I had thought of just looking in on Harriet. I think it will be best simply to meet back at Aethelsham."

"As you wish. In that case you must keep the carriage, and I'll hire one for the return."

"No, Charles, I wouldn't dream of it. You are certain to have a thoroughly stressful day with the restoration committee and your choristers. Harriet will insist on sending me home in her carriage anyway."

They were at the breakfast room now, filled with the eyes and ears of servants and family, so he did not press the matter.

He did try just once more, however, when they entered Canterbury. "Where is this Parisian miracle-worker of yours, my love? I shall have Even take us there first."

"I wouldn't hear of it. You mustn't be late to your meeting, and I've quite a bit of time yet. We must go directly to the cathedral close. Then I'll see to a bit of shopping first."

"Tonia . . ." He grasped both her hands. He wanted to plead with her for the truth. What was it she wasn't telling him? But the frightened look in her eyes cut off any questions. He couldn't bear to think of causing her more dismay.

"Yes, Charles?"

"Have a pleasant day, my love." They stopped just inside Christ Church Gate, and Charles got out.

The carriage rattled away over the rough cobbles. In the Chapter House not even the elegance of the finest barrel roof in England above his head could elevate Danvers's spirits. Instead the coldness of the stone walls and bleached alderwood doors and cabinetry penetrated to his bones.

He looked at the Cathedral Chapter, the administrative body of the cathedral since the Reformation. The gray-haired, bearded dean wore black canonicals with an ornate silver cross on his chest and sat at the head of a highly polished, richly burled table. The four canons, each of whom headed a department of the day-to-day life of the cathedral, sat beside him, two on each side. The rest of the committee ranged around the table.

Danvers tried to concentrate on the lengthy, technical report Randolph Lansing, committee chairman, was delivering. But his concern for Tonia and his intense dislike for Lansing seemed to block any consistent useful focusing. And now Lansing's lewd paintings had distressed her—at a time when she obviously could handle little more stress. If only she would confide in him . . .

"And so, Mr. Dean, you can see from this sketch—" Lansing placed a large drawing on the table "—how the emotional impact of the cathedral will be elevated by the addition of gargoyles to the pinnacles on each corner of the west towers. While at the east end—" another sketch followed "—encircling the entire corona with a ring of flying buttresses . . ."

"Gentlemen of the Chapter!" Danvers brought his hand down on the table far harder than he meant to. "As representative of the Dowager Duchess of Aethelbert, whose bequest to the cathedral initiated this insanity, may I be permitted to point out that the purpose of gargoyles on medieval buildings was to scare away evil spirits—in which bit of voodoo I hope none of the present company believes. And the purpose of flying buttresses was to support the weight of massive stone walls bearing towers and steeples. I might point out that the corona bears the least weight of any part of the cathedral, and its walls show no evidence whatever of giving under the strain of the modest turrets that surround it."

Lansing turned with a smooth smile and placed another drawing on the table. "I am most indebted for your reminder, my lord Danvers. And allow me to say for the Chapter and all the committee how aware we are of our indebtedness to your aunt's most generous endowment. It is our pledge to see that every shilling of her generosity is used to the maximum effect. And that is why—" he pointed to the sketch "—I propose here to cap the corona with a spire that will rival that of Salisbury—a spire, which above all other architectural features is a proclamation of faith."

Danvers groaned and slumped in his chair, but Lansing was uninhibited. "You will note in looking at the present cathedral how the east end simply sinks into anonymity in contrast to the towers and pinnacles of the other end. It has been left to us to complete the addition of this great glory to the mother church of our faith. We can only most humbly submit our poor, unworthy talents, knowing that future generations will be the benefactors. And the glory of the great return to orthodoxy of the church continues inside the building, for the spire is not a mere showpiece but will encompass a lantern as fine as Ely's."

"What? And are we not to have a bit from York? From Durham? Are Exeter and St. Paul's to be slighted?"

Lansing looked at him in open shock, his thin nostrils pinched. "Surely you jest, my lord. The dome of St. Paul's would not fit on Canterbury's corona." He then went on at considerable length to show how his plan reflected five of Ruskin's Seven Lamps of Architecture—sacrifice, truth, power, memory, and obedience.

If Danvers had been less worried about Tonia he might have done a better job of opposing Lansing's mishmash. As it was, however, his obvious distraction and caustic outbursts seemed merely to produce cohesiveness in the others. When the vote was taken, his was the only voice of dissent. Canterbury Cathedral would be "restored" to a dubious glory that none of its builders could possibly have envisioned or desired.

The meeting had gone long, and Danvers was determined not to arrive late for choir practice this time. So in spite of his impatience to be elsewhere in the city, he had no choice but to hurry along.

Already Sam Higgins was there. The brushing he had applied to his curly, rust-colored hair had apparently been somewhat less vigorous even than his streaky job of face washing. But the round blue eyes sparkled. "Been practicin', gov'nor. Want to hear?"

Danvers nodded. His lead boy executed three perfect scales. "You meant what you said last week about choral scholarships, didn't you, sir?"

"Indeed, I did, Higgins. Your voice is quite excellent."

Less could be said for the others, but at least they took their places in some semblance of order. Danvers was thankful not to have to search cloisters or crypt this afternoon.

He dismissed a request that they be allowed to warm up on "Cockles and mussels alive, alive-o!" no matter how popular Hardy's choice had been the week before. Instead he attacked the opening chorus—with perhaps less enthusiasm than he had ever approached a piece of music in his life.

Charles's lack of spirit seemed to communicate itself to his choir. The stone pillars reverberated with the repeated strains of "Restore us, O God; make Your face shine upon us," so off-key that even Charles winced. He wasn't certain what the problem was, but he knew they had it wrong.

He rapped his baton for attention. "All right boys, we'll try that again. Listen to the organ. Listen."

But he could not force his own mind to attention. His vision filled with his last look at Tonia before the carriage rolled off. He had never seen her face so pale, her cheeks so flushed, her eyes so bright. He would have thought her fevered, but he could recall the chill of her hand even through her glove.

He had started to walk toward the door when he realized the choir was still singing.

"And would you be liking me to finish the rehearsal, m'lord?"

"Hardy, where did you come from?"

"You'll recall giving me permission to attend a meeting. Gardiner Simpson, brother of Gladstone and Grace.

Fine speech it was. But as it's finished, I thought perhaps you could be using my help."

Danvers handed Hardy the baton and made his exit. The nave had never seemed longer. It was as if it grew under his feet and he would be trapped here, futilely striding the stone floor forever.

At last he escaped. Then stopped. Who could help him? Who would know the whereabouts of all of Canterbury's merchants and services? *Then he thought, The police station. Surely Constable Miller and his men will know.*

Miller shook his shock of red hair. "D'Arbley, you say? Frenchie, huh? No. Never heard of the likes o' her."

"I understand she's quite new. Perhaps—"

Constable Miller slapped his desk good-naturedly. "Ah, sure, I take your meanin'. Could be one slipped by Constable Miller's nose. Not so sharp, is it?" He jabbed a plump finger at his broad, flat nose. "Well, I tell you true, 'tain't likely. Not likely at all. But to be fair, it's always possible. Always a chance. Best person to ask now would be just three shops along in the High Street. Sell all sorts o' silks and ribbons, finery the ladies take a fancy to. They'd know of any Frenchie modiste."

The bell over the shop door tinkled when Danvers entered. The store smelled of dried rose petals and orange cinnamon pomander. A well-groomed young woman in an elegantly plain, dark blue dress smiled at him from behind the counter but continued her attention to the mother and daughter who were purchasing yards of lace and ribbon for trimming bonnets.

"Oh, Mama, the jet would be quite smart on your puce bonnet. I can imagine nothing nicer. Really, that chenille is very dowdy."

The daughter continued with a sigh and held up two lengths of lace, tossing her blonde curls from side to side as she regarded them. "But I simply cannot decide between the Honiton and the Brussels lace for mine. I think I shall simply have to buy them both."

Mama approved the choices, and at last the shopgirl was able to turn to Danvers.

"Yes, I was advised you would be able to tell me the whereabouts of a French dressmaker—a Madame D'Arbly, I believe?"

The young woman's eyes, as dark a blue as her dress, narrowed as she considered. "No, sir. I know of none, and I do believe all the dressmakers in Canterbury are known in this shop."

"I understand she is quite newly arrived. Perhaps I have the name wrong. Dressmaker for Empress Eugenie, I was told."

Now the young woman's reply was definite. "Oh, no, sir. It is not possible that we would not know of such a one. Most especially if she is new-come. An old established one might have been forgotten, but a new dressmaker—especially one connected with the empress—the whole world would know of her."

At Danvers's downcast expression she hurried on helpfully. "But I can give you references to a most excellent Italian modiste. It is said she has served the nobility in Rome. I am certain she would give satisfaction."

He began backing toward the door.

"But if I might just say, sir, I would recommend Mme. Latour, who was trained by John Redfern, court dressmaker to Queen Victoria. The English style is much admired over all the continent . . ."

Danvers bowed and replaced his hat even before he was out of the small shop. He had known that would be the answer—and yet he had hoped. He still found it impossible to accept the idea that Antonia was lying to him.

He was in the next street when he saw the brooch in the window. It was the size of the emerald that caught his eye. It was the unique octagonal cut that confirmed his suspicion. There could not be two such distinctive jewels set identically with diamonds in gold filigree and having a small fringe of looped gold chain at the bottom.

Tonia was accustomed to wearing the piece on her gold dress with the emerald braid. She had worn the gown just three days ago. And no, the brooch had not adorned its lapel.

Had Tonia been robbed and not noticed the jewel's absence? Or could it be possible she was so desperate for money that she would sell one of her favorite ornaments? It had come to her from her grandmother, so it was hers to do with as she pleased, but he could not imagine that she should have done so easily.

Ugly words sprang to his mind. Blackmail? Gaming debts? Such things simply were not possible to contemplate in tandem with Antonia. And yet there the jewel lay, taunting him.

Danvers went into the shop.

He emerged a few minutes later carrying a small package, but his mind was no clearer. The matter of the dressmaker still made no sense.

What should he do? It would be far the easiest simply to ignore the whole matter. Tell himself he trusted his wife. Decide that the train ticket belonged to someone else and that he had misunderstood about the dressmaker. Or tell himself that the illusive Madame D'Arbly was in Tunbridge Wells. There—a complete solution. Tonia had said she had wanted the whole thing to be a surprise for him.

And yet there were so many things that didn't add up. For his own peace of mind he would gladly let it drop. But what if she were in trouble? What if she needed his help and for some reason was reluctant to ask for it? What if there was danger? Perhaps she was in danger she wasn't even aware of. He must learn the truth for her sake.

He considered going to Harriet Launceston's. It shouldn't be difficult to find directions to her home. Thanington, she had said. And yet, arriving on the doorstep of a respectable country squire, hat in hand, seeking a wife he was forced to admit he had little hope of finding there, was

189

too embarrassing to contemplate. And the idea of actually questioning Antonia's friend was simply unthinkable.

No, he would approach this as he would any other investigation. If Tonia was in trouble he would learn the truth. And he would help her. No matter what it was. He would follow the clues as they presented themselves, objectively and open-mindedly.

He set his mouth grimly and turned back to where the dowager duchess's groom was waiting for him. "To the station, Even."

Now he regretted having burned the ticket. It was possible the attendant could have told him something about it he hadn't noticed, but he would learn what he could.

"This morning, sir? A beautiful woman in a striped dress—purple and black?" The little man behind the counter looked choked in his high, stiff collar and tight black tie. Danvers noted the ticket agent's shiny black hair and sharp, little pencil-line mustache while he searched through his memory.

At last his eyes lighted. "Ah, about so high, sir?" He indicated Danvers's shoulder. "Skin like rich cream, and such hair—the color of the woods in autumn."

Danvers nodded. He could have described Tonia no better himself. "Can you remember where she bought a ticket to?"

The lamp on the counter behind the brass grille highlighted the macassar gleam on the man's hair as he searched his tables and charts. "Yes, she took the nine forty-two to Ashford."

"Ashford?" Danvers blinked. He couldn't even recall where Ashford was.

"Yes, sir, to connect with the ten thirty-eight to Tonbridge."

Danvers nodded. "And then to Tunbridge Wells?"

"I believe so, sir. There is quite a good connection there with the train down from London."

Danvers muttered his thanks and walked away. Tonia must have been determined indeed to get to Tunbridge Wells to be willing to put up with so many tiring changes.

Why hadn't she just taken the carriage? But even as he asked the question, he knew. Whatever it was, she wanted no servants involved. To prevent gossip? To avoid danger to themselves? So there would be no risk of blackmail? No, he would not allow such a thought. Tonia would be incapable of doing anything that could lead to such. He had already determined that, and he would hold steady.

But he had to face the fact that no matter what she was doing, there was something she was not telling him. There was something in his Tonia's life that she could not or would not share with him. How could this have happened? Whatever was wrong must be his fault. How had he failed her?

The ride back to Aethelsham was one of the longest of his life. He kept thinking of questions he should have asked but hadn't. Did the shopkeeper know if there was a Mme. D'Arbley in Tunbridge Wells? And that still left the question, Why go all that distance when Canterbury offered such excellent choices? Should he have gone to Harriet? He could have used the excuse of inquiring about a dressmaker as a surprise for Tonia. And why hadn't he asked the little ticket agent if Tonia had purchased a return?

At least he could answer that one. He had not asked because he could not face the possibility that she might not be coming back. But that was ridiculous. Of course she was coming back.

The sharp black of the winter night, its few stars like chips of ice, covered the cold landscape by the time Danvers arrived back at Aethelsham. In spite of the lateness, however, the dowager duchess had not yet gone in to dinner. Even more astonishing, she called to him from the drawing room. "Charles, I am pleased."

"Oh? I'm amazed to hear that, Aunt Elfrida."

"You have represented me excellently on the committee. As I knew you would."

"Oh?"

The dowager duchess indicated Lansing's drawings spread before her on a low table. "True sentiment. True spirituality. God will be pleased."

"Oh!"

"You may take your time changing for dinner. I told Soyer to put it back an hour. I did not wish to rush my contemplation of such sublime conception. I have told Tonia."

"She has returned?" He hoped Aunt Elfrida didn't catch the note of relief in his voice as he hurried out of the room.

He made it almost to their room when Hardy sprang out of the shadows in order to open the door for his master. "Thank you, Hardy, but I am most capable of turning doorhandles for myself."

"Certainly, m'lord, but I have had a most invigorating day."

Across the room Tonia was seated before her mirror as Isabella arranged her hair.

Danvers crossed to her and dropped a light kiss on her cheek. "I trust your day wasn't too tiring, my love?"

"Thank you, Charles. I'm fine." Then with more determination. "Quite fine."

"Good. And how is Harriet?"

"Oh, Harriet is—vigorous. Unrelentingly so."

He could think of nothing else to ask. Or to be accurate, he could think of too many things he wanted to ask. All of which would be too pointed. He turned to his dressing room to submit to Hardy's rambunctious solicitude. The fact was that with Tonia so withdrawn it was comforting to hide behind Hardy's bustle.

His valet produced a shirt so stiffly starched it could barely be made to conform to Danvers's body, but Hardy was undaunted in his attack with ebony and diamond studs. "Most enlightening meeting today, m'lord. Most enlightening. Two speakers. Most enlightening."

"Hmm? Oh . . . er . . . that's fine, Hardy."

"Oh, yes, a fine thing indeed. It's quite amazing the progress in thought being made these days. Mr. Gardiner Simpson dwelt at some length on all the attention we give to material progress, to the advance of the machine age. But his theory, if you'll pardon my saying so, sir, is that we should be giving more attention to *human* progress. Progress of the mind. Progress of the person. Spiritual progress, if you will."

Danvers nodded distantly, and Hardy continued. "Of course, he was really speaking for the abolition of capital punishment. But give 'im a hearing, I thought." His master's shirt was now securely fastened and tucked and the neck held in place with a silk cravat. He bowed him to a chair where he could attack his hair with a pair of boar-bristle brushes. "Not but what it was the second man you would of liked fine, m'lord. Gladstone Simpson was saying just what you've said—continued his lecture from our last meeting, he did—on the dangers of phrenology."

"Glad to hear it. He sounds a sensible fellow."

"Oh, most sensible, m'lord. Just what you've been saying—great danger in our society. We must take warning before it's too late." He shook his head with the gravity of a preacher warning of hellfire. "Grave danger. People will take the shape of their craniums as their destiny. Use it as an excuse to do evil."

"Just what I said, Hardy."

"Indeed you did, m'lord. So that's why I took what he said so much to heart. But then I expect you've noticed."

"Hmm?"

"You see, the thing is, it's not an excuse at all. It's an opportunity to be warned of the darkness in our souls."

Danvers waved off the energetic hairbrushing and stood to take the coat Hardy had hung out for him. "I was under the impression that the Bible does that quite adequately—far better than any phrenologist reading cranial bumps, I'm quite certain."

The valet outreached the master and held the coat for him to slip into. "Well, yes. But if you'll be so good as to forgive a personal reference, we could be taking my own case for example. I must be confessing to you, m'lord." The jacket slid smoothly over Danvers's shoulders. Hardy moved in front of him but hung his head. "I must confess. My diligence bump is much underdeveloped, while the general roundness of my forehead reveals a tendency to sloth and carelessness."

Before Danvers could reply, Hardy's eager face split in a smile. "If I may presume to hope, sir, you might just have been noticing a few small improvements in my service. Just a wee touch here and there."

"Yes, Hardy, I've noticed."

"Ah, well, there it is then, sir. You see? Knowing my tendency, I'm forewarned. I then have the knowledge I need to work extra hard to overcome my deficiencies. Such knowledge, so far from being an excuse to apathy and dilatoriness, can be my very salvation."

"Hardy!" Now his man had Charles's full attention. This was not something he could pass off with careless assent. "I will not have you speaking of achieving salvation by your own works. I can only hope that was just your Irish hyperbole, but I will not tolerate such heresy." He knew that he sounded fully like Aunt Elfrida's nephew at the moment, but he was undeterred. "You're washing the outside of the cup."

Hardy appeared lost in the face of metaphor.

So Danvers added another. "Can a leopard change its spots? You can't change your soul or the shape of your skull by polishing the leather off my shoes or brushing the hair out of my scalp—although I might say you've worked vigorously enough to add a few bumps to mine." He picked up a white silk handkerchief and turned to the bedroom door, where he could see Tonia waiting for him. "Salvation is all a matter of God's grace and our faith, Hardy. And not a bit of it about pressing and brushing suits. And there endeth the first lesson."

Danvers glanced over his shoulder just in time to see Hardy leaning toward the mirror and running his fingers carefully over his skull. Then he offered Tonia his arm.

When they were in the hall she looked up at him. Deep lines were drawn between her eyebrows. "Charles, what you said about grace. It is true, isn't it? For all of us."

He put his hand over hers. "Grace and mercy and the goodness of God. It's all any of us has to hope in."

"Yes. Grace and mercy—from God."

Why did she sound so dejected? he wondered. "And from one another as His children, I should hope," he added.

She turned her hand over to clasp his fingers and held on very tightly all the way to dinner.

16

For the third time that afternoon, Tonia caught herself walking in circles. For the past two days she had felt like a caged animal. If only this drizzle would stop and she could go outside. Then she could walk in a much wider circle around Aethelsham's gardens and orchards, and her actions would not attract the attention that pacing round and round in a small room would if someone should walk in on her.

Charles had already gone into Canterbury to see that everything was in readiness for the concert at evensong. She glanced at the rain dripping down the tall leaded windows of the library. It would put a sad dampening on the children's lantern parade if the weather didn't clear up. But at least Charles was fortunate to have something to occupy him.

She looked down and realized she had completed another half-circuit of the room. If she didn't find something to occupy her she would go crazy. Wait. That had been the verdict. Wait and see. She could do nothing more for now. But Tonia was not good at waiting.

On Tonia's third circuit around the chamber the door burst open. She turned quickly to grab a book off the nearest shelf to hide her aimlessness.

She needn't have bothered, however. Eleanor was in no state to notice another's mood. "Oh, Tonia, thank goodness I've found you. What am I to do?"

Tonia put an arm around the distracted girl and led her to a chair by the fireplace. "You're cold, Eleanor. Sit here and tell me what has you so agitated."

"I've just been talking to Aunt Elfrida. I didn't know —Randolph is to be in her party this evening."

"Oh, dear. How awkward for you. But we can contrive that you needn't sit by him. I understand there are to be several present—her architectural committee, my friend Harriet Launceston, Gil—that is, Dr. Morris. Anyway, quite an adequate number to keep between you and anyone you don't want to see."

Eleanor did not respond.

"Nelly, you don't *want* to see him, do you? I thought you'd quite changed in your feelings."

"Well, I have. But then I haven't. That's why Aunt Elfrida says I must just go ahead."

"Go ahead and what?"

"Let her announce our engagement." Eleanor began twisting her hands in her lap. "That's what Randolph wants. And Aunt Elfrida says that, since the committee has accepted his sketches, he shall be thoroughly established now, and I really have nothing to wait for."

"But Aunt Elfrida isn't your guardian."

"No, but she says that as my mother is dead and she's a near female relative, she'll be quite happy to take charge for me."

"I think you have no need to worry. Charles can handle that nonsense. He sees matters quite clearly."

Still Eleanor didn't cheer up. "Yes, but you see—it's not just a matter of my saying no to Randolph." She twisted her hands quite violently, then stopped with a hiccup. "The truth is, I wrote some very silly letters."

"Oh, my dear." Tonia took the shaking girl in her arms. "What a very silly thing to do indeed. But that's all it is—just silly. You may be rather embarrassed if evidence of a misplaced infatuation is circulated in society. But it will quickly be replaced by the next nine-days' wonder."

Eleanor shook her head. "Charles will be embarrassed . . . the family . . ."

Tonia jumped to her feet and began her pacing again. "It always comes to that, doesn't it? The family, the family, the family. Well, assuming you've been honest with me about the state of affairs between you and Randolph . . ." She looked at Eleanor for the confirmation she expected.

"Oh, yes, yes. Truly, Antonia!"

"That's as I thought. Then you have nothing to fear past a little embarrassment, Nelly. And Charles will agree. I don't understand Aunt Elfrida. This seems too high-handed even for her. Come on now—" she pulled Eleanor to her feet "—let's go pick out just the right dress for you to wear to the concert. And I'll contrive to have a word with Randolph Lansing. Perhaps if I tell him how little control you have over your fortune . . . or perhaps I could bribe him to return the letters. The matter warrants considerable thought."

Eleanor's shining face was almost frightening. Tonia couldn't stand the idea of letting Nelly down if her ill-formed plot failed. Still, she was confident she could think of something.

"Now, we must choose something very warm . . ." She approached Eleanor's wardrobe.

"I had thought of my pink silk."

"No, my dear. Not in the rain. You'll want something much heavier if we're to view the lantern parade." Tonia pulled a soft blue-gray velvet cloak from the back of the tall, mahogany chest. "This looks perfect."

Eleanor sighed. "Yes, it's quite the warmest garment I own, but the hood makes such a mess of my hair."

Tonia considered for a moment, then plucked a long, white silk scarf from the top shelf of the wardrobe. "Here

—drape this loosely over your hair. It will protect it from the hood."

Eleanor did as she was told, then turned to Tonia, the white silk scarf curving around her face, the soft blue cape covering her shoulders. "Pity it's Lent rather than Christmas. I look like a Madonna in this."

Tonia took one look at the girl, then shivered. "Take it off, Nelly. It won't do at all."

Eleanor's eyes grew wide at the note of aversion in Antonia's voice. "I'm sorry, Tonia. I didn't mean anything irreligious. I just thought—"

"No, Nelly, it's all right. But your green wool will be most appropriate."

Tonia turned toward her room to get ready, but all the time Isabella was dressing her in her favorite rust-brown velvet suit, Tonia kept trying to remember what it was that Eleanor had reminded her of—and why she had reacted with such repugnance to the scarf and cape.

It was more than two hours later, when the dowager duchess's party had assembled just inside the Christ Church Gate, that Antonia found the answer she had been badgering her mind for.

The rain had quit and left a freshness in the cold air that even in February hinted a promise of spring. The heavy clouds hung low, adding to the sense of comfort in the night and reflecting the glow of the gaslights lining the street. The damp, mellow stone buildings reflected the ambient light, and the square panes of glass in the bow-fronted shop windows sparkled.

The booming of a small brass band made people crane their necks. Then down the street Antonia could just catch a glimpse of flickering lanterns. At last the words of an old Lenten hymn reached her ears, sounding especially sweet on the crisp air: "Begone, ye powers of evil with snares and wiles unholy! Disturb not with your temptings the spirits of the lowly."

The Lenten Charity Choristers came first. Their white surplices bulged over the layers of jackets and jumpers underneath, their mouths were open wide, the light of their lanterns, swinging from the ends of long poles, reflected on their faces.

Tonia smiled at the sight of the tall, thin man walking in the midst of his choir, singing as heartily as any of the children. "Depart! for Christ is present, beside us, yea, within us; away! His sign, ye know it, the victory shall win us." Danvers gave a small wave to his family.

The choir was escort for the robed archbishop, carrying his staff of office—a simple shepherd's crook. Behind him came the seven- or eight-piece band, sounding like two or three times their number, and then came the people following along behind, some singing, some just walking and smiling.

It was hard to say what, in all that warmth and good feeling, should have brought to Tonia's mind the worrisome answer she sought. Perhaps it was the glow of lanterns against the dark—recalling her lamp glowing in Lansing's closet—so soon after having seen Eleanor dressed like a Madonna. Perhaps it was the fact that Randolph Lansing stood only a few yards away while Eleanor sheltered on her other side. Perhaps it was that they were following the crowd into Canterbury Cathedral, where so recently she had seen the staring eyes, bloodstained hair, and slit throat of the maid Lily—looking so different from what she had in Lansing's paintings that for days the likeness had remained unrecognizable in Tonia's mind.

Her feet followed the dowager duchess up the nave, but her mind followed quite another pattern. It was perfectly clear now. She should have thought of it sooner, especially when Higgins showed her the ring—one of those Lansing had painted on Lily's finger. Perhaps her modeling fee?

The cathedral was warm with candles and humanity, but Antonia shivered. She was thinking how whoever had so viciously slit Bessie's throat, while she and Charles were next door having their portrait painted, had later applied the same but fatal treatment to Lily. But now she had her weapon against Lansing.

She smiled as she ascended the steps toward the choir and entered under the row of shield-bearing angels. The artist had worried that the fact of a murder occurring next door might discourage his society patrons. What would it do to his trade if it became known that one of his models —a model of whom he had painted very rude pictures— had come to such an end?

The return of Eleanor's letters would be a small fee to buy Tonia's discretion. Of course she would have to tell the police. But Futter could be the soul of diplomacy. His knowing would be nothing compared to what would happen in society if Agatha were handed that weapon against a man she already disliked vehemently.

Confident, Tonia tugged at Lansing's coat sleeve just as he was about to enter the row of seats behind her in the section that had been reserved for the Dowager Duchess of Aethelsham and her party. "I have something most particular to say to you."

Lansing stepped back into the aisle and made a sweeping bow. "Indeed? Then please, say away, dear lady." His thin mustache curled in a parody of a smile.

Tonia recoiled at his oiliness. She had no desire to hold private speech with this man. And yet she had promised Eleanor. "Something of a private nature. Perhaps we could just step into the transept. It should be a few moments before the introit."

The cathedral was nearly full, but a shuffling of feet and chairs still sounded above the strains of the organ prelude, and she knew it would take Danvers, and Hardy who was assisting him, some time to get their choristers reordered after the invigorating procession. They were robing in one of the chapels.

The north transept was empty.

Tonia faced Lansing. She had one goal—to transact her business as quickly as possible and get out of his company. "Sir, you have something of value to my family. I have information you would not want widely disseminated. I propose a bargain."

His features looked sharper, his eyes paler in the shadowed light. "Indeed?"

Just then a group of people entered the adjoining aisle looking at the tombs of the archbishops there. Lansing took her elbow and drew her out of the way. "Now, perhaps we shall be undisturbed here."

Tonia did not like being in a dark, deserted passage with this man. Her knees evidenced an alarming tendency to tremble, but she would not let her chin quiver. "That day in your studio when I observed your paintings on my own. I saw more than those on display, if you take my meaning."

"Ah, my closet. Yes, I thought some of the canvases appeared to have been moved. Good likenesses of the girl, don't you think?"

"I hardly think you would find it to your liking that the existence of those pictures should become known, any more than Eleanor wishes for the letters she unwisely sent you to be known.'

Lansing's narrow eyes darted from side to side. "What do you propose?"

"I suggest that you return Eleanor's letters, and I will refrain from divulging what I know about your relationship with Lily."

Now the wolfish eyes were still, frozen on her. "What do you mean, my 'relationship with Lily'?"

The door at the far end of the cloister opened and the skipping clatter of a pair of young feet came toward them up the stone passage. Swiftly Lansing seized Tonia and thrust her backward farther into the transept. Surprise more than fear made her cry out.

He shoved her through a doorway, and the heavy, wooden door creaked shut behind them. A scraping sound of metal on metal followed.

"What are you doing? What do you mean shoving me like that?"

"What do you know about Lily?"

Tonia caught her breath. She knew only that the girl had posed for Lansing. But she suddenly realized from the violence of his reaction to her ill-chosen words that there must be a great deal more to it than that. Then she remembered. "Lily was pregnant."

As soon as she heard her words, Tonia realized her folly. She had no time to work it all out, but in a horrifying flash she knew who had fathered the child Lily carried. And who had silenced her.

It was too late to pretend now. "What did you do? Get her into the crypt on the excuse of posing for one of your religious paintings?"

"Something like that."

Tonia put her hands to her throat and began backing up.

Wherever they were, it was a very narrow space. Three backward steps brought her flat against a rough stone wall. She groped with her right hand. A stairway? A narrow, curving stone stairway leading sharply upward. Lansing lunged at her. In the semidark his aim was unsure.

Something grazed her shoulder. Not a knife. Something heavy.

Instinct rather than planning caused Tonia to bring her knee up hard just as he lunged again. Lansing staggered backward. She heard a sharp crack. Perhaps he had struck his head against the edge of the stone stairs.

She turned and groped for the door. Her fingers found the heavy iron hinges. She fumbled desperately for the doorhandle.

Lansing moaned behind her. He was dazed, but he would be on his feet again in a moment.

She pulled back for an instant when she caught a sliver in her finger. Then she found the latch. She pumped at the thumb plate above the cold handle. It refused to move.

Of course, that was what Lansing had attacked her with—the heavy, ancient iron key to the tower.

Then she knew. She was locked in the Bell Harry Tower with a murderer. He had murdered Lily. Now he intended to murder her.

17

Danvers surveyed the seething roomful of energetic boys in varying degrees of undress. The Lady Chapel had withstood centuries of weather, fire, and martyrdom. He could only hope it could withstand the Lenten Charity Choristers as well.

"That's right, boys." He rapped on a reading table for attention. "Pile your coats and mufflers in the corner. Then the red robes on first. White surplices on top again. Hardy here will come around to check that your hands and faces are clean and your hair respectable."

Perhaps the four or five closest boys heard him. The next two had got as far as removing their knit jumpers and were whipping each other about the head and shoulders with them.

"If I might just say a word to the wee lads, sir?" Hardy offered.

"By all means. Please." Danvers stood back.

Hardy more bounced than strode into the fray, grabbed each boy by the scruff of the neck, and cracked their heads together. Danvers rubbed his own forehead in sympathy, but the action had as efficacious an effect on the rest of the choir as on the two Hardy held. All froze as if a gunshot had rung out.

"There now, my lads, I'm knowing that smarts a bit. At least it did when my dear mam did it to me. But it never failed to get my attention. Now, if you'll just be putting these lovely robes on we can be getting lined up. Fine thing, the lantern parade, fine. And now you'll be wanting to do as fine for the service."

Danvers shook his head in amazement. The boys were lined up in less than two minutes. All except his lead boy.

"Where is Higgins?" Danvers shouted and pointed at the glaring empty space. "He was here for the parade. Has anyone seen him since?"

A short boy in the front row looked up at him from under a thatch of blond hair. "Gorn to the privy, sir. Private like. 'iggins is very partic'lar."

Danvers listened. The organist had just finished "Sheep May Safely Graze." "Sleepers Awake" would be next. Then the processional. They should be in line at the west porch now, ready to serenade the archbishop, dean, and all the canons in stately procession up the nave.

"Hardy, take them out through the cloisters and in the west door. I'll look for Higgins."

He strode across the transept and yanked open the door to the dimly lit cloisters. Where could the boy have gone? Fine time for him to turn shy. He'd never known of a street boy being so desirous of privacy.

Which way should he go? Where should he look? In the distance he heard the slamming of a door. Behind him the choir crossed the transept to enter the cloister as he had instructed Hardy. The rest of the passage was deserted. He paused, trying to think what to do.

"Gov'nor, you better come—quick!"

Danvers looked up at the red-robed urchin running toward him. "Higgins. About time you showed up. Go to the back with the others."

"No, no, sir. It's not the singin'. It's the lady. The pretty one—your wife."

"What?" Danvers sprang toward the chorister.

"In the tower, I think. I was comin' from . . . outside." The child waved vaguely. "I heard her cry out like—I think 'e knocked her about a bit—but the door's locked."

He grabbed the thin shoulder. "Show me."

His small guide scuttled across the aisle, around a corner, and pointed to an iron-studded door.

"My wife is in there? You're sure?"

Danvers didn't wait for Higgins's nod to lunge at the door. Several people walked by staring, but he didn't care. He pulled on the thick, twisted brass handle, but it wouldn't budge. He pounded.

To his amazement an answering thud came from the other side.

"Tonia?" He would have shouted to the vaulted ceiling and not worried about the congregation filling the cathedral, but he knew he would have a better chance of being heard if he put his mouth to the door and cupped his hands on either side. He tried it. *"Tonia!"* Then he pressed his ear against the unyielding wood and listened.

He was certain he heard her voice calling his name. Then, "Lansing's here. Lansing killed Lily!" Could that possibly have been what she said? "Lansing's here." At that moment the organist pulled out a full bass stop. The cathedral vibrated with sound. There was no more talking through the door.

A key. Apparently Lansing had one. Perhaps the only one? Even if there was another, it could take forever to locate the verger. Then by the time he found a duplicate key . . .

He had to get into that tower. He racked his mind to recall the architectural drawings he had studied for the committee. The Bell Harry Tower. At the crossing of the western transepts at the top of the nave. He looked up to where the gold-embossed fan-vaulting of the underside of the tower reflected light from below. Above that hung the

Great Harry Bell, rung only for the death of a monarch or an archbishop.

He forced his mind back to the drawings. In the wall of one corner there had been a narrow, circular stairway leading up to the bell tower. That would be this one. But were there others? Did the south transept hold a staircase as well? Could he go up another way and reach Tonia by crossing to the tower and coming down? Perhaps. He couldn't remember, and he couldn't afford to waste time. What was happening to Tonia behind this locked door while he stood here trying to think?

At the back of the nave the procession started. The procession he was supposed to be leading. "Are there any other staircases?" he hissed at Higgins.

"St. Anselm's the only one I ever climbed." The child pointed to the staircase tower in the angle of the eastern transept.

It was just possible. A mad scheme. But it might work. Thank God it had quit raining. "Go sing." He gave Higgins a shove toward his choirmates progressing in stately manner up the center aisle.

Then Charles darted up the side aisle. At the next transept he grabbed at the doorhandle of the staircase tower, refusing to consider that it might be locked. The door swung open.

The pie-shaped stairs were too narrow to take his whole foot even at the wide end. And they spiraled so steeply it was more like ascending a ladder than a staircase. The stone was treacherously slick. No light penetrated the black shaft above him. Danvers determinedly kept a picture of Antonia in his mind and climbed upward toward that vision. Around and around. His hands pressed against the rough stone on each side to help maintain balance.

And when he reached the top—what then? The upper section of the tower was ornamented by three—or was it four?—rows of narrow, arched openings that in the day-time would provide some light. Could he get onto the roof from there? The window slits were narrow. And covered—with metal grilles? stone tracery? glass? He couldn't remember. How terrible it would be to have to smash glass that had survived from the twelfth century. But he would do it without a second thought to save Tonia.

He lurched around the final turn and out onto a flat surface. A few gaslights burned in the cathedral close hundreds of feet below. A few stars shone through the clouds above. These were enough to turn the landing from impenetrable black to murky gray. Enough to show the outline of a door.

Of course there would be a door. The purpose of the tower was to provide an exit to the roof. Opening it, he saw that a narrow walkway ran the length of the building. From directly below he could hear the choir singing. "In those days and at that time I will restore the fortunes of Judah and Jerusalem."

The wind flung the words against the Great Harry Tower. "In that day I will restore David's fallen tent. I will repair its broken places, restore its ruins, and build it as it used to be."

Danvers inched forward along the walkway, feeling the ridged lead roofing under his feet. His right hand ran along the stone balustrade above the celestery windows, the fingers of his left hand brushed the lead strips of the steeply rising roof. The wind buffeted him. He fought an impulse to run—a careless step would cost far more in time than controlled progress.

"The Lord will restore the splendor of Jacob like the splendor of Israel, though destroyers have laid them waste and have ruined their vines." *Oh, Lord, restore Tonia to me. Protect her from the destroyer.*

When he reached the great central tower, he again held his breath, hoping he could find yet another door, hoping it would be unlocked. He did. It was. *Thank You, Lord.*

Inside he edged around a narrow wooden walkway toward where he judged was a staircase that should take him downward. Had the two in the tower heard or seen him enter? Did Tonia know he was on his way? Did Lansing know to beware of him? Tall windows let in enough gray light to reveal the heavy beams that filled the tower with supporting framework—and a narrow, wooden stairway leading to the bell chamber at the very top of the tower.

But Charles sought a stairway that would take him down, and he found it in the corner. It was only slightly larger than the one in St. Anselm's Tower, and going down was more treacherous than going up. One misstep would send him plummeting, and Lansing would have no need to crack his skull for him.

Hands braced firmly against the stone shaft on either side, he spiraled downward. He was more than halfway down when he heard a sharp cry from Tonia. A sharp cry, then a cracking sound followed by a gasp and moan.

Did that mean he was too late? To have come so close and failed? He lunged forward. He missed a step. His feet flew out in front of him, and he skidded downward on his back. Worn though they were, every step still cut sharply at his shoulders before sending him along to the next bruising, scraping edge.

He descended with a muffled bumping that seemed loud to his own ears. But perhaps it was covered by the pealing organ below and the gusting wind above.

He collided with Lansing about three turns from the bottom. A tangle of arms and legs, the two fell together, each grappling more for some sort of solid grip than to defeat his enemy.

Danvers landed at the bottom, winded and sore. Lansing's departing kick struck just below the small of his back, or the chase might have ended there. As it was, the blow to his spine stunned and slowed him. He looked upward in the dim light just in time to see Lansing gather up something—a cape? a body?—and sling it over his shoulder before disappearing up the stairwell.

Was he carrying Tonia? If so, she must be grievously hurt to hang so raglike. Hurt but alive. Why else would the man bother? Danvers glanced about the tiny chamber where he lay but could see nothing. He thrust himself to his feet, somewhat unsteadily, and began the spiral upward once again.

He tried to make sense of what the artist was doing. Surely Lansing had the key. Why hadn't he simply escaped through the door? But no, he would have heard Tonia calling to Danvers. He may have thought the door guarded. So he was racing upward to escape over the roof.

Charles gasped for air and shook his head to try to steady it as he clambered upward, around and around. And why would he take Tonia with him? The chill he felt at the answer served to clear his head.

The man would leave no witness. He had killed before. He would not hesitate to do so again. Danvers had to keep Lansing from reaching the roof—would he throw her down?—if he ever hoped to see Tonia again. A surge of energy spurred him to greater speed. Around the next turn he glimpsed Lansing's feet disappearing just ahead of him.

Faster. But don't misstep. One more spurt. There was Lansing's leg. Danvers grabbed for the man's ankle. He felt the fabric of Lansing's pantleg slip through his fingers. They must be almost to the landing.

With supreme effort Danvers hurled himself upward. Just when he was within grabbing distance again, Lansing sprang out of the stairwell. He kicked once again at his pursuer but did not take time for a follow-up when his aim fell short.

Now Charles had the advantage. He had just been here. He knew where the door was. Lansing turned to his right, but Danvers sprang across the landing and blocked the exit.

He could see now that the object over Lansing's shoulder was indeed merely a cape. Had he slung it there to entice Charles upward and away from Tonia? Or was he merely providing himself with protection against the weather? Did the fact he had left Tonia somewhere behind mean there remained no worry that she could testify against him?

Lansing reached the wall. Finding no door, he spun around. Three strides brought him within arm's length of Danvers.

Charles lunged and struck. But instead of the solid blow he expected to feel, his fist tangled in the voluminous folds of the cape Lansing flung at him. He flailed with both arms to get the thing out of his way.

Lansing dodged past him and leaped at the wooden staircase leading to the trapdoor in the floor of the bell chamber. The man was up the steps by the time Danvers reached the foot. Danvers was no more than three steps up when Lansing pushed up the trapdoor and sprang through it.

The heavy wooden planks fell back into place with such a thud it almost knocked Danvers backward. Then he heard the scraping of something heavy being dragged across the door.

Lansing's words slammed out of the dark. "Give it up, Danvers! You're too late. Your fine lady's dead. Skull cracked like an egg. That's your aristocratic breeding for you." His laughter was a hysterical shriek.

Charles refused to listen, refused to feel the pain the words struck. Later. He would feel it later. If that beast had killed Tonia, Danvers would not stop until he had dealt with him.

He pushed futilely against the planking overhead. Whatever Lansing had placed there was effective. But what could the man hope to gain? There might be a ladder that would take him out to the top of the tower. But that would afford no escape. Did he think to use a bell rope to let himself down the outside? The idea of rappeling down hundreds of feet of wet stone in the dark was sheer folly.

Possibly Lansing had acted from panicked instinct and had no plan. Danvers could hear him moving about on the bare wooden floor above. Did the man know what a dangerous place a bell tower was? Even an experienced ringer could tangle in a rope if not careful. The heavy bells were always left cocked upward, ready for the first ring. This meant tons of iron balanced at the end of loosely coiled rope. On the other hand, if Lansing knew what he was doing, it might be possible to booby-trap such poised weapons to deal with anyone who came unawares after prey he thought safely caged.

Rested after his pause for reflection, Danvers took a deep breath and again pushed up on the trapdoor. He would proceed cautiously, but he would proceed. If this man had killed Tonia, there was nothing he wouldn't do to see him captured. There was no risk he wouldn't take.

This time he shoved against the trapdoor with greater strength and felt a slight give. Apparently, whatever Lansing had put over it, the door was not locked in place. The weight could be lifted or jarred off. Given enough time and strength. If only he had something to work with.

He descended the wooden stairs and groped about the landing. If only a careful canon might have decreed stowing fire-fighting tools here, he could even hope for a hatchet. He was unable to locate such a thing in the uncertain light. How long had he been at this? Twenty minutes? An hour? Was the service about to conclude? In his lofty isolation it seemed impossible that hundreds of people were congregated in worship, surrounded by light and music, directly below him.

His foot struck something and scraped it across the floor ahead of him. He dropped to his knees and groped. Just a stick. A length of building lumber, probably left by a workman seeing to any weakened beams in the tower. A primitive but sturdy tool.

213

Once again at the top of the stairs, he pushed with all his might on the trapdoor. It seemed that it opened farther this time. One more shove, and he managed to insert his stick in the opening. Now he could alternate pushing and prying. In a short time he had the door opened several inches.

What was Lansing doing? He could hear nothing above him now. Was he waiting for his adversary to spring through the trapdoor opening? Waiting with a heavy instrument to cudgel him? Waiting to throw him down the shaft of the tower where he would land broken somewhere amid the maze of criss-crossing support beams?

But he could not think about danger to himself. Not when he was Tonia's only hope for survival. If there was any hope left for Tonia. He used the desperation of that thought to lend momentum to his next shove. With a rasping and grating, whatever was balanced on the door slid aside. One more push and he was through, letting the heavy door slam shut behind him.

The crash of the thick planks was accompanied almost simultaneously by a wild cry from Lansing, who came lunging out of the darkness.

Danvers sidestepped.

Unable to halt his momentum, Lansing hurtled forward, then tripped over the rope chest he had shoved over the trapdoor. His feet tangled in the spilled ropes, and he plunged onward toward the spot to which he would have pushed Danvers.

Charles turned just in time to see it. The bell rope that should have been coiled safely on a wall peg was looped like a snare on the floor, waiting for an unsuspecting victim to trip it.

In a desperate attempt to avoid stepping into the trap he had laid for his pursuer, Lansing seized the rope. And Great Harry toppled from his carefully balanced upright position. As the enormous bell swung downward, Lansing —clinging to the rope—was flung upward toward the grinding gears of the wheel that controlled the movement of the huge bell.

Some of the monarchs whose death Great Harry had tolled had been murderers. But this was the first time Great Harry tolled the death of a murderer who was no monarch.

Stunned by the clanging, which made the whole tower vibrate, and the swiftness and horror of what he had witnessed, Danvers stood immobile. Holding his breath, he waited for the body to fall back to the floor.

He had focused his energy on the man's capture, had put his own life in danger to bring it about, but he could have wished such a grisly death on no one. He brushed away a drop of rain.

Then he realized it wasn't raining. At least not inside the tower. A drop of blood had fallen from the mangled body hanging above him. Thoroughly enmeshed in the workings of wheels, ropes, and pulleys, Lansing's body would not be falling to the floor.

Danvers turned to make his lonely descent back down the three levels of the Great Harry Tower. What would meet him at the bottom? Was the sight there to be far worse than the one he left hanging in the belfry?

18

T onia was not there. How could that be? The door stood as firmly locked as ever. He groped again about the small chamber, covering, he thought, every inch of rough, cold stone on his hands and knees. "Tonia? Tonia!" The tightness in his throat would let no more words out.

Then he heard a small moan in the far corner under the spiral of the stairs. In his haste he must have brushed past her the first time around. He turned in such haste he struck his head against the wall, but he barely felt the impact. His hands closed on the warmth and softness that was Antonia.

He gathered her into his arms, crying her name incoherently over and over. After all he had been through, his enormous relief at finding her alive and regaining consciousness was almost too much for him.

"Charles?"

"Yes, my love. Everything is all right."

"My head hurts."

"Shh, just rest." He tightened his arms around her, and she snuggled into his embrace.

The peace of the room filled with the strains of the closing anthem of the cantata. "The God of all grace who called you to His everlasting glory in Christ will restore His beloved to Himself. Dominion be His throughout the ages. Dominion and glory be restored." The organ pealed the final chorus.

Danvers bent his head and kissed his beloved. "Tonia, thank God. If I ever lost you . . ."

She pushed herself to a more upright position and put a finger over his lips. "Don't, Charles. You don't know . . . you might have to . . . might be forced . . ." Tangled in her own words, she buried her head against his chest.

A moment later the postlude began with such vibrato it rattled the tower door. But then he realized it was not the music shaking the door. Someone was there. Still holding Tonia, he struggled to his feet and helped her to cross the floor with him. He pounded back and shouted, "Yes! Who's there?"

"And would you be wanting any help, m'lord? Wee Higgins here thought you might be in a spot of bother, but if we're intruding—"

"Hardy, don't you dare leave! Just get the verger—or someone. There must be an extra key." He said to Tonia. "Where's the key Lansing had?"

"I'm not sure. It was on a huge iron ring. He tried to hit me with it. Then I kicked him . . . I don't really remember. I rather think he might have flung it at me. Do you suppose it could have landed on a ledge up there?" She turned her face toward the inky stairwell.

"It's likely. That could explain why he was dashing upwards when I was coming down."

"Coming *down?* Charles, what—"

"I'll tell you all about it later. Now what about you? Your head . . ." Her hat had long ago come off. Now the coils of hair fell loose in his hands. He had to resist the impulse to run his fingers through the silky, sweet-smelling strands.

"Ooh." She winced when he touched a lump just

above her left ear. "He shoved me, and I hit my head. He probably thought I was dead."

Danvers nodded, his face still against her hair. "I know. So did I."

Renewed rattling at the door announced the return of their rescuers. And then, arms tight around one another, Lord and Lady Danvers blinked at the brightness of the candlelit nave, now almost emptied of its congregation.

They nevertheless still had a considerable audience. Behind the black-robed verger, holding his key ring, stood Hardy along with Higgins, jumping up and down beside him, clapping and shouting, "See, I told yer so. I told yer, didn't I?"

But before the jubilant chorister could be congratulated, Gil Morris and Constable Miller, who had been summoned by Hardy, pushed forward. Danvers surrendered Tonia to Dr. Morris's medical expertise and explained briefly to Constable Miller what had happened.

"Grisly affair up there. You'll need men with ladders and lanterns to deal with it."

Miller's face blanched as white as if it had been covered with the flour that generations of his ancestors had produced. "Er . . . rightly so, m'lord. Would you be thinking it might be the right thing to do to get on to Inspector Futter first? What with the deceased being from Chatham and all?"

Danvers smiled. "I can see no harm that could come from waiting. As a matter of fact, I'll be glad to give a full statement, but I'd like to get my wife home tonight."

Tonia added only a few sentences to his explanation before allowing Gil to lead her away.

Charles had started down the aisle behind Tonia and Morris when he felt a tug at his sleeve.

"Pardon, Gov'nor, but did yer hear any of the concert?"

"Very little, I'm afraid, Higgins. And that from some distance. But I'm sure it was a great success."

The eager face fell. "But not enough that yer could be recommending me for the school?"

"Certainly—" he began.

Tonia turned and held out her hand. "Sam Higgins, I don't think the King's School is quite the right solution, do you?"

"Well . . ."

"I shall see what I can contrive that will be more suitable."

"Thank you, I'm sure, yer ladyship." Higgins gave a whoop and skipped off down the nave.

"Tonia . . ." Danvers began uncertainly.

But she shook her head. "It's been a long day. It can wait till tomorrow."

Danvers took a deep breath. A long day indeed. A murder solved—more too, but he couldn't sort it all out right now—and Tonia restored to him. And his debut as choirmaster a resounding success. He lifted his face and as much shouted as sang, "The Lord their God will care for them; He will restore their fortunes."

The next morning at breakfast Charles's jubilant spirits rose yet another notch when the dowager duchess accosted him.

"It will not do, Charles. Not one scrap of it." She pushed at a stack of Lansing's architectural drawings with the tip of her walking stick, knocking them off the sideboard and scattering them over the carpet.

Soyer, in the act of placing a silver platter of eggs on the buffet, stepped on one. It crumpled under his foot with a sharp crackling.

"And a very fitting end to it too," Her Grace pronounced with a satisfied sniff. "Architecture reflects morality. Canterbury Cathedral could not be restored with designs drawn by an immoral artist. It's all quite unthinkable. I'm surprised at you, Charles. I expected more discrimination of you."

He bit his lip to preserve his gravity. "You're quite right, Aunt Elfrida. It was unthinkable of me to promote such a scheme. I was also quite mistaken in thinking my sister should encourage the fellow's suit."

"Well, you should have listened to me. I always said he was up to no good. The Barony of Crofthurst—a jumped-up affair—title no more than two hundred years old. It wouldn't do at all."

Danvers winked at Eleanor seated on the far side of the table. "Don't know how I could have been so wrong-headed."

"Quite. And now that you are thoroughly chastened, there is another matter I wish to speak to you on." Three raps of the ebony walking stick demanded attention. "Something really must be done about the succession, Charles. You can't let the family down. We're all relying on you. I have spoken to Antonia very precisely on the matter. She thoroughly understands her duty in the scheme of things."

"Yes, Aunt Elfrida." He turned to serve himself from the sideboard, rejoicing in the dowager's words about the cathedral. Another problem solved. It was amazing. The murder of an archbishop had built much of the glory of the cathedral. The murder of a maid had saved that glory from desecration.

It wasn't until late afternoon when he and Tonia were sitting with Futter in the drawing room, recounting the details of the night before, that he realized not everything was solved.

"Been over that studio with a fine-tooth comb. Especially that locked closet you told Constable Miller about, Lady Danvers." Futter paused, cleared his throat, and blushed to the roots of his hair. "Those paintings in there —cool your soup, they would, or boil it, as the case may be." He shook his head. "And right next to paintings of the Virgin Mary—sacrilege, that's what it is. The man must have been sick."

"So Lily posed for him—and more—but when she and her condition became inconvenient, he murdered her." Danvers shook his head. "I suppose she was badgering him to marry her and give her child a father."

"We'll never know, but that seems likely. Bad timing on her part, when Lansing thought he was about to catch an heiress." Futter looked down at his ever-present notebook. "Which brings us to the matter of Mrs. Bacon's valuables. Orson went over the studio with me. He recognized a good many of Lansing's artist's props as items that had belonged to Catherine Bacon."

"You're certain about his identification?" Danvers asked. "After all, Orson's an interested party, so to speak."

"No question about it. He even showed me a small painting Mrs. B. had given him of herself several years ago. Guess what? She was wearing that slide bracelet and holding that fancy fan."

"So do you think Lansing murdered Mrs. Bacon when she caught him stealing from her?" Tonia asked.

"Don't see how he could've, ma'am. Considering his alibi."

She nodded. "Yes. Charles and I were both with him at the time of the murder."

"And he didn't leave the room for any length of time while you were there, did he?"

Tonia thought back. Then Charles answered for them both. "No. He didn't leave it at all. Besides, Bessie would have recognized him."

Futter rubbed the top of his pale head. "Aye, there's a sticky one now. Haven't got that one figured out yet. Bessie has to be involved in the robbery some way—at least in the pawning. Three local pawnbrokers have identified her positively."

"But she couldn't have stolen anything that morning," Tonia said. "While the murderers cleared out the engraved silver, she was lying on the floor beside her dead mistress, bleeding from a cut throat." She shuddered.

"Or was she?" Danvers asked. "Maybe there wasn't any robbery at that time. We've only assumed those things were taken then because Bessie said she figured the 'dustmen' were there to rob. What if all the items had been stolen earlier by Lansing and Bessie working together?"

"You mean no robbery connected with the murder?" Tonia frowned. "But then what was the intruders' motive? "

"If there *were* any intruders." Danvers spoke softly, as to himself.

But Tonia heard. The idea was so startling she was unable to react for a moment. "You mean—"

"I'm not sure what I mean. But nothing about the dustmen theory really makes any sense. And none of it is borne out by any evidence—apart from Bessie's story."

"So you're suggesting maybe there was a falling out between the thieves, and Lansing attacked Bessie and her mistress, but Bessie didn't want to accuse him because that would mean admitting her own guilt?" Futter's normally soft voice took on confidence and volume as he spoke. "Now that's a right fine theory." He began looking back through his notes. "Yes, I like it. I like it. Certainly explains a lot if we can throw out the notion of unidentified intruders. Chances are Bessie opened the door to Lansing herself."

"While he was painting our portrait?" Danvers asked.

Futter deflated like a balloon. "Oh."

But Antonia picked up the idea. "Wait a minute. Bessie said she went unconscious after they slit her throat— that's why the killer thought he'd left her dead. Maybe she was out considerably longer than she thought."

And Danvers picked up on that thought, "You mean maybe Lansing beat and slashed two women, then nipped back through the garden gates and spent the rest of the morning calmly making pleasant conversation while he sketched our portrait?" He drove his fingers through his hair fiercely. "I can't believe even he could be that cool."

Tonia reflected for a moment. "It's horrible to think of, but he did keep us waiting a bit, if you remember."

222

"Well, yes, just to wash his hands . . ." Danvers held out his own long fingers and looked at them, palms up first. Then he turned them over. "Red paint it was—all over his hands . . ."

"Right." Futter rose to his feet abruptly. "Time we had another wee look at our artist friend's studio. We'll get to the bottom of this yet."

"I'll just get my hat and cape." Tonia rose, and Danvers sprang to assist her.

"Tonia, are you sure you should go today? After that bump you took last night? Perhaps a quiet day resting?"

"Nonsense. Fresh air will do me good."

He watched her go. He would be delighted to have her companionship. But she still looked pale and drawn, although she had been looking that way even before yesterday's adventure. And as much as he disliked thinking about it, Aunt Elfrida was right. He had failed in his duty toward Tonia—and the family.

The years of their marriage had sped so happily it was hard to realize how long it had been. But it was time and past that they should have produced an heir. Perhaps a trip abroad when this matter was cleared up. Italy or the south of France, where it would be warm and Tonia could relax. She had seemed so tense lately . . .

19

Careful, Isabella." Antonia winced as her maid applied too much vigor tying on her bonnet.

"Oh, my lady, your poor head. You should not go out today—all that jostling in the carriage."

"Don't be silly, Isabella. I am quite well."

"But, my lady, you could have been murdered."

"Well, I wasn't, was I? Besides, being so intimately involved in the whole affair makes me even more determined to see it to its conclusion." She fastened the frogs holding the front of her cape while her maid dithered.

"At least take your drops with you. Just in case the pain worsens." Isabella held out a small brown bottle.

Tonia slipped it into her reticule. The fact of the matter was that her head hurt considerably more than she cared to admit, but she had never found giving in to a headache to be of much help. She certainly had no intention of spending the day in a darkened room with the laudanum drops Gil had prescribed. Applying herself to the puzzle at hand would be far more beneficial.

And most of all she wanted to spend the time with Charles. She didn't know what the future held. But she wanted to spend as much of it as possible with him.

He seemed to reciprocate her mood, and he held her hand in the carriage all the way to Chatham. Futter had gone ahead in his hired conveyance, so they were alone. They talked little during the ride, but it was a comfortable, companionable silence that seemed to bring them closer than talking might have. It was as if, after yesterday's terrors, they each needed assurance of the other's presence. Tonia was sorry when the brougham pulled up at Ordnance Terrace.

Hardy handed them out of the carriage. "If you won't be needing my services for a little while, m'lord, there is just one call I'd like to be making."

Danvers shook his head. "Another of your phrenological society acquaintances, is it? Cranium cronies, I suppose you might say. Well, be off with you then, but be quick. I don't expect this to take long."

A black bicycle parked just inside the front gate of Number 7 showed that a member of the local constabulary was keeping an eye on things indoors.

A white-faced Mrs. Gillie answered their ring. She started to give Futter a sharp reply, then saw Lord and Lady Danvers. "You better come in," was the best she could do even for his lord- and ladyship.

"He was a good master, he was," she announced staunchly as soon as they were in the parlor. "I don't care what other people say he got up to, he was always good to me. It was that great-aunt of his what cut his father out of the will—it was all her fault. Ruined his chances before he was born. I ask you, is that right? People shouldn't cut their own flesh and blood. It's not natural. If he'd had what was his by rights, he wouldn't never have been driven to get tangled up in any of this."

"That's as may be, Mrs. Gillie," Futter interrupted. "I was brought up chapel—taught that we're responsible for our own decisions—but that's neither here nor there at the moment. What we want to ask you about is the morning Lord and Lady Danvers here came for their first sitting."

225

"Yes?"

"What had Mr. Lansing been doing that morning—before we came? Can you remember, Mrs. Gillie?" Tonia leaned forward in her chair, hoping to placate the woman's defensiveness with a gentle voice.

"Same as he always does—did." Mrs. Gillie shrugged her thin shoulders. A few strands of gray hair escaped their haphazard pins.

"Could you be more specific?" Futter prodded.

"He painted, didn't he? Morning light was best, he said. He was always in his studio by first light. Course, that's none too soon in the winter. He always goes—always went—straight up to work. I'd take his breakfast up to him on a tray. Toast and coffee, that's all he ever takes—took."

"And that's what you did the morning we came?" Tonia asked.

"Just said so, didn't I? I'd no more than brought his tray back down when you came."

"Do you just happen to remember what he was painting that morning?"

"Course I do—couldn't forget it if I tried. Huge canvas in the very center of the studio. Why a woman the size of Mme. Florizelle would have herself painted in red satin is more than I could say. Still, what can you expect of an opera singer?"

"Thank you, ma'am. We won't keep you from your duties any longer." Futter stood. "With your permission I'll have a look at Mr. Lansing's papers in this desk here. I think Lord and Lady Danvers would just like to take a look at the studio. I believe my man's up there now."

"Can't stop you, can I?" The housekeeper hunched her already stooped shoulders. "But if that young fellow up there damages any of Mr. Lansing's paintings, you'll be responsible."

Danvers took Antonia's arm and led the way to the stairs. "You don't mind going up, Tonia? After last time?"

226

"Certainly not. Just so the Chatham constabulary has had the delicacy to face those paintings to the wall."

Inside the studio they paused before the painting of the rubescent soprano. Danvers shook his head. "Poor Mrs. Gillie. Apparently, she didn't know about the paintings in the closet either."

"Do you believe Mrs. Gillie? Would she lie for him?"

"I'm certain she would. The question is whether there was any need for her to do so in this instance."

Tonia walked slowly around the large room, then paused in front of the portrait of Charles and herself. "It really is an excellent likeness, Charles." She shook her head. "What a pity to misuse a talent like that."

He stood behind her, his arm around her waist. "Yes. He captured your skin tones perfectly. The light from the window falling on you is quite wonderful. What should be done with it, do you think?"

"Charles, would you forgive me if I didn't have a fit of maidenly vapors and faint at all the ill associations connected with the painting? In spite of everything, I quite like it."

He bent and kissed her cheek. "Tonia, darling. I was so hoping you'd say that. I would hate to part with such a lovely representation of you."

"Oh, Charles . . ." She caught her breath. Had she said entirely the wrong thing? Would it make it all even harder for him when . . .

She looked again at the painting, and it was as if the morning dawned. How could she have been so slow? Why hadn't she noticed before? "Look, Charles!" She pointed to the right side of the canvas.

Then she walked to the long window that filled the back of the studio from floor to ceiling, overlooking Lansing's garden and much of his neighbor's. She moved back again to the painting. "Yes, that's exactly what it was like. Don't you remember?"

Danvers frowned his puzzlement. "The view out the window? Yes, that's as I remember it. Just all white—fresh snow. Nothing else."

"That's right. Nothing else. No footprints in either garden. Charles, if Lansing had nipped over there and slit Bessie's throat and dashed back to do our portrait, there would have been tracks in the snow."

"Yes, but he would have hardly painted such incriminating evidence if tracks had been there, would he?"

"Of course not. But I sat there for—what? two hours, maybe? I am certain there were no prints in the snow. But more important—there were no dustmen. I would have seen anyone in Mrs. Bacon's garden."

"Which means that if there was an intruder, he—or they—would have had to have come and gone long enough before our arrival for all traces of footprints to have been covered by the falling snow."

Tonia nodded. "That's exactly right. Which means the paint on Lansing's hands must have been—just paint."

"I wonder if Bessie could have been unconscious that long—say three hours at least?"

"Seems she would have bled to death in that length of time, as much as the cut was still bleeding when we saw her." Tonia shuddered. "Let's ask Gil." She was happy for Charles's arm around her as they went back downstairs.

Futter listened to the report of their discovery, then gave a shy smile. "If you'll pardon a bit of pride, seems I've come across something rather useful here as well." He held out a piece of paper with writing covering three-fourths of the page.

"Unfinished letter. Appears Lansing got interrupted and forgot about it—or didn't have time to get back to it. Dated two weeks ago, it is."

Danvers took the paper the inspector held out to him and pointed to the direction at the top. "To Baron Crofthurst. Oh, yes, the distant relation. I suppose he must be notified of all this, poor fellow. Well known for his charitable work. He may take this quite hard."

"I doubt it, sir." Even Futter seldom blushed as brightly as he did this time. "That is . . . er . . ."

"What are you trying to say, man?" Danvers snapped.

"Well, thing is, seems Lansing acquired some of his artistic taste from his uncle. Uncle collected naughty pictures. He apparently had expressed interest in buying some of Lansing's . . . er . . . more exotic ones. Lansing was apparently trying to get more money out of the old man." Futter pointed to a paragraph halfway down the page. "Rather looks like he might have been trying for a bit of extortion—rather veiled reference there about knowing his uncle wouldn't want the extent of his amatory collection to become known . . ."

Danvers read aloud, "'Knowing the value you place on the good of the family name, even to supporting Cat Raddison in cutting my father out of her will. Well, Uncle, here's your chance to make a bit of that up to me and keep your own name unsullied—as well as acquiring some very fine paintings peculiar to your rarified taste.'" Charles lowered the paper. "The little snake. He was attempting to blackmail his own uncle."

Tonia grabbed his wrist and took the crumpled paper out of his hand. "But look—that next paragraph—'speaking of my dear, dear great-auntie, you will be amazed to hear that I have taken a terrace house right next door to hers in a neighborhood quite crawling with respectability. Should I call on our dear relative, I wonder?' That must be another threat. I—"

Tonia stopped and looked at the letter again. No, there was no mistaking. She felt warm and tingly as she always did when she gained a certain insight. She had learned to trust those perceptions. "Cat Raddison—that's *Catherine Bacon*. Remember, old Mr. Dalrymple mentioned the name 'Raddison.' And he kept on about someone named 'Cornhusk.' I'll bet he meant Baron Crofthurst."

Her words had tumbled out as quickly as her mind could form them. Now she spoke slowly, emphasizing each word. "Catherine Bacon was the long-lost great-aunt who disinherited Randolph Lansing's father for marrying an actress."

"That's right. Not respectable enough for the likes of her, I wasn't."

Tonia, Charles, Futter, all wheeled about at the housekeeper's voice.

"Mrs. Gillie . . . you're . . . Randolph's mother."

The bent-over little housekeeper straightened and tossed her head. Before their eyes she transformed into quite another person as she flung off her apron and crossed the room with a subtle seductiveness. "Mrs. Gillie, Mrs. Lansing, Sybil Stallington. Pity you're so young—" she looked at Danvers "—you'd have liked my Cleopatra. The toast of London I was in those days. You wouldn't credit it now. But one night a whole regiment of Hussars came together—bought out the whole theater. Afterwards we drank champagne from the regimental silver—a bowl so big I could hardly get my arms around it. Cleopatra, Juliet, Desdemona—I played them all. But Cleopatra was the best."

Danvers crossed the room to take her hand. He bowed over it. "Sybil Stallington, allow me to greet you for my father. I have heard him speak of that night. Your performances gave great pleasure."

She sighed. "Yes. But it was all long ago, long ago. And now I've played Mrs. Gillie so long I hardly remember any other role. Still—they were grand days."

"Madam, I am sorry to be asking painful questions just now . . . but under the circumstances . . . that is . . ." Futter cleared his throat and tried again with more determination in his soft voice. "Do you know if your son identified himself to his great-aunt?"

230

"No. No, why would he do that? Never wanted to have anything to do with us, she didn't. Better this way, it was. Just got his rightful due, and no one the wiser. Very nice arrangement. It could have gone on and on if it hadn't been for those dreadful dustmen."

Before Tonia could stop herself, she gave a gurgle of laughter, then clapped a gloved hand over her mouth when she realized how inappropriate her reaction must seem. "Forgive me, Mrs. Gillie . . . uh . . . er . . . Mrs. Lansing . . . er . . ."

"Miss Stallington would be nice to hear again."

"Miss Stallington. I do apologize for my outburst. But you see, the enormous irony of the whole thing is that Mrs. Bacon had her lawyers searching for years to find her great-nephew. She wanted to restore the relationship."

The woman pressed on, disregarding this information. "My son wasn't stealing, you understand. He was just taking what should have been his inheritance."

"What *was* his inheritance," Danvers corrected. "It was all there, waiting to be given to him. Only he didn't claim the relationship. He chose to do it his own way instead." After a pause he added, "So that's why you took such good care of Bessie. You were looking out for your son's interests by keeping an eye on his partner in crime."

Miss Stallington tossed her head. "The girl's a thief. She helped Randolph with what was rightly his, and he paid her well enough, but she had her own game going on the side, don't think she didn't. I let her know in no uncertain terms that nothing more was to leave that house until Randolph could consult a solicitor. But now it doesn't matter . . ."

A look of wild desolation swept over her face as if she suddenly realized her son was dead. "It doesn't matter now. Nothing matters."

Sybil Stallington stumbled to the center of the room as if on center stage. "We drank champagne from a silver bowl this big—" she circled her arms "—a whole regiment of Hussars."

She bowed unsteadily, swept the fringed drape from a table, and flung it around her shoulders like a magician's robe. "'Our revels now are ended . . . the actors . . . are melted into air, into thin air, and like the baseless fabric of this vision, this insubstantial pageant faded, leave not a rack behind. We are such stuff as dreams are made of, and our little life is rounded with a sleep.'"

She ended on a note of hysterical laughter.

Tonia went to her. "Come, Miss Stallington. You've had a terrible shock. Let me help you to bed."

The woman yielded to her urging, and over her shoulder Tonia directed Charles, "Bring the brandy."

In a few minutes the actress-mother-housekeeper was merely a distraught old woman who made hardly a bump under the comforter and yielded readily to the laudanum drops from Tonia's reticule administered in a glass of brandy. "Sleep now, Sybil. I'll send Dr. Morris to you."

Hardy waited at the end of the walk with the carriage.

"I hope Gil is in his surgery." Tonia rubbed her own throbbing head.

"Tonia, your head?" Danvers turned to her in concern.

"No, no. Only the slightest headache—no more than to be expected. Sybil needs him far worse. Actually I was thinking about Mrs. Bacon," she continued when she was settled in the carriage. "It doesn't seem that Lansing would have killed her even if he could have."

Futter answered. "All her valuables next door to help himself to—good as money in the bank."

Tonia nodded. "That's exactly what I was thinking. Unless he somehow found out about the will, of course. And there doesn't seem to be any indication of that."

Danvers agreed.

"So does Constable Orson inherit now?" she asked.

He nodded. "That's right. The terms were that the nephew had to be living to inherit."

Futter shook his head. "The intended heir rejected his inheritance, so it goes to the one who loved her like part of the family. One who would accept the invitation, so to speak."

Gil was indeed in his surgery. Or rather Dr. Benson's surgery, where he was still on locum. "Tonia, you shouldn't have come all the way into Chatham. I was coming to see you." He led her to a chair. "How's the head?"

She untied the brown satin ribbons of her bonnet. "Still rather sore."

He gently examined the lump.

She winced when he touched it.

"Sorry. Headache?"

"Some," she admitted.

"And you wouldn't take the laudanum drops, I suppose."

"Truly, Gil, it wasn't that bad." She told him how she had administered them to the woman who turned out to be Lansing's mother, the actress forced to play her ultimate role in order to live with her son next door to the woman who had hated her.

"I'll call round on her this evening. But first, let's get you something you will take." He turned to several rows of pots and jars in glass-fronted shelves. He took a few grains of calomel and an equal amount of antimonial powder, mixed them with soft bread crumbs and formed the whole thing into two pills by rolling them between thumb and forefinger.

"One now." He handed it to her with a small glass of wine.

She swallowed obediently.

"And one at bedtime." He slipped the other into a small white envelope and gave it to her.

All the time Gil had been attending to Tonia, Hardy and Danvers sat quietly in curved-back oak chairs across the room. That is, Danvers sat quietly.

233

Hardy shuffled through the journals and papers on the table that served as an extension of Gil's desk. Now he held out a black-and-white sketch showing the profile of a woman and some medical notes written across the bottom of the page. "Is there any chance you would be allowing my friend Gladstone Simpson to make a copy of this, Dr. Morris?"

Gil looked at him in surprise. "That patient sketch? Whatever for?"

"Ah, Gladstone Simpson, as a man of science like yourself would be knowing, is amassing the world's largest collection of phrenological evidence. Amazing gallery he has—I was just by way of visiting him today as a matter of fact. He received a new batch of daguerreotypes from Australia. An entire compendium of horrid murderers from New South Wales."

"Hardy!" Danvers growled warningly.

"Ah, yes. Thing is—" Hardy pointed to the prominent forehead in the sketch "—you'll note the strong frontal crest of this subject. Prime identifying mark of a criminal, that is. And—" he indicated the jutting chin "—combined with a prognathous jaw, I'd say we have here a clearly identified criminal type."

Gil raised his blond eyebrows. "Would being the *victim* of a criminal count?"

"What's that?" Hardy asked.

"That's my sketch of Miss Elizabeth Law. You'll note my documentation of the entry of the knife, the depth of the wound, and the angle of the cut." Hardy moved his hands, which had been covering the lower part of the page. "Also my notes on the treatment of the cut and the patient's progress. I doubt that would be of interest to your phrenological friend."

"One matter of great interest though, Gilchrist." Danvers plucked the sketch from his man's hand and dropped it back on the table. "'Outstandingly fine, head of an intellectual, superior cranial development'—I believe that's how you characterized our friend Lansing," he said aside to Hardy.

Then he turned back to Gil. "Elizabeth Law's wound —how long had it been made when you saw her?"

Gil referred to his notes on the case. "Copious bleeding. Fresh blood." He shook his head. "Impossible to say exactly. No more than an hour certainly. Probably not nearly that long. Beyond that, the blood would either have congealed, or she would have bled to death."

Tonia thought carefully, feeling that familiar tingle at the top of her head but forcing herself to be logical, to think of other possibilities. No one entered Mrs. Bacon's house from the back, she was certain of that. She had no oil-painted record of the front to refer to. Yet the scene was imprinted clearly in her memory. There had been only the would-be shovelers' tracks in the deep snow leading to the door. Could intruders have lurked in the house for hours before attacking and then hidden themselves again afterward? It seemed unlikely—nearly impossible when she considered how carefully the house had been gone over after the discovery of the murder.

She took a deep breath. "Gil, could Bessie have slit her own throat?"

The question hung in the air while the young doctor looked again at his notes and examined the drawing.

Tonia felt foolish at the very sound of her suggestion. She recalled vividly the blood and horror of the scene. With a shudder she imagined the feel of a steel blade at her own throat. Drawing the razor edge across. Knowing that cutting a hair's width too deep would end everything. How had she the audacity to suggest such a thing? Of course Bessie couldn't have done it.

Antonia jumped as Gil smacked the back of his hand against the page he was holding. "Yes. Elizabeth Law *could* have battered her employer to death and then cut her own throat to cover it up."

235

20

You're looney! Completely round the twist, you are." Bessie put one hand protectively to her throat and held out the other as if to ward off a lunatic. "You're looney, or you think I am. Why should I want to kill myself?"

Inspector Futter shook his head. "We don't think you wanted to kill yourself, Bessie. But we're absolutely convinced you desperately needed to make it look like somebody else wanted to kill you."

Tonia wondered whether the fear that came into Elizabeth Law's eyes was the fear of arrest—which even an innocent person could feel—or fear that stemmed from guilt, an uncovered guilt that she thought successfully hidden.

"Supposing I did, how would you ever prove such a thing? Did you think of that before yer come in here scaring a girl to death? I'd as soon face a dustman with a knife as a looney policeman, I can tell you."

"All right, Bessie. That's a good try," Futter said. "Can't blame you putting a brave front on it, but we've got the right of it, and you know it. Best you remain silent. Only fair to warn you, anything you say now can be taken down as evidence and used against you."

"What? You think you're going to trick me into a ruddy confession with your fancy words, do you? Well, just you try, because I've got nothing to confess, I haven't."

Futter stepped forward and snapped handcuffs on her large-boned wrists. "That's enough, Bessie. Just you come along now. Where's your cape? Cold out it is—you'll need it." He ushered her toward the door, where a long, dark woolen mantle hung on a peg. He draped the garment over her shoulders and led her out to the waiting black vehicle.

Just as she entered the carriage she gave a laugh that chilled Antonia far more than the February wind. "You're wastin' your time. You'll never prove a thing."

As the hollow clump of the horses' hooves rang down the street, taking Bessie Law to "Tom-all-Alones"— the prison outside of town—Tonia indeed wondered how successful the crown would be in proving its case. The accused herself was the only witness. The evidence seemed to be more a lack of evidence: no dustmen, no footprints in the snow, no indication of theft except that by Bessie and Lansing.

Tonia believed that Bessie possessed the brashness to steal and murder, then inflict a grievous wound on herself to cover it all up. But would the jury believe such a thing?

She would know in a few weeks.

Lord and Lady Danvers were back in London at their Grovesnor Square residence when Hardy presented them with a pristine copy of the *London Times* at the breakfast table. The paper had been carefully pressed and the pages cut by his own hand, as any well-trained gentleman's gentleman would do. It still smelled of printer's ink.

"I believe you'll find a most interesting item on page seven, m'lord." Hardy had been behaving with remarkable restraint since his vagary with the phrenologists.

Danvers opened the paper, took a sip of his morning coffee, and read aloud: "'The Murder at Chatham. The girl Elizabeth Avis Law, charged with the murder of Mrs. Bacon at Chatham, yesterday was examined before the county magistrate at Rochester. The evidence was much the same as that given before the coroner. Major Henry Boys, the magistrate, who received the statement made by the prisoner that the murder had been committed by two men, deposed to the fact of having taken that statement. Two pawnbrokers proved that the prisoner had pledged property belonging to the deceased. The magistrates committed the prisoner for trial.'"

Tonia sighed. "So we shall soon be returning to Kent for the assizes."

Danvers checked his pocket diary. "I believe they sit in Rochester in late March. We have a few weeks to wait yet."

Tonia nodded. Wait. Yes. That was what everyone told her to do. Wait. And then the verdict. The verdict at Rochester. The verdict at Tunbridge Wells. "I suppose you shall be required to give testimony. I hope they will not ask it of me."

Charles took her hand. He did not comment on how cold it was, but he continued to hold it. "I certainly shall testify. You must be present, I'm afraid. But I shall try to shield you from the necessity of a public appearance."

Dear Charles, always so good. She forced a smile.

On Thursday, March 22, 1855, the case of Regina vs. Elizabeth Law came to trial at the Rochester Assizes.

Tonia, in a sober black dress and properly veiled hat, took a seat beside Danvers in the timber-ceilinged, stone courtroom. "I'll be so glad to have this whole squalid affair behind us." She heaved a sigh. "Do you think the trial will run long?"

Danvers raised one dark eyebrow as he looked about the room. "Not if our friend Futter has anything to do with

238

it. He's been on tenterhooks for days now, expecting word from Mrs. Futter."

"Oh, I'd forgotten." Tonia raised a black-gloved hand to her mouth. "It is near her time, isn't it? Poor man, he must be beside himself."

She looked to the front of the wide chamber where the inspector's pale hair accented his bright pink cheeks. Usually so calm, he sat today on the edge of his chair. Whenever the door at the back of the room swung open, he jerked around to see who had entered. After a few moments of watching, Tonia began to wish that the traffic would stop or that Futter would reposition his chair before he severely dislocated his neck.

At last the clerk appeared droning, "Oyez, oyez, oyez," and all stood for the entrance of the black-robed, bewigged judge. He took his place behind the elevated bench and perched a pair of wire-rimmed spectacles on his small nose. He peered around the courtroom like a nearsighted ferret while everyone resumed their seats.

Bessie Law clasped the railing of the dock with her rough, coarse hands. Her wiry, rust-colored hair was skewered firmly into a bun at the back of her neck. The white collar of her gray deal dress framed her freckled face and green eyes.

The clerk read the charge that Elizabeth Avis Law had, with malice aforethought, on the twenty-ninth of January last, at Chatham, murdered Mrs. Catherine Bacon.

"How does the prisoner plead?" the judge asked, looking at the accused over the top of his spectacles.

Elizabeth Law raised her chin just a fraction.

Tonia wondered if it was a conscious movement to exhibit her scarred throat to the jury.

Her voice was bold and unwavering. "Not guilty."

Tonia groaned inwardly. The woman was obviously guilty. The evidence, though circumstantial, was so strong. Did Bessie mean to face it out to the last? *Let justice be done, Lord,* Tonia prayed. Then added, *And quickly.*

Elizabeth Law maintained her defiant stance while Counsel for the Crown, Mr. Prendergast, also appropriately robed and wigged, gave the opening statement for the prosecution.

"Gentlemen of the jury—" he made a sweeping gesture that stopped just short of bowing to the twelve severe-looking men in the jury box "—you have heard that the prisoner is indicted for the crime of willful murder. You will naturally ask, What motive can the prosecutor assign for such a crime as this? A question natural and reasonable. And I will say to you that we will prove in the course of this prosecution that the passion which ruled Elizabeth Law to bludgeon her mistress to death and then attempt to cover up her crime by slitting her own throat was none other than that most elemental of the cardinal sins—simple, overweening greed.

"Elizabeth Law had, for a period of many months, been routinely stealing from her employer and selling her ill-gotten gains in local pawnshops . . ."

Mr. Prendergast's curly, gray hairpiece tipped slightly to the right as his voice marched on, each well-enunciated word echoing off the stone wall behind Tonia. She found herself tipping her own head to the side to compensate for the slippage.

The prosecution was doing a careful job of laying out its case—telling the jury what it was going to tell them. And when the witnesses had finished telling those things, Mr. Prendergast would then tell them what he had told them. A thoroughly competent job. Even for Tonia, who knew the facts far more graphically than she wished she did, the ringing words painted fresh scenes in her mind.

"Picture with me the accused, under the cover of a snowy, predawn morning, sneaking as quietly as possible into the respectable premises of Mrs. Bacon's terrace home. The maid who should have spent the night in Christian slumber, now heavily under the influence of the deep drinking which she had engaged in with her companions, stealing into her employer's home, thinking to deceive her employer yet another time as she had so many times before. But this time Catherine Bacon, small and aged but not willing to be taken advantage of, accosted her wayward employee and upbraided her for her misconduct."

The opening statement continued, explaining how Bessie had taken the coal shovel at hand in the cellar and ruthlessly battered the elderly woman. Tonia, who had seen the blood-spattered storeroom, shuddered. She knew the importance of laying out a careful case, but she did wish they would get on with it. If only the trial were over.

Mr. Prendergast then began listing the pawnbrokers who would give evidence of Bessie Law's selling Catherine Bacon's property to them.

Tonia began calculating. If each witness was to take, say, ten minutes (the pawnbrokers, the policemen, the doctor, the publican) . . . then there would be the evidence for the defense (she supposed some of Bessie's friends would testify for her) . . . then the closing speech for the prosecution . . . for the defense . . . then the summing up . . . And how long would the jury take to deliberate?

Could it be done today? And if not—if she were forced to sit in this chilling, damp-smelling courtroom another day and miss her rendezvous—what then? Would another day matter? Could she contrive to send a note? Would he still be there?

Tonia glanced at Charles sitting tall and stalwart beside her. He must have sensed her gaze because he turned toward her. Immediately his craggy features softened, and the corners of his eyes crinkled in a tiny smile. He picked up her gloved hand and tucked it in his arm, warm and secure.

Tonia swallowed hard. Dear Charles, so kind, so good. He had been so loving of late, especially since her abduction by Lansing. She blushed as she thought of the warmth of his fervor. And yet she still had not dared tell him. When they first came to Kent almost two months ago,

241

she had thought the time away from London would provide the perfect opportunity for her confession. She couldn't have been more wrong. They had immediately been plunged into the murder, the details of which Mr. Prendergast was describing so graphically for the jury, and then there had been the tangle with Lansing, the cathedral committee, the Charity Choristers—

She sat up with a start. That was it! She had been worrying for days what legitimate excuse she could give Charles tomorrow, assuming the trial was over and she was free to undertake this final step, and there it was. The perfect excuse because it wasn't an excuse at all. It was an obligation she must see to.

She had promised Sarah Higgins she would arrange something for the girl's education. So far she had done nothing. She must see to the matter. Sarah had essentially saved Tonia's life. And the child had a rare gift of music and intelligence. Tonia would make arrangements for her before she did whatever she must do about her own life.

What time was the first train to Canterbury in the morning? She would be on it. If only this trial would be over.

Apparently Hardy, sitting to her left, noticed her distraction, for he turned from his scrutinization of the jury, which she noticed had absorbed him since first they took their seats. He shook his head with the expression of a soothsayer who had found a very bad portent in the entrails spread before him. "Criminal-looking lot up there. I don't like it at all. Mark my words."

"Who?" Tonia whispered back, glad for a diversion from her worrisome thoughts. "Bessie's witnesses?"

It must have required considerable emotive energy for Hardy's cherubic face to take on the dourness it now assumed. "Nay, not them. The jury. Can you not be seeing it?"

Tonia looked. The twelve men, most of them in cheaply cut black suits, wore a variety of styles of neckties around their stiff white collars. Probably clerks and shop-keepers, she judged. Three in the tweeds and soft-collared, colored shirts of laborers. Most with their hair uncomfortably brushed, but few, she guessed, with overly clean nails.

She shrugged. "I don't see anything out of the ordinary."

"Ah, that'll be because you're not knowing how to look." He pointed. "Third from the left, front row. I'm not liking that bulging forehead—bad sign that is. And next to him—massive brow, small compressed mouth, villainous expression—known criminal phrenology, that is. Three up there with jug-handle ears. Two definite sugarloaf types . . ." He shook his head. "Strongly characteristic of degeneration."

Tonia smiled. It was rather nice to have Hardy back to his old self. "Hardy, you're not suggesting we're in danger for our lives sitting in Her Majesty's courtroom?"

"I'm suggesting justice is in danger. Grave injustice to Her Majesty's law and order."

"Nonsense, Hardy. This is England."

She returned her attention to the proceedings before her as Prendergast continued.

"This is a case of unusual subtlety. Therefore you, men of the jury, good men and true, must be acutely aware of the evidence that is to be presented before you. You must listen carefully, weigh each statement in the light of reasoned common sense, evaluate closely the veracity of all you see and hear. The eyes of your countrymen are upon you. This great charge, I know, will be no hindrance but will make you more anxious to discharge your duty and to adhere to that great golden rule of human conduct—to do one's duty and to brave the consequences."

Questioning and cross-examination of the witnesses first on the scene began. Danvers was sworn in and gave careful testimony to all that he had seen that fateful morning. Tonia watched him carefully, following his every word, the pride she felt in him warming her throat. He was so

243

precise, so exact and clear in his descriptions and answers. He did this with the care and perfection with which he did everything. Each duty received his best attention.

Duty, duty, duty. Always it was there. No duty too small. And, Tonia knew with a chill, no duty would be too great.

Thankfully, he was able to answer all questions to the satisfaction of the prosecution. And the defense, wisely enough, wanted to hear no more of the extent of the battering of Catherine Bacon, so Antonia was not called to take the stand—although she would have been willing if it were necessary to see to the full carriage of justice.

The questioning continued with Constable Orson. "Yes, sir, knowed the deceased for many years, many years. Let's see, must be getting on for eleven years now—more like twelve maybe. One of the first people I got to know when I was just a young cub on my beat. I remember the first time I saw her. Little bit of a thing with her hair all done up tight under a lace cap. One of the worst nights I ever remember in these parts, it was—cold rain sluicing down. Then the wind whipped it right up off the pavement and blew it back at you a second time.

"'Come in for a nice cuppa cocoa, won't you, Constable?' That's what she said, just as bright as if she was standing here right now—which I wish she was. Don't know whether she was just taking pity on a poor drowned creature or maybe she was feeling a mite uneasy with the storm howling around so, but—"

"Ha! Invited the devil right in, didn't she? Was that when you decided you wanted to get your hands on her valuables?"

The whole courtroom gasped at the outburst from the prisoner.

The judge gaveled vigorously and turned to reprimand Bessie, but she would not be silenced. "Don't think I don't know who profited by Catherine Bacon's death. Clever

Dick, weren't you? But just how clever? What do you know you aren't telling?"

The courtroom buzzed until the judge threatened to have the chamber cleared. Tonia shifted uneasily. They were wasting time. At this rate the trial would go on all week.

Orson was visibly shaken, and Tonia observed him carefully. No, she would not judge that his reaction showed either fear or guilt. It seemed more that he was hurt that anyone could make such a suggestion. He hung his massive, dark head and shook it slowly.

Bessie subsided, and the trial continued, but Tonia's attention was next taken entirely another direction by Hardy's tugging urgently on her sleeve. "There, the one in the back row, next to last."

Tonia looked. "What is it, Hardy? Not another sugar-loaf cranium surely? That man looks perfectly harmless."

"No, no, fine head. Idealism bump highly developed. Can see it from here. Makes it all the stranger I didn't notice sooner."

"Notice what?"

"Gardiner Simpson he is." When Tonia looked blank at this supposedly astounding announcement, he continued. "Brother of Grace and Gladstone Simpson, the phrenologists. Surely you'll be remembering my telling you about their fine meetings I've been attending."

"I've heard little else from you, Hardy. But what about this brother?"

"He spoke at a meeting—certain I am I was telling you about it. Fine crusading fellow—given his life to promoting the cause, he has."

Tonia shook her head. "I think your phrenology is more of a disease than a cause."

"No, no. Not phrenology. That's the other two. No, Gardiner Simpson's cause is the abolition of capital punishment. Given his life to it, he has."

245

Tonia frowned. A true-believing crusader against capital punishment on the jury in a murder trial? "Well, let's just hope his respect for human life extends to issues of murder as well as of punishment."

And justice, she thought. *Presumably the man opposes capital punishment on the grounds that there might be a miscarriage of justice. Surely one so dedicated would not choose to be a party to so blatant a failure of justice as refusing to convict Catherine Bacon's killer would be.* And yet she worried. *Justice quickly, Lord,* she repeated.

Next on the stand was Owen Dorset, in whose pawnshop Tonia had spotted the engraved silver urn from Catherine Bacon's grape-patterned set.

"And is the woman who sold this piece to you in your shop present in the court today?" Mr. Prendergast asked.

The pawnbroker clearly identified Elizabeth Law and vowed that she had represented the urn as having been in her family for years. "Before they got down on their luck, she said. Course if I'd had any notion the piece was nicked, I wouldn't of had anything to do with it."

Two more pawnbrokers gave similar testimony, which proved unshakable in the face of cross-examination.

Then the publican from The Three Bells testified that Bessie left his establishment deep in her cups on the night in question. "Remember it clearly, I do—not as I'd remember every night back as far as two months ago, you understand. But that was the night that snowstorm was blowing up, and we had sailors in from three ships—all up and rowdy 'bout the weather, whether or not it'd affect their sailing and did they just have time to go off with some girls on account of delayed sailing. That sort of thing. Made for a right lively atmosphere in The Three Bells. One of our best nights all year. What's not so good for other folks is often very good business for us publicans. Seems to be the nature of the business."

Tonia began to fear the jovial host would go on forever, but Mr. Prendergast brought his witness back to the matter at hand, and she heaved a sigh of relief when the prosecution rested.

The opening remarks of the defense took a strong stand for the apocryphal dustmen, as unwaveringly testified to by Bessie Law. At least their existence was unwaveringly testified to, even if their description seemed to be different every time the subject was approached. Poor little Miguel would likely be on trial for his life right now rather than on his way back to his family in Madrid if Bessie's identification of him hadn't been so botched.

Witnesses for the defense consisted solely of Elizabeth Law's friends, who insisted that Bessie was a good girl who liked her bit of fun but had no harm in her.

Under cross-examination each admitted that, yes, Bessie had often complained loudly and vehemently against her employer. Yes, Bessie often had more spending money than most girls in her station—more than any of *them* had, that was certain. And yes, in the wee hours of the morning of January 29 Bessie had departed from their company a fair bit more than three sheets to the wind. And no, Bessie did not care overmuch for her employer . . . well, yes, I suppose you could say she hated her . . . despised her at least. No, Bessie wasn't a violent woman . . . no more than most, that is. Of course there was the time she knocked Mamie's teeth out in a fight—but she was drunk then, and she didn't mean no real harm.

Tonia held her breath. It had been a long morning and was now well into the afternoon. Would Judge Rolfe, undoubtedly longing for his dinner, adjourn court and require them all to return tomorrow? Although her testimony had not been called for, she would have to remain available should a question arise—no matter how inconvenient that might be.

It seemed that Mr. Rolfe was asking himself those same questions. He surveyed the courtroom, peering over the top of his silver spectacle rims from his elevated position. Tonia sighed with relief and settled back against the hard seat when he nodded at Mr. Prendergast to proceed.

The prosecution cleared his throat and adjusted the white bands at the neck of his robe. "Gentlemen of the jury, I have a very invidious duty to perform in calling your attention to the evidence which has been laid before you . . ."

He then proceeded to remind the jury of Elizabeth Law's strong motive and unlimited opportunity to perform the crime with which she was charged, as well as the complete lack of any evidence to support her claim of unknown intruders.

Tonia had come into the courtroom convinced of Bessie's guilt. Now she was doubly certain. Every dark corner of the case had been thoroughly delved into, and the best efforts of the defense had served only to strengthen the Crown's position.

"I will say no more on this matter," Prendergast concluded. "I will only add to you, as jurymen, the charge to do your duty and pronounce your verdict." He gave a half bow to the jury and sat down.

Do your duty and pronounce justly, Tonia thought. The closing remarks of counsel for the defense did nothing to shake her conviction that Elizabeth Law was guilty.

Only the judge's summation remained. Then how long would the jury deliberate? She looked out the window. The gray of the late March afternoon hung thick in the air.

Mr. Justice Rolfe adjusted his lopsided wig. "Gentlemen of the jury, it is my duty to remind you that your decision in this case must be founded exclusively and entirely upon the evidence you have heard detailed. Anything you might have believed about this case before you came to your position of weighty trust in this courtroom, anything you might have thought or heard, must be left outside as surely as you left your cloaks in the cloakroom. The evidence before this court, and this evidence only, must influence your decision."

The judge then reviewed the evidence as it had been placed before the jury. "Looking at these facts, public duty makes it your imperative duty to say if the accused standing before you is guilty. If there was anything in the evidence so presented which leads you to the conclusion that the prisoner is innocent, then you must find her not guilty.

"But let me remind you that, in this sacred duty you hold, it is not permitted to any body of men acting as jurors to conjure up doubts or to say that there are doubts if from the bottom of your hearts you feel there are none. Let us see justice done."

The jury retired to a side room. All stood as the judge retired from his bench. Then the courtroom erupted in a buzz of chatter and rustle of crinolined skirts and frock coats as people who had been sitting for the better part of a day were freed to move about.

Lord and Lady Danvers strolled into the foyer, and Charles paused at the long glass door at the end of the corridor. The silvered landscape without looked invitingly crisp and clear.

"Tonia!" He turned with a flourish and seized both her hands. "Let's celebrate. Tomorrow—please Lord that this trial is over—let's make an ascent!"

"Oh . . ." Tonia fumbled for words. She fervently shared his wish that the trial should be over. And the idea of a balloon ascent was the perfect solution to keep him occupied while she went about her business this one last time. But celebrate? Would there be anything for them to celebrate tomorrow—or ever again? "Yes, that would be perfect. Of course you must go for a fine flight. Only—"

"Yes? Only what?"

"Well . . . I know you didn't bring your balloon."

"No, of course I didn't. I thought you'd heard me mention—Laver Esherwood, one of the finest aeronauts in England, lives just a few miles from Aethelsham."

"Oh, yes. I think I do recall you mentioning something about it." Tonia fought to think clearly. She was losing control of the situation. Tomorrow was crucial. "Well, I certainly hope it will be a fine day for you."

"Surely you mean for *us*. You'll come too, won't you?"

Her shiver was not entirely for effect. Her laugh was. "I know all aeronauts are quite mad. But sailing through air that is little more than gaseous ice is not my idea of a celebration. Besides, I must see Harriet tomorrow. I've been shockingly remiss on my promise to arrange for Sarah Higgins's musical education."

"Who?"

"Oh, Charles, didn't I tell you? I must have forgotten in all the excitement. Your lead boy soprano is a girl." Tonia drew her story out in as much detail as she could. And when she concluded, the danger of discussing tomorrow's activities was past. For the moment. But she knew it would come again.

Hardy joined them with the report that there was no activity in the courtroom. Supper had been taken to the jury, and the clerk who carried it in said that they were deep in debate.

"Oh, Charles, what can they be debating? It's so obvious she's guilty."

His answer was to suggest they look for a respectable eating establishment—which would perhaps be more easily found here in the cathedral city of Rochester than around Chatham's naval yard.

They ate slowly and well. Tonia had not realized she was so hungry.

Afterward they stepped out into a chill, inky night, and she glanced at the crystal brightness of the stars cutting through the black. "Do you suppose they're still deliberating?"

Charles put his arm around her for warmth and led her to the waiting carriage. "I don't see how they could be.

It's been hours. There simply wasn't that much counter evidence. The defense hardly had a case."

She nestled under three rugs. "Charles, they couldn't possibly fail to convict, could they?"

"I don't see how, but we'll soon know." The horses trotted briskly through uncrowded streets back toward the courthouse. "At least, I hope we will."

But when they got inside, the clerks and police officers half dozing on the uncomfortable wooden benches lining the hall told Tonia they had missed nothing here. Futter and Orson shared a long bench, each leaning heavily on a wooden arm.

"Is this going to go on all night?" Danvers asked.

Futter shook his head, saw Antonia standing, and stumbled to his feet. "Don't know when I've ever known a jury to take as long over such a simple case. Suppose we might as well go on home. There isn't much likely to happen now. Jury probably went to bed hours ago and forgot to tell anyone."

Tonia's heart sank. "Charles, do you think we—"

Just then, behind them the doors of the courtroom swung open.

"The jury has reached a decision." The word went the length of the corridor. "We've got a verdict!" "Come into the court."

Everyone was on their feet, yawning, stretching, hurrying forward, in spite of a few sleepy staggers.

When all were in their places, Mr. Justice Rolfe squinted over the top of his spectacles and the Clerk of Arraigns turned to the jury.

Tonia tried to read their expressions. Did they look happy with their decision? Would the judge in a moment be placing a black cloth on his head to pronounce the death sentence? Besides the dazed sleepiness that was only to be expected, it seemed to Tonia the jury looked oddly downcast and confused. None would meet the eye of the judge or of anyone else in the courtroom.

"Has the jury reached a decision?" the clerk asked.

Hardy made a growling sound when Gardiner Simpson stood as foreman.

"We have, Your Honor." Gardiner Simpson, inveterate campaigner against capital punishment, looked neither sleepy nor confused. He looked invigorated and triumphant.

"Have you found the prisoner guilty or not guilty?"

"Not guilty."

The words echoed off the stone walls and seemed to hang over the jury box. Gardiner Simpson was the only juror who would look up.

Tonia glanced about her. Everyone else seemed to be as stunned as she was.

Except Bessie Law and her friends. They erupted in cheering and made a jubilant rush for the nearest exit.

People around her began to get up, but Tonia didn't feel she could move. She relived again every moment of that terrible morning in Ordnance Terrace: the pitiful sight of Catherine Bacon, the trail of her blood through the house, Orson's grief over the woman's death. She thought of the friends who would miss her, the charities she had supported faithfully. And her killer was to go free?

Then she thought of all the investigation, all that had gone into the prosecution of Elizabeth Law, of Futter's sacrifice of being away from his beloved Marianne so near to the time of the birth of their child. Had it all been for nothing?

She went once more over the evidence. Was she certain there were no footprints in the snow? Was she positive no one had gone into or out of Number 9? The more she asked, the more convinced she was of the rightness of the charge. Had British justice miscarried?

She looked up at the long faces of Futter and Orson, who had just joined them, and she knew she was not the only one asking such questions.

252

The constable seemed the most downhearted. "I promised her. I promised Catherine Bacon as on the grave of my own granny, which she was next to being. I said I'd avenge her. I'd get the person who did that to her. And I failed."

Tonia held out her hand to comfort him. She knew that also at the back of Orson's mind had to be the fact that he had been publicly accused. And now, with no conviction and no other suspect, Constable Orson, legatee of the murdered woman, would bear the brunt of popular suspicion and rumor. It was likely his career was over. The thing he mourned, however, was not what this would mean to his profession but the fact that he had failed in his duty to the victim. Tonia thought it likely he would resign his position even if rumor did not drive him from it.

"And you've all been so kind, all worked so hard to help. I feel I've let you all down, being on my patch as it was." It seemed that even Orson's square, bristly black beard drooped. "Ah, but I'll have one final pleasure before you go, and I'll have no nay-saying." The smile was weak, but he did smile.

The constable reached into his pocket and turned to Futter. "I recall hearing you say it'd be a thing of great pleasure for you to give such as this to your wife, who is about to present you with something far more precious." He placed in Futter's hand the delicate slide bracelet and matching rings that were Orson's by inheritance but had been held in custody as evidence. "Perhaps this will help make up to both of you for your being away from her for so long. I only wish I could have the pleasure of seeing it on her wrist."

Futter blushed and stammered.

It was Danvers who bowed to the constable. "Exceptionally thoughtful of you, Orson. I'll say thank you too. Your act gives us all pleasure."

"Sort of a thank-you to the inspector here, it is. A real

253

support he was when there was some as thought different about me." His head ducked, Orson looked up at Danvers.

"Oh, Constable . . ." Tonia started to say more, but Orson turned to her.

"And Lady Danvers. So brave you were, and so caring for us all. There's a crystal paperweight that always sat on Mrs. B.'s desk. Maybe you noticed—painting of an eighteenth-century lady on the bottom—her hair all up, roses across her . . . er . . . below her neck . . . well, thing is she reminds me of you. If I could be so bold, my lady, I'd be highly honored if you'd accept that."

"I'd be delighted." Tonia would have hugged him if it hadn't been so shockingly improper.

"Thank you, my lady. Awkward thing is, I don't have it with me. Would it inconvenience you terribly to stop by Ordnance Terrace? Or I could have it sent on to Aethelsham in the morning, late as the hour's getting . . ."

"No, of course not. Ordnance Terrace isn't at all out of our way. Come in our carriage, won't you? Both of you." Her invitation included Futter.

A few moments later they drove up Rochester High Street, which ran into Chatham High Street, and up the long incline to where Ordnance Terrace stood on the brow of the hill.

On the way Tonia told the men what Hardy had told her about Gardiner Simpson. "I'm convinced he ignored the judge's charge to decide only on the evidence presented in the trial. I'm sure he browbeat the other jurors into what was essentially a political decision—you could see it on their faces. Can't something be done about that? Couldn't you get the Crown to bring a charge of mistrial? I'm certain the other jurors would back you up."

Futter and Orson both shook their heads.

Charles answered. "Only if you could prove perjury on the part of one of the witnesses. That's the only basis for retrial."

"Protection against double jeopardy—goes back to Magna Carta. Can't be tried more than once for the same crime," Futter said.

"But the foreman—" Tonia protested.

"Might have an argument if you could prove jury tampering—if he'd been bought off, or bribed the others, or something," Orson said. "But I doubt anything like that went on."

Tonia had to agree. Gardiner Simpson would deny he had been motivated by political beliefs. And she herself doubted any actual coercion beyond the force of a strong personality. So Catherine Bacon's brutal murder would go unavenged, local gossips would whisper and point fingers at whomever they chose to suspect, and a callous murderess would roam free.

They pulled up one last time before the long row of tidy, brick terrace houses with their tiny front gardens looking out toward the gray-brown Medway and the dockyard.

Tonia was thankful it wasn't snowing. But in spite of the dark of night and the lack of snow, the scene still strongly recalled that day the door of Number 9 had been opened by a frantic woman bleeding copiously from a slit neck. So little had changed on the outside, yet all was entirely different inside. Both houses at this end of the terrace had seen theft, violence, and deception. Now they stood empty.

Not quite empty. Was that the flicker of a candle behind the heavy curtains?

Tonia was still several strides from the door when she heard harsh laughter from within. She paused and looked up at Charles.

His frown told her he had heard too. He put a finger to his lips and signaled Futter and Orson to follow him. Gently he cracked the door.

"A right old party we'll have! Throw some more coal on the fire! Fill the glasses again, Edith. Got plenty to celebrate, we have." The gravelly voice of Elizabeth Law, harsh

255

with liquor, rang clearly from the small dining room where she and her friends sat around several nearly empty bottles.

Through the partly opened door Tonia saw the one called Edith splash more drink in each glass, then plop herself into the lap of one of the men.

"But Bessie, you're just making that up, aren't you?" Edith squealed and shivered, either from horror or in excitement. "Ooh, to slit your own throat! You couldn't have!"

"Oh and couldn't I, really?" Bessie shook her mane of long hair, which now fell loose over her shoulders, and stretched her neck to display her scar. "And who says I couldn't? Anyone here think I'm a coward? I could do something far worse than that if I had do. Ain't nothing Elizabeth Law can't do. Just leave it to Bessie. She can get away with anything!" She threw back her head with a shout of triumphant laughter.

Orson was the first through the door, raging like a mad bull toward the woman who had murdered his surrogate grandmother and now flaunted her guilt. "You'll not get away with this, Bessie Law! I'll—" His bearlike hands lunged toward her throat.

For the first time Tonia saw fear in Bessie's eyes. She took a step backward and stumbled against the sideboard.

Orson gripped her. "God help you, girl—for you'll get no other in this life."

Then the usually quiet, diffident Futter inserted the authority of Scotland Yard between murderess and avenger. "Elizabeth Avis Law, I'm arresting you in the name of our sovereign Queen Victoria on the charge of robbery."

Orson, still breathing heavily, stepped back and let Futter snap the handcuffs on Elizabeth Law. The iron click echoed in the suddenly silent room. Bessie's friends looked on in frozen horror.

Bessie broke the tension with an attempt at defiant laughter, which came out more as a snarl. "Oh, robbery is it now—theft and larceny. My oh my, ain't we particular!

Took the old bat's silver, did I? Course I did. Paid me beans, she did. She deserved everything she got."

"And you deserve everything you'll get." From behind Futter, Danvers spoke quietly.

"Sure, do your worst! What'll it be—six months for nicking the Chelsea porcelain?" she taunted.

Danvers nodded. "Yes, that's about what the sentence is likely to be." His voice was still level.

Bessie laughed. It was clear she would have spit on them all if her mouth weren't so dry.

"But that's not the end of it, Bessie." Danvers's careful enunciation gave weight to his words.

"I know my rights. The law—"

"Yes, that's the best we can do under the queen's law."

"See! A puny six months—outsmarted you all, I did!"

"Not quite, Bessie. There's one you didn't outsmart. There's one more court you'll face someday. You won't deceive that one."

21

Danvers bounded out of bed the next morning and threw the drapes open before Hardy could arrive for his morning ritual. "Look at that, Tonia—sunshine!"

She pushed back the covers and crossed the floor to him, squinting at the bright light flooding in the window.

He flung one arm around her and gestured toward the landscape showing just the faintest promise of spring green under the insistent morning sun. "A quite glorious day! And we've so much to celebrate, Tonia. Come with me. How can you refuse the thought of sailing through such radiance? Oh, Tonia, I do love you."

He felt her shrink from him. What had he said? Yesterday she had declined the flight, but surely with a little encouragement . . .

"It won't be overly cold—not anything at all like that flight across the Hebrides. I'll loan you my warmest cloak—" He looked down at her, and his enthusiasm stuck in his throat.

Her face was so drained of color he thought she was going to faint. "Tonia, are you ill?" He swept her into his arms and placed her on the bed.

She struggled to sit up.

He could see she was making an enormous effort, and he backed off. Whatever it was, he wouldn't make it more difficult for her by arguing.

"Charles, I explained yesterday."

"Yes." He nodded. "Sarah Higgins. Arranging schooling for her. Most admirable of you."

"She's absolutely brilliant, you know, and so talented —besides all I owe her. It would be very wrong of me to fail in this duty."

"Duty. Yes."

"And just two days ago I received a letter from Harriet. It's all settled. I can't think why I haven't told you about it. Anyway, I must go to Canterbury to arrange it all. Sarah will have lessons with Harriet's daughter Lavinia. The companionship will be excellent for Lavinia, and she has a most excellent music teacher . . ." Tonia's words rushed on.

Danvers frowned. Yesterday she told him she had completely forgotten about her promise to Sarah Higgins. Now she said she had a letter two days ago, and all was settled. "Surely, if it's all settled you could—"

"No, Charles. Please, I must do this."

He hadn't thought it possible for her to look any paler. Now she was whiter than the linen sheet she had pulled up under her chin. Her face was drawn, her cheeks thin, her eyes wide and overbright.

"You must have your ascent, Charles. I'll have Even take me to Canterbury. There's no reason at all for you to change your plans. There's nothing lovelier than Kent in the spring, is there? Well, coming on spring at least. I won't hear another word about it." She held up her hand as if to prevent his speaking, threw off the covers, and fled from the room.

Was she running from him? He took two steps toward her dressing room, then stopped. Whatever it was, he mustn't intrude.

Danvers turned to the top drawer of his chest. From under his cravats and silk handkerchiefs he pulled the small package he had obtained that day in Canterbury. Tonia's emerald brooch. What did it have to say to all this mystery? He considered giving it to her now to see what she would say.

But no, she was clearly in no state for a confrontation. He started to put it back in the drawer, then on impulse stuck it in his pocket.

A few minutes later Hardy bustled in with his breakfast tray. "Only brought yours, m'lord. Isabella said she was seeing to Lady Danvers."

"Yes, that's quite right."

Hardy set the tray on the table in the corner by the window and bustled about arranging the proper attire for his master's ascent. "You'll be pleased to know I bestirred myself early this morning. Been to Esherwood's and back already, I have. Course it's just a skip and a shout away. Anyway, everything's arranged. Canterbury's best place to get coal gas, he said. Wished he could go with you, he said, but has a fellow coming down from London today. Said he'll look forward to visiting with you when you return."

Danvers let Hardy talk. What a comfort the man was. Did he notice Tonia's absence? Danvers's tension? If so, he gave no hint. But cool as Charles hoped he appeared outwardly, inwardly his mind was churning, urging him to follow paths of unthinkable thoughts.

Tonia's beaded reticule lay on the dressing table. As clearly as if he were reliving the scene, he saw the white card flutter to the floor, felt its unbending slickness between his fingers, and saw the black letters *Tunbridge Wells.* Yes, the agent in Canterbury had said, train runs regular—two changes, but good trains. But why? Why, why? He looked at the small black bag as if it could give him the answers to the questions its contents had evoked.

And then, as Charles abandoned any pretense at eating breakfast, he had to admit that the questions were more than mere questions. They were suspicions. Almost accusations.

Yet that was impossible. There was nothing he could accuse Antonia of. Nothing in their three-and-a-half years of marriage he could reproach her for. Nothing—until this.

A vague idea began to form in his mind. It was too sketchy to call a plan. More a proposal it was—an outline of a direction. But whatever name he put on it, he knew he could not live with this fear and doubt that at first niggled at the back of his mind and now began clamping cold at his stomach.

He pulled his watch from his pocket. What had the ticket agent said? Was it the 9:40 to Ashford? Surely something close to that. Then change at Tonbridge . . .

Could they make it that quickly? It would be an hour's drive to Canterbury in the lumbering farm cart that carried the balloon. He shoved impatiently at Hardy who moved implacably through the process of making his master presentable. "What are you dawdling for, man? It'll take a good hour to fill that silk bladder—more, maybe. Let's get on with it." He almost ran toward the door.

"Two hours at the least, I should think, m'lord." Hardy reached for Danvers's hat and gloves. "Plenty of time we have."

"Plenty of time? Two hours? That's far too long—I'll be too late—"

Hardy puffed at his heels as Charles sped down the stairs. "Don't know what your rush is, m'lord. There's little sense in breaking our necks here when it'd be much finer to do it on an ascent. No sense either that I can see in getting to Canterbury before the balloon's filled, and I only sent it on an hour ago. Didn't think I should be getting Laver Esherwood out of bed, even considering what early risers aeronauts tend to be."

Danvers slowed his step. "Sent it ahead? It's being filled now? Good man, Hardy." Although Danvers's feet stopped racing, his mind didn't.

Hardy had been right in his estimate of time. The balloon was no more than two-thirds filled when they ar-

261

rived at the city gasworks. The plant that provided gas for the city's lighting system was situated near the train tracks, and Danvers started every time a black-barreled iron horse puffed down the tracks trailing a cloud of steam over the cars behind it. *Is Tonia on that one?* he asked himself each time.

He fully believed she had gone to Harriet Launceston's as she had said. Nothing had been an outright lie. But how long would she require to settle the business of Sarah Higgins—half an hour? An hour? Two? No more than that. It could have been settled by letter. What was she doing now? He felt certain he knew where she was going. But why?

"What a beauty she is, m'lord." Hardy's voice broke in on his grim thoughts.

"What? Tonia?" Then he realized Hardy referred to the blue-and-red-striped aerostat tugging at her moorings, now ready to ascend on the bright morning air. "Yes. Fine. That'll do fine, Hardy." He moved mechanically to the gondola and accepted Hardy's hand as he stepped over the high wicker side.

Then Hardy gripped the rim preparatory to springing in.

But Danvers held up a hand. "No, Hardy. Thank you, but not today."

His man started to protest.

Danvers shook his head. "No. I have to do this alone."

His teeth clenched, his face set, his hands so stiff he could hardly manipulate the valves, Danvers set off on his cold solo flight. This was the first time in his experience as an aeronaut that he hadn't enjoyed ballooning.

All the more reason to do it carefully, he told himself. Perhaps he had been foolish to leave Hardy behind. His man was expert at instrument reading and charting. Now he must do all the navigation himself. And he must do it correctly. Getting lost would do nothing to resolve the situation.

He looked down on the towers and pinnacles of Canterbury Cathedral. The sun gleamed dully on its ridged, leaded roof. The sight brought back the memory of being on that roof such a short time ago. The desperation he felt then to get to Tonia welled up in him again. He had always wanted to protect her from harm. And now she was in some sort of danger again. He knew it. He had protected her before. Could he do it again?

That time she had wanted protecting. She wanted him. Did she want him this time? With all the care she had exerted to keep her actions secret, he could only think she did not want him.

He floated over the leafless trees lining the streets of Canterbury's residences and headed out over the surrounding fields, brown and fallow now but soon to spring to verdant life. He checked his instruments and adjusted the flaps on each side of the gondola. Esherwood's invention these were, an excellent improvement. Easily manipulated, they enabled him to catch a strong air current to the southwest. He checked his map once more to ensure he was on course. Was that Chilham or Chartham below him? Either way, he was making excellent time. But toward what?

His course set, Danvers had no other distractions for his mind. His thoughts drifted to memories of Tonia before they married. How lively she had been—the toast of society, moving from the London season to one country house party to another. When they fell in love, she had professed she was more than happy to give up the artificial existence demanded by society.

But had she found life with him intolerably dull?

He was older than she, quiet and philosophical by nature, not handsome, not a good dancer . . . there was little reason she shouldn't find him a dull dog.

But if she had found another . . .

No, he wouldn't accuse her without proof. And even then it would be nearly impossible to believe such a thing.

It was all too easily imaginable that one could fall out of love with him . . . but it was unthinkable that Antonia should be capable of being untrue.

He gritted his teeth and checked the instruments again. The aereostat seemed to be moving more slowly than the clouds overhead. He let half the sand out of two ballast bags. The balloon ascended and caught a swifter current. The new sense of speed was satisfying, although he was not certain he wanted to hurry to the answer that awaited him at the end of this journey.

He continued to wrestle with his imagination. But in the end he lost. A lifetime of rigorous adherence to intellectual honesty was too much to overcome. The question had to be faced. What would he do if Tonia were false? What if she were meeting another man? What sort of man? A lover? Or one who meant danger?

He felt the package in his breast pocket. He didn't know what had prompted the impulse to bring the brooch, but there it was. What could have made Tonia so desperate she would have pawned it? He could think only of blackmail. And yet she could be guilty of nothing that would leave her vulnerable to that.

He returned to the idea that she had taken a lover.

The thought was incomprehensible, yet the evidence was so strong. Circumstantial, only circumstantial, he argued. Yes, but the evidence against Elizabeth Law had been only circumstantial. And it had been right.

It would be easier to think Tonia guilty of murder than of adultery, and still . . . what would he do? How would he confront her?

Divorce was unthinkable. But if she had found another . . . if her happiness was truly at stake . . .

And always there was the duty to his family to consider.

His mind whirled round and round, forming no clear thought, making no sense. At last he tried to pray and found it as impossible to form words to God as to himself.

But at length he was able to quiet somewhat the turmoil in his mind.

He marked off two more villages on his map. Wait—that one was no village. That was a town. Ashford. And there was a train just puffing out of the station, headed straight west. Was Tonia on it?

He pictured her sitting on one of the high-backed, deeply tufted seats, her face turned from the window and the light falling on her pale cheek. She would be sitting a little sideways, as the stiff crinolines required all women to do on narrow train seats. Perhaps she was reading. Or talking to another in her compartment. Or thinking. Thinking of him or of the one she would meet in Tunbridge Wells?

He tried again to pray. No words came. No answer came. But a Scripture did come. Not a Bible verse as such, but a story—a whole book. The story of Hosea.

Hosea, who had married the beautiful Gomer and was betrayed by her time and again. And yet Hosea had taken her back. Nor had he merely taken her back—he went out seeking her, and he cared for her when she was sick and fallen.

Hosea had been a great prophet. He had been ordered by God to such action to demonstrate God's love for His people. He was an object lesson of how God would restore Israel. That was all very fine. A beautiful parable and of course an exact image of God's unending love, His grace, His restoration.

And yet Hosea had been a man. A man with feelings for his beautiful wife. A man who must have known anger, hurt, confusion, all the things Danvers had known or imagined. And Hosea had restored Gomer to her place as his wife, not acting as a prophet but acting as a man. A man who loved and forgave.

It was beautiful. But could he do likewise? Danvers wondered.

He mused long, and the wind was stiff. His approach to Tunbridge Wells came up so suddenly he might have flown right over it. Checking his maps of the town, he began valving furiously. He must let out just the right amount of gas to bring the balloon down but not so much as to cause it to fall on a building or in trees as he had once done. The aerostat must remain buoyant to be stable and navigable. There were always sharply shifting air currents near the ground, which made landing especially tricky. This was complicated today by the fact that he had never before made a descent into Tunbridge Wells and that the town was built on a series of steep hills.

He oriented himself by the train tracks almost directly below him and marked Mount Ephraim, Lime Hill, Mount Pleasant, and Mount Sion on his chart. Tunbridge Wells Common spread green and open before him. That would be the perfect place to set down if he could achieve it.

To his right he caught a glimpse of streaming billows of steam. Would that be Tonia's train? Would she see him? Of course she wouldn't recognize Esherwood's balloon. Still . . .

A treetop rushed by him, and he narrowly grazed a branch. He had taken his mind from his navigation with near-disastrous results. He had time only to grab his sheath knife and hack at the ropes holding two ballast bags. The lightening of the load increased his buoyancy and slowed the descent. He hit the ground hard, but at least he had avoided an actual crash.

Immediately the balloon was surrounded by a swarm of small boys who had been playing cricket on the nearby oval.

Now Danvers realized how rash he had been in leaving Hardy behind. He had no one to care for Eshwerwood's aerostat. He tossed out two grappling hooks.

A tall lad in cricket whites, older than most of the cricketers, secured one of them and directed a mate to do the other.

"Thank you," Danvers said and pulled out his wallet. He took out a pound note.

The fellow's eyes got large at the sight of the princely sum.

"What is your name?" Danvers asked.

"Pembury, sir."

"Well, Pembury—" Danvers tore the note in half "—take good care of this balloon for me and the other half of this shall be yours."

"Right-o. No fear, sir. Fine gentleman I can see you are. No one'll mess with Pembury." He shoved his rolled sleeves above well-muscled forearms.

Danvers saw he had chosen well.

The train he had spotted from the air now steamed into the station just up the street from the common. Danvers moved toward the depot with a strange sense of hurry and yet a dragging step. Would someone be there to meet Tonia? Someone he had no desire to see her with?

He wished he knew what she was wearing today. He had not seen her since she had run from their bed in her white nightgown. His vaguely formed plan had been to follow her from the train station. If he missed her now, he might have made this mad journey for nothing.

And surely it was mad. Surely there was a perfectly simple, innocent explanation. Did Tonia have any sick relatives who might be convalescing in this spa town? Someone awkward or difficult that she had no desire to saddle him with? Yes, surely that was plausible.

Tunbridge Wells must be filled with octogenarians who tottered to the healthful springs every day and whose one pleasure would be a visit from such a ministering angel as Antonia would be to them. A distant relative—or an old servant. Tonia's old nanny, perhaps. Odd that she wouldn't have spoken of it, and yet that offered a perfect explanation. That was why she needed money. That was why she pawned the emerald.

He was so enamored of his explanation that when he saw a familiar gray-blue dress and bonnet moving across the platform he almost shouted at Tonia and rushed to her.

267

Just in time he stopped himself. Lovely story as it was, he knew she would have told him if it had been anything so simple. Well then, not an old, decrepit servant or relative—but surely someone who had come here for nursing. Perhaps a woman of fame and beauty, someone from Antonia's past in high society whose position demanded secrecy. Yes, someone of the aristocracy. Someone who had sworn Tonia to secrecy, so that she must sneak off to minister to her.

As if to prove the correctness of his rationalization, at that moment a young lady of great beauty indeed, with startling white skin and golden curls, wearing a fashionable gown of magenta and pearl pink, waved to Tonia and hurried to her. Yes, a younger sister of the great lady, perhaps. Danvers peopled his story with a noble family suffering in secrecy.

Of course he would remain hidden. Allow them to believe their secret was safe from all.

The two women entered a fashionable carriage, and Charles signaled to another cab, which pulled forward for him. He was no more than seated than he remembered Tonia's own explanation for her earlier disappearances. The story of delight and fashion she had used to pawn him off. It had been complete fabrication.

How could he have forgotten her carefully woven tales of Madame D'Arbly, dressmaker to Empress Eugenie? What had happened to the gown she was having made in honor of his role as charity choirmaster at the cathedral? The great surprise she had promised him? The night of the concert she had worn a dress almost two years old. And in the excitement of her abduction and Lansing's death, all such mundane matters as new gowns had been forgotten. But now he knew she had lied to him.

For whatever reason, there was no Madame D'Arbly, no new gown. He had to face the fact. Antonia had lied.

22

The carriage stopped so abruptly Danvers thought there must be some trouble. "What is it, driver?"

"You said follow them, sir. Appears we're here."

Indeed, it did appear so, although it was odd that Tonia's escort should have bothered with a carriage to go such a short distance. Perhaps the steepness of the road explained it, for they were at the top of the elegant Calverley Development, where houses in the grand style sat amid landscaped gardens above a fashionable shopping promenade.

Tonia and the young woman entered a large, red brick house. Its multitude of gables, towers, and turrets were garnished with ornate black iron like lace on a lady's gown. It stood in the middle of a garden filled with trees and bushes and surrounded by a tall, wrought-iron fence.

Danvers paid his cabby and turned to the ornate, double gate. His movements were stiff and jerky. He dreaded facing the secrets that house must hold. Yet he was driven to know the truth.

He was reaching out to push the gate open when a well-polished brass plate on the ivy-covered fence caught his eye. "Madame D'Arbly, modiste by appointment."

Charles's relief was so great that he blinked to be certain he was reading the words correctly. He read them two more times, stifling his impulse to trace the engraved letters with a finger. There *was* a Madame D'Arbly. It was her assistant who had met Antonia at the station. He had merely misunderstood.

The dressmaker was in Tunbridge Wells, not Canterbury. It was a long way to come—but undoubtedly worth it for a dressmaker to the empress. It all made sense now. The money had been to pay the expensive French courtier. She had wanted to surprise him. The dress had not been ready in time for the concert, so she would now wear it for him in celebration of the trial's being over. *Oh, Tonia, forgive me. How could I have doubted you? Forgive me.*

He felt a song welling within him. He could now sing with Figaro, "Come to my arms; embrace me! May sorrow pass our door . . ." He started to rush in to her, then paused. She would be in the midst of her final fitting. He must wait. When she came out he would surprise her and bear her off in his balloon.

But he was far too impatient to stand and wait. With long strides and the energetic speed born of relief and joy, he went for a walk across the green park, where darker green shoots coming up through the grass promised a bed of daffodils in a few weeks.

When he reached the far side of the gardens, however, he was tugged with the concern that he might have gone too far. He might miss Tonia. He didn't want her to have to take the stuffy, uncomfortable train back when she might travel aloft in the fresh, golden air with him. It would be unthinkable to let her make the journey alone when she had come all this way to secure a surprise for him.

He almost ran down the cobbled walkway toward Madame D'Arbly's, then stopped suddenly as the gate swung open with a clang.

He caught his breath at the sight. He had been right. The new gown was stunning. The gold-and-russet stripes of gleaming silk ran vertically, emphasizing Tonia's slim height. The wide, crinolined skirt was so daringly short in front it showed the tips of her shoes, but as she turned away from him he could see that in the back it fell to a graceful, brief train. The new gown was sensationally right for her. She was dazzlingly beautiful. He started to call her name.

Then the words stuck in his throat.

This time Antonia's escort was not the girl who had met her at the station. It was a strikingly handsome man with polished manners. He paused to close the gate behind them, then turned with almost a bow to offer his arm solicitously. She took it with a smile.

After only a few steps the man handed her into an elegant, shiny black carriage that had not been there earlier. Danvers heard her trill of laughter as the vehicle rolled away.

There were no hackneys in sight. He ran to the corner, keeping an eye on her carriage and praying there would be a cab. There was. He could just point out the carriage he wanted to follow.

Then he sat back against the cold, leather seat. He had only glimpsed the man, but even so quickly he had seen the glimmer in his eyes—and the answering one in Tonia's. How long had it been since he had seen such happiness on her face? The man was younger than himself and more graceful. Undoubtedly more charming, more . . . fun.

Charles's mind filled with a hundred questions. Where had she met the fellow? How long had she known him? Who was he? Was he a scoundrel—someone who preyed on lonely women that places like this fashionable resort would attract? *Oh, Tonia.*

Then his thoughts shifted from the occupants of the carriage ahead to himself. Angry words filled his mind as he felt the pain of her faithlessness. For a moment all was black before his eyes. When the carriages came to a halt he would tell her how he felt, call her to account, upbraid her for her deception.

But even as his mind pictured himself doing that, he knew he would do no such thing. He must be at least equally responsible for whatever had gone wrong in their marriage. And he still loved her terribly.

Even as words of accusation rang in his mind, he knew. As Hosea had taken Gomer back, as the heavenly Father would always take a wayward child back, so he would take Antonia back. No matter what. Unconditionally.

A new fear gripped him nevertheless. Tonia might not choose to come back. He would never reject her, but she might reject him.

The gleaming, sleek carriage in front stopped at the top of the fashionable, tiled walkway. The promenade was bordered on one side with charming, colonnaded shops and on the other with a grove of trees showing a budding of pale green behind a white picket fence. Danvers watched the man hand Tonia out of the carriage and offer his arm.

He hung back, but as soon as there were enough people between them so that he could follow with ease, he dismissed the cab.

The warmth of the sunshine reflected off the red clay pantiles underneath and the white trim of the galleried buildings. Such a day, signaling the end of winter, seemed to have brought out all who came to the spa for health or for pleasure.

Even this early in the year there were many who patterned optimistically the example of Lord North, who had founded the spa 250 years earlier after its waters had ostensibly cured him of a consumptive disorder. And North was followed by such royals as Catherine of Braganza, who came here seeking a cure for her childlessness, and Queen Anne, praying for relief from the tragedy of her numerous miscarriages.

Danvers was so deep in thought he nearly passed Tonia and her escort before he realized that the couple had stopped before the ornate iron railing surrounding the healing well. A dipper stood there, dispensing glasses of hopefully miraculous waters from the chalybeate spring.

Tonia raised her tumbler of yellowish mineral water as if it were the finest French champagne. The flared oversleeve of her dress, trimmed with its fringe of tiny amber beads, caught the light as it fell back from her elbow. She tipped her head and gave a trill of joyful laughter.

With a cramp of intolerable pain Danvers knew he had never seen her look more beautiful, more radiant, happier. He could not stop himself. "Tonia!"

She gave a small cry as she saw him. The glass slipped from her fingers and smashed on the tiles. She flew into his arms.

"Charles! Oh, Charles! How wonderful! How perfect! Oh, Charles, how did you find me? How did you know?" She clung to him laughing and sobbing.

A small boy from the dipper's well ran to sweep up the shards. Tonia's escort stood apart, smiling.

At length Danvers pulled her gently away. He couldn't begin to admit to himself how wonderful she felt in his arms. "Tonia, I don't know anything. Tell me. I don't understand."

"Oh, Charles." She drew a handkerchief from her reticule—a new one, beaded all over with amber and gold. "I was so afraid. I despaired, I really did. I thought—but then Dr. Penthurst—" She turned to indicate the man benignly observing them.

"Doctor! Oh, Tonia. You've been ill? You came to the Wells for a cure? But why didn't you tell me? Let me help?"

Dr. Penthurst indicated a relatively secluded bench in the grove where they could talk more privately, without the curious stares they were presently garnering from several people gathered around the dipper.

They crossed the pantiles, and Tonia sat as close to Charles as her crinoline would allow.

The doctor stood. "If you would allow me, Lady Danvers, I might just give Lord Danvers a brief medical background of the case."

"Oh, yes, please, Doctor. There's so much to tell, I don't know where to begin. And I was so afraid—"

"Quite, my dear, and not without foundation. Many cases such as yours have not had so felicitous an outcome."

"What—" Danvers began.

"You see, my lord, when your lady wife was quite young—at the age of five years and three months, to be exact—she was diagnosed to have contracted tuberculosis."

At the dreaded word Danvers grabbed Tonia's hands. "Antonia!"

"As she was so young and otherwise healthy, the case a light one, the diagnosis made early, and the treatment thorough—and as there had been no recurrence of the problem in all those years—it was quite a reasonable assumption on her part and on her physician's that the cure was complete and there would be no harmful . . . er . . . complications. Do not judge your wife too harshly, Lord Danvers. I must emphasize that her position was entirely in line with the best medical opinion. Conyngham House in Ramsgate is one of the best in the kingdom. She had complete rest in the purest sea air; bathed in both hot and cold seawater regularly; was most obedient in matters of the kelp and seaweed diet. There should have been no adverse consequences. Unfortunately—"

"Tonia, tell me! Are you ill? We'll go to the south of France, to Italy, to the best spas. Germany, that's it. Marienbad—would that be best, Doctor?"

Dr. Penthurst shook his head.

Tonia broke in. "No, no, love. That's what he's trying to tell you. Dr. Penthurst, come to the point. Charles, darling, you are going to be a father. I've just learned. I feel as if I've been holding my breath for months. If the treatments had failed . . ."

Danvers shook his head as the astounding news struck home. "I don't understand."

Dr. Penthurst cleared his throat and continued at his maddeningly deliberate pace. "As I was explaining, sterility is a usual consequence of tuberculosis. But as the now Lady Danvers's case was so light and so well treated, she was perfectly reasonable in believing herself capable to carry out her duties as the future Countess of Norville. When, however, after several years of marriage, there had been no . . . ah . . . results, it was equally within reason to believe the earlier doctors had been too optimistic in thinking her capable of producing an heir. It is, however, my very great privilege to congratulate you, sir, and assure you that the succession appears to be quite safe." Dr. Penthurst bowed and walked away, leaving the couple to their privacy.

Tonia laughed. "Isn't he the most positively maddening man? And terribly expensive too. But, oh, isn't it the most absolutely wonderful news imaginable?"

Danvers slipped his arm around her, hoping their seclusion would remain uninterrupted. "It is, my love. It's— stupendous. But I still don't understand. Why did you sneak off? Why didn't you just tell me?"

"Oh, Charles, I was so frightened. I thought when you learned I'd married you under false pretenses—when you learned I'd deceived you into thinking I could give you an heir and then couldn't—well, I know how important your duty is to you . . ." She hung her head and spoke so softly that for a moment the words didn't register. "I thought you would divorce me."

"Tonia." He grasped her shoulders and blinked at her, unbelieving. "Tonia, how could you think that? How could you trust me so little?"

"Not you, Charles—never you. But all the others I'd let down—the family, the title, all of England, really. I know how important family loyalty is to you."

"But don't you see—*you're* my family. Far and away, you're the most important part. Loyalty to you comes before any of the others."

She caught her breath in a little sob. "Oh, Charles, I've been so stupid." Her lip quivered, but her eyes were bright.

"Yes, you have been, rather. Odd, isn't it, how that just makes me love you more." He kissed her, then looked around to be certain they were unobserved.

"Oh—" he drew the package from his pocket "—and I have something for you."

She opened it, and her eyes grew huge and as bright green as the emerald. "Charles! How did you find it? How could you have known? But I'm so happy to have it back!"

"A rather long story, I fear. I'll explain later, my love. But first, tell me why did you come all this way alone? Isabella, Hardy—why didn't you take someone with you?"

"You know how even the best of servants gossip—or let things fall by accident. If the treatment worked I wanted to be the first to tell you. And if it failed . . . well, I didn't know what I would do. But I didn't want to involve anyone else." She put her hands to her cheeks. "Oh, Charles, I'm so happy, so thankful. The succession—"

"Not the succession, Tonia. You, my love. That's what's important. You and the baby. The succession can go to Jericho!"

She put her hand over his mouth. "Shh, darling. Not in front of the baby."

He threw back his head and flung out his arms. "The baby! Yes, the baby." He began in a faltering voice somewhere between Figaro's baritone and Count Almivara's tenor, "Come to my arms; embrace me! Now to be joyful!"

"And so my sorrows past, my joyous days begun, I'm free and happy-hearted, for now and time to come," Tonia joined him, for once equally off-key. "May love and joy eternal, all sorrow now behind. May smiling heaven send us bright skies forever more!"

They ended in an embrace.

276

Afterword

The exploits of Elizabeth Avis Law are historical and have been as accurately depicted as I could make them. References to the case are found in *Victorian Studies in Scarlet,* by Richard D. Altick (W. W. Norton & Co.: New York, 1970).

Thank you, Donna Hansen, University of Idaho Reference Library, for searching the *London Times Index* for me; and Laura Pershing, Idaho State Law Library, for introducing me to the tricks of researching dusty British legal tomes.

The rest of the story is fictional but reflects attitudes and beliefs of the time. Phrenology enthusiasm such as Hardy's is recorded by Havelock Ellis in *The Criminal* (Montclair, N. J.: Patterson Smith, 1973) and in *Psychology's Occult Doubles* (Chicago: T.H. Leahey and G.E. Leahey, Nelson-Hall, 1983).

A very helpful book discussing the work of A.W.N. Pugin and the successes and failures of Victorian architectural restorations is *A History of Western Architecture,* by David Watkins (New York: Thames & Hudson, 1986).

And finally, an excellent biography of Charles Dickens describes his time at Chatham, even in residence at Ordnance Terrace, about thirty years before the Elizabeth

Law incident: *Dickens,* Peter Ackroyd (New York: Harper Collins, 1990).

The effigy of the Black Prince was indeed painted black by Victorian restorers. It was restored in the early 1930s, quite to the amazement of those who found gleaming bronze under the thick coat of paint.

Danvers's lines from *The Barber of Seville* are loosely based on translations by George Mead in *A Treasury of Opera Librettos,* edited by David G. Legerman (New York: Doubleday & Co, 1962).

Moody Press, a ministry of the Moody Bible Institute,
is designed for education, evangelization, and edification.
If we may assist you in knowing more about Christ
and the Christian life, please write us without obligation:
Moody Press, c/o MLM, Chicago, Illinois 60610.